THE
RELAXISTS

For information about permissions to reproduce selections from this book, translation rights, or to order bulk purchases, write: info@therelaxists.com.

Cover design by Oliver Michael Robertson

Spencer, Alton
The Relaxists
979-8-218-00806-2

1. Fiction / Visionary & Metaphysical. 2. Fiction / Literary.
3. Philosophy / Metaphysics.

Elowah Press

Printed in the U.S.A.

THE
RELAXISTS

ALTON SPENCER

THE
RELAXISTS

The Book of Aten

A strange sensation overcame Edward Slowbe as he peered out of his bedroom windows at a crescent moon resting on the horizon. He glanced over at his clock. It was 3:22 a.m. Everyone else was asleep and dreaming, he thought. In the silence that surrounded him, it felt as if the mysteries and secrets of the universe were creeping tantalizingly close to his personal space. He had just finished writing a poem, one whose words had seemed to pour onto the pages of his notebook almost spontaneously, and he was reflecting upon its true meaning—and upon the true meaning of poetry itself. Slowbe turned and walked quietly out of his room. He made his way down the flight of stairs, through the living room, and down a short hallway, until he came to the place where his mother kept her books, heirlooms, and old photographs. He was hoping to find a clue, an opening, some sort of guide that would help him lift the veil on the unknown worlds and hidden places that seemed to be whispering to him in the night. The yearning had been there in one way or another ever since he was a child, and unexpectedly, in the present moment, he felt certain there was something in his mother's library that would offer a pathway. The notion of looking there hadn't occurred to him before, and he wasn't sure why it had on this particular evening.

Slowbe turned the doorknob and entered the small, rectangular room. He closed the door behind him and pulled a thin metal chain that dangled from the ceiling. Illumination. Slowbe looked to his right at the several open boxes, each full of pictures, that were sitting on the floor. To him, there had always been an enigmatic quality surrounding his mother's old photographs—especially the ones of his grandmother, Helen. Like her husband, Solomon, she had died from alcoholism long before Slowbe was born. They were both dead by the time his mother was ten years old. The pictures of Helen always sent a slight chill up his spine. She looked like a dead person, he thought, like she had always been a dead person, always a ghost, looming. He'd even once had a nightmare about her, when he was a little boy, of her apparition-like figure floating up the staircase toward his bedroom. Some of the pictures of Helen were framed, and there was one whose glass covering was cracked.

A copy of Botticelli's *La Primavera* hung from one of the longer walls, and across from it was a brown bookcase with eight shelves. To the left of the bookcase was a thick, heavy wooden chest with two leather straps over the top and a metal latch. Inside the chest were a coarse blanket and a rustic, three-foot-long peace pipe. According to the story Slowbe was told by his mother, the pipe and blanket had been passed down on her side of the family from a Cherokee woman who was his great-great-great-great-grandmother, but there was no other information about her. Despite the distance in time, and the shroud of mystery surrounding her, he felt a connection to the woman. The peace pipe, in particular, made her real to him. Slowbe surmised that she would have likely been born in the 1850s or early 1860s. He'd come to this conclusion by counting six generations from himself to the Cherokee woman, estimating that a generation was about twenty-five years. He multiplied 25 by 6 and subtracted the product from 2007, the year of his birth.

Slowbe stood in front of the bookcase. None of the texts looked like they had been read in ages, and he wondered why it seemed as if he'd never seen them before. He'd observed them from this very position many times. Something was different. Slowbe started at the top left-hand corner of the shelves and carefully scanned the rows of books, sliding his finger over each one, stopping briefly at a few—*God Is an Idea, and All Things are Ideas*; *Science Is Eternal*; and *Consciousness and an Infinite Multiverse*—whose publication dates and synopses he quickly glanced over. In the fourth row down, almost all the way to the right end of the shelf, his finger stopped at a medium-sized paperback entitled *The Book of Aten*. "Aten?" he whispered. He was familiar with the name. Aten was a sun god who'd been worshiped in ancient Egypt, albeit only briefly. Slowbe had written a report on this period for a history class.

In 1353 BC, Amenhotep IV, son of Amenhotep III, came to power in Egypt as the tenth pharaoh of the eighteenth dynasty. He ruled for seventeen years with his wife, Nefertiti, and was the father of Tutankhamen. In the fifth year of his reign, he'd done the unthinkable—he'd abandoned all the traditional Egyptian deities and had established, by decree, a monotheistic religion across Egypt that was based on worship of a new sun god: Aten. The priesthoods of all other deities were disbanded, radically altering the political and religious structure of Egyptian society. The pharaoh then changed his name to Akhenaten, meaning "effective for Aten," or "he who is useful to the Aten," and built a new capital in central Egypt called Amarna, which replaced Thebes as the center of government and religion. Tens of thousands of Egyptians were relocated to the new city. This social, political, and religious upheaval was accompanied by a radical shift in artistic style, later called the Amarna style, or Amarna art, that depicted more realism and movement than had previously been the convention.

Twenty-first-century scholars described Akhenaten's movement as the first appearance of monotheism in world history, the first conception of belief in one god; but within ten years of his death Egypt returned to the old polytheistic belief system, to the old traditional gods that had been worshipped for over two thousand years: Ra, Isis, Osiris, Horus, Thoth, Seth, Mut, Bastet, Ptah, Wadjet, Hathor, Anubis, Maat, and others. The memory and images of Akhenaten and his one god, the eternal sun god Aten, were destroyed. He and the Amarna Revolution, as the episode was later called, were lost to history until twentieth-century archeologists discovered the site of his city. On January 6th, 1907, one century before Slowbe's birthday, to the day, Akhenaten's tomb was unearthed.

Slowbe pulled *The Book of Aten* from the shelf and looked at the cover. There was a portrait of a woman with short brown hair seated at a slight angle so that while both of her eyes glanced to the left, she was looking directly at the observer. Shadow surrounded her face and her ambiguous expression resembled that of the *Mona Lisa*. Above the title read "Aten, an entity from another plane of existence, communicates via the consciousness of modern-day oracle Najera Strebanore."

This was it, the treasure. Slowbe immediately claimed the book as his own and quickly made his way back upstairs to his bedroom. As he sat cross-legged on his bed holding the book in his hands and looking at the cover, he considered what was to him the very strange coincidence that the Egyptian sun god and the personality channeled by Strebanore had the same name. He remembered that he'd heard somewhere that the sun symbolized the soul. He opened the cover of the book and noticed that the publication date, the ISBN number, and any information on the publisher had completely faded. This, too, struck him as peculiar.

He began to read, and the words and passages flowed into the crevices of his mind like water pouring into a dry riverbed. There was something authoritative, rational, and intuitive about what Aten was saying to him. Slowbe read page after page, effortlessly, as if he were floating outside of time. And the more he read, the more he became convinced that not only did he have the potential to perceive and experience planes of reality outside of what he was accustomed to with his five senses, but that within him existed a conscious system, of which he was a part, that extended interminably beyond the constructs of ego and body. When he'd read the last word of the last page, he walked across his room and placed the book on his dresser. He looked out his windows and noticed the crescent moon still resting on the horizon.

Slowbe awoke from his dream. It was 8:34 a.m. on Sunday, September 24th, 2023. He lay in his bed in a sort of awestruck imperturbation. He'd never had such a vivid, conscious dream before; and for the first time in his life he felt a sense of seamlessness between his dream experience and his waking experience. He remained in bed for close to forty-five minutes, thinking about his dream and observing his surroundings. His room seemed somehow animated.

Slowbe leaned over. Usually, there were a few books that he'd checked out from the school or public library lying on the floor next to his bed—often books on medieval or ancient history, or art history books full of colorful, glossy pictures— and several more scattered across his dresser. He'd recently discovered Ralph Waldo Emerson and Henry David Thoreau, and copies of *Nature* and *Walden* lay within reach, along with a copy of the Upanishads that he'd found in his mother's library the previous week. He loved being surrounded by these types of books: art, history, philosophy, and religion. Slowbe looked at the three book covers for a moment and then returned to lying on his back. Across from his bed, in the corner near his dresser, were a set of bongos, a bass guitar, an acoustic guitar, and a small amplifier. The room had a walk-in closet, a small desk and chair, and the floor was covered with tan carpet. On the walls were posters of women in bikinis; rock icons Jimi Hendrix, Led Zeppelin, and the Beatles; and one of Machu Picchu. The bedroom was on the third floor of a brown Tudor-style house on a tree-lined street in Chillicothe, Ohio. A roof jutted out from below his windows—perfect for resting under the hot sun, or for feeding the neighborhood birds (mostly crows, blue jays, chickadees, doves, and cardinals) in the early morning.

After finally getting out of bed and eating breakfast, Slowbe spent the rest of the day mowing the lawn, riding his bike, playing his bass guitar, and reading from the Upanishads. Around 9:00 p.m. he settled in to study for an exam he had in the morning. He sat down at his desk and opened his quantum mechanics book to the chapter on the behavior of subatomic particles. As he reviewed the chapter, he cross-referenced several worksheets and study guides, as well as the notes he'd taken in class. Just before 11:00 p.m. he placed everything in a stack on the left side of his desk and turned off the lights in his room. He closed the curtains across his windows and slumped down on his bed. He turned onto his back and propped his head on his pillow.

Slowbe lay there in the nearly pitch-black room with his eyes open, thinking about the dream. He decided to try an experiment. He closed his eyes and placed his right and left middle and index fingers on his eyelids, right on right, left on left. Even though the room was dark, and his eyes were closed, placing his fingers over them somehow reinforced the sense that he was intentionally directing his focus away from the external reality, away from the world around him. Slowbe saw what most people see when they close their eyes: blackness, a black veil. He began to concentrate. Slowly but surely, he took his attention off the facts of the environment that surrounded him—the walls and ceiling of his room, the world outside his windows. He turned his attention entirely to his sense of himself within himself, as if he was within a capsule outside of which nothing existed, and away from the dominant paradigm of human perception in which sight and sense are almost exclusively outward-focused experiences. For the moment he assumed a belief that everything that there was to be aware of was inside, and only seen by his mind's eye. His focus became more and more crystallized, and eventually, for all intents and purposes, the world around him faded far into the background. In his mind he began repeating the statement, "I am calling out to my inner self, please make yourself known to me, I beseech you to make yourself known to me."

Slowbe repeated this statement over and over again, for almost fifteen minutes. An intense wave of energy suddenly surged throughout his body, causing him to gasp. A few moments later a cascade of colored balls of light—red, orange, yellow, green, and blue—appeared in his mind's eye, flowing down from the top of his field of vision. The balls of light rushed before Slowbe like a waterfall, each one robust and distinct, bright, but with splayed edges, like the sun. After less than a minute, the surging energy subsided, the black veil and the balls of color were gone, and Slowbe was looking out into a scintillating violet-colored expanse. The reality facing Slowbe was akin to a three-dimensional experience of being surrounded by a blue sky, with nothing but the sky in one's central and peripheral vision—the remarkably notable difference being that, one, he was witnessing a vast expanse of violet space, not a vast expanse of blue space, and, two, his eyes were closed.

Slowbe could hardly believe what was transpiring, but, overwhelmingly, he knew that the experience was stunningly, undeniably, resplendently real. It was the most beautiful and exciting, and shocking, thing that had ever happened to him: an instantaneous paradigm shift rising unexpectedly out of the blackness.

Ostensibly, the experience was a direct response to his implorations, and to his acceptance that knowledge of other planes of reality and other dimensions of consciousness were, simply by virtue of his own true nature, available to him. Nonetheless, there was an element of cognitive dissonance with regard to the encounter he was having, as he had been well-conditioned, like most people, into an orientation that revolved exclusively around the five senses and the physical world. He lay there observing, in awe at the great unknown. He began to notice lucent pulses gliding across the inner skyscape in rhythmic, repeating patterns. He heard no sound, no voices. No figures or familiar images appeared before him, simply the violet expanse.

After about thirty-five minutes, Slowbe opened his eyes. He got out of bed, turned the lights on, and stood by his door for several moments looking around his room. He turned the lights off and returned to his bed. When he closed his eyes again, the violet expanse was gone, and all he saw was the blackness. He rolled over onto his right side, pulled his blanket above his shoulder, and eventually drifted off to sleep.

While Slowbe dreamt, white smoke began to emerge from the chimney of the Sistine Chapel in Rome. Shortly afterward, a slightly built cardinal named Paolo Alighieri appeared on the central balcony of St. Peter's Basilica and announced, "Habemus Papam!" ("We have a Pope!"). The large throng filling St. Peter's Square (disproportionately crowded with men, women, and children from the United States) cheered the widely anticipated selection of Andrews Norton as Pope. The first pontiff born in the U.S., Andrews had been the archbishop of Boston for fifteen years, a cardinal for twelve, and would now be Pope Leo XIV: the fifth Pope of the twenty-first century, following John Paul II, Benedict XVI, Francis, and Urban IX.

At noon Central European Time, Leo emerged from the chapel balcony to deliver his Apostolic Blessing to the world. A light rain fell upon Vatican City, and there was a thick fog. "I speak from the seat of Peter," he said in his low, authoritative voice, "and I reaffirm the decree of papal infallibility. Our world is troubled, and I implore you to hear me, to do as I say when I tell you, now, repent for your sins." The new Pope went on, calling for peace in the Holy Land; encouraging acts of charity; and warning his flock not to stray, commanding that they reject the seductions of the secular world and commit themselves to spreading the Gospel. "Satan is trying to destroy the church," he told the rapt and increasingly wet crowd, "but I will not let him, and neither will you."

When Slowbe awoke in the morning, his mother, Isabella, whose maiden name was di Mariano, was watching video of the papal ceremony. She was a devout Catholic, although one who strayed from tradition in certain respects. For example, she believed that the Buddha and Jesus Christ were "two sides of the same coin," as she put it; and she theorized that both had studied the Upanishads. Also, she referred to God as a "She," despite holding firm to a belief in the Trinity. Furthermore, on several occasions, she had told Slowbe that she was a witch. He didn't see any reason not to believe her, although he didn't quite know what to make of her assertion. Isabella's favorite saints, of whom she hung pictures in her room, were Cecilia, Monica, Lucia, and Catherine of Alexandria.

From the time Slowbe was a small child, Isabella had insisted that he attend mass with her; but earlier in the year, a couple weeks after he turned sixteen, with no warning whatsoever, she told him that attending mass would be his decision. He'd paused for a second out of surprise. A feeling of excitement and relief filled him. He told her he would prefer to stay home on Sundays.

Slowbe had never liked going to church, even though there were three features of the experience that always amused or pleased him. First, he enjoyed listening to the congregation recite the Lord's Prayer, not because of the content of the prayer, but because of the way the "s" sound resonated throughout the nave during their recitation of the passage "... as it is in heaven. Give us this day our daily bread, and forgive us our trespasses, as we forgive those who trespass against us, and lead us not into temptation, but deliver us ..." The passage "our trespasses, as we forgive those who trespass against us" was where the "s" sounds really jumped out and pervaded the space. It caught his attention every Sunday, and he waited for it with anticipation. Then there was the wafer and sip of wine during communion.

But above all, mass was a countdown to the donuts and coffee (which he always drank with cream and sugar) that were served afterward. Slowbe did, in fact, feel a sense of affinity, even mystical fascination, for the Nazarene, although he somehow never felt like a real Christian.

Slowbe's father, Leonard, was a tall, imposing man who'd grown up in the Black Baptist church in Atlanta but who had become disdainful of religion in his adulthood. Slowbe didn't have many memories of him, and those he did have were negative. This was mainly due to the fact that Leonard took delight in emotionally abusing the little boy. Often, the abuse would occur in the form of a diabolical, wide-eyed stare that Leonard would give his son. Time and again, when Isabella was away at her jazz gigs or consumed by drugs and alcohol, Leonard would stare wildly at the boy, unexpectedly and for no apparent reason, and the boy, like a deer in headlights, could only stare back, in horror, crying hysterically. Leonard would begin to laugh, aroused by his power to shake his child so profoundly, as if it were a game. When Slowbe was six years old, he found Leonard lying in the bathtub with a self-inflicted stab wound to the chest, drenched in blood. The searing image compounded the internalized fear he already had around his father. Following Leonard's death, Isabella spiraled further into a pattern of addiction, from which she never returned.

Slowbe, carrying a bowl of cereal, walked into the living room, where Isabella was watching the events that had transpired in Rome. As he sat down, he glanced at the slight crack in the bottom left-hand corner of the glass coffee table, where he'd placed his bowl. He wasn't sure how the crack had gotten there, but he knew it had happened during a party he threw the month before, while Isabella was in Cleveland visiting her aunt. The party had been a hit, or so his friends told him, but Slowbe had missed almost the entire occasion because he drank over half a bottle of rum before most of his classmates arrived. He was conscious until 10:00 p.m. or so, when he passed out on Isabella's waterbed. When he woke up the next morning, he swore he'd never drink again. Isabella knew nothing of the party, at least not to Slowbe's knowledge. No questions had been asked about the crack.

"I told you if you skipped doing the dishes again you were going to be grounded," she said matter-of-factly. "One week, Edward."

"But Mom, I was up until almost midnight studying," Slowbe exclaimed.

"You should have done them right after dinner, like I've said a thousand times."

"I shouldn't even have to do them, I work harder than you do," Slowbe said. "I go to school from eight in the morning until three thirty, then I have soccer practice until six; I come home and eat dinner and then I study all night."

"Watch your tone, Edward," she said. "You had plenty of time to do the dishes last night."

Slowbe had considered telling Isabella about his experience from the night before, but instead, because of her castigation, he excluded her. He finished the bowl of cereal, grabbed his backpack, and left the house without saying goodbye. It was drizzling when he got outside. He opened the garage door to retrieve his bike. He pulled it off its rack and began the fifteen-minute ride to school. The air was clean and cool. The sky was a smooth, uniformly pale grey.

Four blocks from his house, near the intersection of Laurel Street and Stafford Avenue, Slowbe spotted a large raccoon appearing from behind a rhododendron bush. He clenched his brakes and came to a stop. Slowbe crossed paths with raccoons somewhat frequently at night, but he'd never seen one during the day in his neighborhood. The raccoon immediately noticed Slowbe, and the two creatures watched each other carefully from a distance of about twelve yards. On the telephone wires above them, three crows had their eyes on the situation. The raccoon made a quiet chirping sound and then crept into the bushes. Slowbe cautiously pedaled toward the rhododendron bush to see if he could get another look. He didn't see the raccoon, so he continued on his way to school. By the time he arrived at Chillicothe High School, the rain was coming down hard. He locked his bike and ran up the wide staircase to the front entrance of the school. He was ten minutes late for his first-period quantum mechanics class, but despite being tardy he was able to finish his exam with time to spare.

At lunch he met up with his best friend, Seven. "Hey Sev," Slowbe said, placing his tray at the edge of a long table. The din of hundreds of chattering teenagers filled the cafeteria.

"Hey, Slowbe," Seven replied, lifting his eyebrows and smiling, his mouth partially filled with french fries. "Dude, last night I finished recording the lead guitar parts for that song I was telling you about. Man, I'm psyched, this shit is sweet. I'm gonna throw in backing vocals this weekend and then do some mixing."

"Awesome," Slowbe said with moderate enthusiasm.

"Can you come over Friday night and jam?"

"Sweet, yeah, I can come over...well, shit, I don't know. This morning my mom said I was grounded because I skipped doing the dishes."

"Again? Damn dude, you're always grounded."

"I know, it sucks. I might be able to get out of it, though. I'll let you know."

"Cool," Seven said.

The two high school juniors, who'd known each other since second grade, regularly got together to play music in a special basement room in Seven's house, affectionately known as "the womb," whose walls, ceiling, and floor were covered entirely in shag carpet. The space was filled with musical equipment: a digital keyboard, a drum kit, three guitars, a bass, microphones, amplifiers, and a PA system, all courtesy of Seven's parents, who actively supported his preternatural talent as a musician, singer, and songwriter.

Although Slowbe was Seven's most ardent fan, and playing music with him was a highlight of his life, he struggled with the lingering thought that his own musical skills, while considerable, were marginal or unimportant by comparison. "I'm the better poet and writer," Slowbe would say to himself—which, in fact, he was. Nonetheless, at the time it seemed a small consolation. Slowbe also knew in his gut that Seven was going to be rich and famous someday, and he wanted that for himself as well, but he didn't have the same gut feeling about inevitable prosperity regarding his own future, even though he often dreamt of mansions and expensive cars and of being a philanthropist and giving away large sums of money.

There was a slight, brief lull in the cafeteria din. Seven pulled his laptop out of his backpack and went to the Guitar Center website.

"I like this new Stratocaster—seventieth-anniversary model. I was playing one down at Good Luck Music on Saturday. The anniversary is next year, but I guess they started hitting the stores last month. I'm thinking about getting one," Seven calmly stated.

"That *is* nice," said Slowbe. "You think you might get it?"

"Yeah, maybe, I'd like to. I got some money saved up," Seven said, as he and Slowbe looked admiringly at a picture of the twenty-five-hundred-dollar guitar. Over the previous summer, Seven had started performing at bars and clubs in the Columbus metro area, about an hour north of Chillicothe. He was quickly becoming in demand in the state's capital and largest city, and he was making money.

"What do you think of those poems I emailed you?"

"They're awesome, Slowbe," Seven replied as he smiled encouragingly at his friend. "I showed 'em to my mom too. She loves your stuff. You've been prolific with the writing lately."

"Yeah, I'm writing a lot. I'm pretty glad about it. Definitely feeling connected...to something." Slowbe looked out the window. The rain was still coming down ceaselessly. "I had a weird experience last night."

"What happened?" Seven asked.

Slowbe paused. It's raining really hard, he thought to himself. He could almost feel the vibration from the sound of the rain falling against the trees, the houses, the ground, and the school. The world outside the cafeteria windows was grey and green. "I did an experiment," Slowbe said.

"What were you trying to find out?"

"I'm kind of...well...it's hard to...I'm not sure about the words. You ever heard of the Gnostics?"

"No."

"I've been reading about them lately. They were some of the earliest Christians, from the first and second centuries, but they were unique because they didn't adhere to the institution of the church. Their main idea was that they could have real, direct contact with 'God' or the divine, just like you and I are having real, direct contact with each other right now—you know, legitimate, down to earth. The Gnostics thought this experience was available to them by nature, like a birthright, or just something inherent. I think they believed that because they were connected to 'God,' like 'God' was within them, they could know a reality beyond the physical senses. The church considered the Gnostics a threat because if the Gnostics found knowledge, wisdom, or spiritual power, or whatever, without having to go through the church, it would limit the church's power and influence. It would hinder the church's ability to control and define what is and what isn't truth. It was all about power: power the Gnostics felt existed within versus worldly power the church sought to exert."

"Never heard of them. And so what was your experiment?"

"I wanted to see if I could discover something beyond my five senses, like a soul, or another reality."

"That sounds pretty weird, Slowbe. Well...what happened?"

"So, it was around eleven at night and I turned the lights

off in my room and closed the curtains, so it was like almost pitch black. I lay down on my bed and propped my head up on my pillow and placed my fingers over my eyes like this." Slowbe put his left index and middle fingers over his left eye and did the same with his right hand and eye. "I was lying on my back and I just started to concentrate on ignoring...I guess you could say I was ignoring what was around me. And I just started concentrating. I concentrated on being within . . ."

"Being within? What do you mean being within?"

"I was focused on what I was seeing with my eyes closed, and not on anything else, like my room. So, when you close your eyes you're kind of inside yourself, you can't see anything around you. I just concentrated really hard on being inside myself."

"I don't really get that, but go ahead."

"I started saying, 'I am calling out to my inner self, please make yourself known to me.' I said it over and over again, and I was in the blackness, the blackness that you see when you close your eyes. I kept saying, 'I am calling out to my inner self, please make yourself known to me,' for about ten or fifteen minutes, and then all of a sudden out of nowhere this rush of energy totally surged through my body. It surprised the hell out of me. And then these balls of light, different colors, started... started pouring down in front of me, and my eyes were closed. They were pouring down for like forty-five seconds. And then, after that, the blackness was gone and there was this whole...I don't even know what to call it. It was like I was inside another world. It was like looking into the sky, but my eyes were closed. It was three-dimensional. There was depth, but my eyes were closed. And it was violet; the whole thing that I was looking at was violet, like a violet sky, or a violet reality. It was crazy, unbelievable. I just lay there and watched...for like a half hour...I don't know. You should try it, Seven."

Seven's silence and indiscernible expression made Slowbe nervous.

"What do you think?" Slowbe asked. "You should try it."

"That's...I don't know...that is really weird. I've never heard of anything like that before, Slowbe. What do you think it was?"

"I don't know," Slowbe replied.

"Well, I need to get going to study hall, dude," Seven said. "Mr. Jaworski said if I'm late again he's gonna make me stay after school, and I need to go to my locker first and get some stuff."

"Ok. I'll see ya later," Slowbe said.

Slowbe sat at the cafeteria table looking out the window. He had history class next period.

When Seven and Slowbe got together to play music four days later, Slowbe asked his friend if he'd tried the experiment. Seven said no. Slowbe didn't bring up the subject again with him, or anyone else, for a very long time after that.

Through the remainder of his high school years, Slowbe performed the nighttime experiment on a regular basis. After his initial experience, he never again saw the cascading balls of light. It was as if they represented the opening of a gate, which had now been passed through. No longer would he need to call out to his inner self in order to enter into the violet realm. All of the other procedures he would continue to follow: the inward concentration and intention, the blocking out of external stimuli, the clearing of his mind, the lying on his back with his head propped, the placing of his fingers on his eyes. Usually after about ten to fifteen minutes of inward focus the surge of energy would come about and the expanse would open up before him. Eventually, the surge of energy became a less frequent part of the experience.

Within the violet realm he began seeing visions and images with regularity. He would see landscapes, seascapes, and skyscapes filled with stars; personages, faces, or eyes looking back at him; villages and cities that seemed to be from the past, perhaps from another life, he thought. He would see various other scenes, like an image of a mountainous desert where a grown man was kneeling down to a young boy and pointing up at the stars above. On occasion, cloud-like images would form and dissipate in repetitious fashion upon the violet backdrop, and at other times they would simply float before his field of vision, just as normal clouds float across the sky. Much of what he saw when he was within the violet realm was indescribable, defying any sort of comparison. Most often he would simply see a vast open space characterized by dark or light shades of violet. Sometimes, he would have the sensation of falling, and of weightlessness. There was nothing more beautiful or fascinating to Slowbe than the grandeur and light of this inner reality. But he also feared it in a way—the power of it, the vastness of it. And he noticed that he had to stay relaxed in order to have, or maintain, the experience. If he began to tense up, the violet realm would begin to recede or would simply disappear.

Grace Market

As Slowbe drove along the Scioto River toward U.S. Route 23 out of Chillicothe, he was pleasantly surprised to see a full rainbow to the west. He viewed it as a good sign, and it provided him a welcome respite from the somber mood he was experiencing following Isabella's funeral, which had taken place the day before, on October 20th, at St. Mary's Catholic Church. Slowbe hadn't been to his hometown, or spoken with his mother, in the seven years since he'd graduated from Harvard in 2029, and it'd been only a few days since he'd received a call from Father William Berkshire, a priest he'd known most of his life, who'd informed him of Isabella's passing and had persuaded him to attend the funeral. Interesting, Slowbe thought to himself after the call had ended. He was as taken by the timing of the funeral as by the death itself. Earlier in the year, he'd made arrangements to move from New York City to Portland, Oregon, in large part so that he could be in closer contact with his mentor, the writer, philosopher, and mystic, Toussaint Riviere. Slowbe was scheduled to leave New York on October 19th. He'd decided he would take his time driving across the country, traveling only during the day so that he could see everything, and the route he'd mapped out had him crossing through Ohio. He wouldn't have thought to stop there had it not been for the call from Father Berkshire.

Slowbe had been living in New York City since November of 2029, and for several years he was almost entirely supported by Seven, living rent-free in his Park Avenue penthouse, regularly traveling with him on tour, and working for him as a session bass player on several recordings. In 2033, he published his first volume of poetry, *Follow Me to Your Favorite Colors*, which he referred to as his "new poetry." He'd been working on the collection since early 2030, and it made a name for him virtually overnight as a poet whose writing was both original and breathtaking. Slowbe's correspondence with Riviere began shortly after the release of his volume, and the two quickly developed a meaningful bond. Eventually, Slowbe decided to move to Portland so he could be immersed in the flourishing artistic culture that had emerged in the Pacific Northwest, so he could enjoy the natural wonders of the region, and so he and Riviere could engage in more frequent discussions on art and metaphysics. When Slowbe mentioned his interest in relocating, Riviere offered him use of the guest cottage on his property.

Although it was late October and heavy snow was in the forecast for the upper midsection of the country, Slowbe was determined to take a northerly course to Portland in order to avoid the Great Plains, an area he'd traversed once before. He thought they were stunning, in their own way, in their rolling endlessness and homogeneity, but one time across was sufficient for this lifetime, he thought; anything more would be excessive. And he wanted to explore some new territory. Once he was out of Ohio, the remainder of his itinerary would take him through Indiana, Illinois, Wisconsin, Minnesota, South Dakota, Wyoming and Yellowstone National Park, and Idaho, then finally into Oregon and Portland.

Slowbe drove west on U.S. Route 35 to Interstate 75, then to Interstate 70 and onto Interstate 65, until he finally reached Interstate 90 heading west, which, before long, merged with Interstate 94. Just over six hours after having left Chillicothe, he saw what looked like a huge monolith rising on the horizon, appearing out of an otherwise perfectly flat landscape. So, this is Chicago, he thought to himself.

As he got closer to the city, the highway opened up to six lanes. Slowbe hadn't owned a car, and had rarely driven, during his years in New York, and now he was entering Chicago near the peak of rush-hour traffic. It seemed as if hundreds of cars suddenly appeared, swirling around him, darting left and right as they shifted lanes, shooting in front of him and closing in on him from behind, moving unreasonably fast; a dizzying mass of impatient and self-interested drivers. His heart raced and he gripped his steering wheel tightly. He leaned his torso forward, closer to the windshield. His eyes were wide open as he focused intently on navigating the perilous terrain that felt like a real-life video game. An old grey car honked as it pulled around his left side. Slowbe turned his head quickly and glimpsed a young man's angst-ridden face yelling at him. He couldn't watch the actor for long. Slowbe glanced at his speedometer. He was going forty-five miles per hour. He started to speed up. A few moments later, it occurred to him that he'd lost reception to the radio station he'd been listening to, leaving nothing but the loud, crackling static of cosmic background radiation from the beginning of time, from the Big Bang. He moved his hand toward the volume knob of the radio and turned it all the way to the left until there was absolutely no sound being emitted. The sense of frenzy diminished a bit, and he took a deep breath.

Slowbe was looking for the sign that would inform him of the point where Interstate 90/94 split into separate highways, where 90 veered west and 94 continued north. He knew it was in the vicinity. Was he in the right lane to stay on 90? If not, would he be able to switch lanes fast enough once he saw the fork? Would he veer off in the wrong direction? Would he crash? He felt a clenching sensation in his abdomen. Finally, he caught sight of a green sign that provided the confirmation he was looking for: one and a half miles to go before the I-90/94 split. I-90, left lanes. He looked to his left, then back to the car in front of him, and then to his rearview mirror, as he nervously prepared to cross four lanes of insanely dense traffic. He would have to gun it and hope that the person in the car diagonally behind him was driving defensively. Unwittingly, he held his breath. Slowbe shot into the lane directly to his left. The maneuver was successful. He rolled his window down slightly to get some air. The sound of the highway roared. He glanced at the speedometer again, which was settled right at fifty-five. Thirty seconds later he moved sharply into the next lane, and then the next. Finally, the end was near. He could see where the highways diverged. Slowbe dashed into the lane furthest to the left and continued on toward Interstate 90. "Damn," he said, as he exhaled deeply. He took another deep breath and let it out.

It was 4:50 p.m. when Slowbe emerged from the morass of traffic. At 5:13 p.m. he noticed an ominous, pitch-black band of clouds brooding on the horizon directly in his path. The sun hovered serenely above them. A dark-red glow fanned out across the space between the setting sun and the rising swarm of clouds, lacing the storm's edge with a thin line of fiery, pulsating light. Slowbe's breathing became shallow and rapid and his stomach tensed up again. Soon, the sun dropped out of sight, leaving much of the sky a warm, evening blue. For a while, orange-red rays of light rose from behind the black clouds. The storm front continued to expand on the horizon, taking up more and more of the sky. By 5:45 p.m. the environs were completely subsumed by the rumbling, tumultuous black clouds and the torrential rain they brought with them.

Slowbe felt compelled to keep driving, even though he noticed other cars pulled over onto the shoulder of the highway. He could barely see the road ahead, except for the faint red taillights of the eighteen-wheeler that was traveling fifty to sixty feet in front of him. All he had to do, he told himself, was go straight and stay focused on the taillights—close enough to see them, but not so close as to be overwhelmed with spray from the tires. The truck was moving at a speed he could keep up with in these conditions, under fifty. Other eighteen-wheelers didn't seem to be experiencing any difficulty, and when they sped by in the left lane, which happened several times, Slowbe's car was doused, and his visibility temporarily went to zero.

Almost mindlessly, Slowbe trudged forward, resisting the option to pull over and wait out the storm. His body was rigidly angled forward, inches away from the steering wheel. His eyes were peeled and completely fixed. The windshield wipers, set on the highest speed, raced furiously back and forth in a vain attempt to keep the water at bay. Slowbe hoped that because the storm had moved in so fast, and because he was moving in the opposite direction, it would pass by him in a reasonable amount of time; and it did. In about thirty-five minutes, the storm was in his rearview mirror and he could look up and see a smattering of stars in the nighttime sky. He drove for another hour, intent on making it across the border into Wisconsin on the first leg of his journey. He pulled off the highway at the first town he came to once he crossed into Wisconsin: Janesville, a good stopping point after a long day of driving.

Slowbe entered the parking lot of the Red Lion Motel, a half mile off the exit. There were a dozen or so other cars in the parking lot. As he eased into an empty space, his headlights illuminated a large lavender bush and the reflection of his car shone in the windows of a ground-floor room. Slowbe turned off the lights and the ignition and sat motionless for several moments. He rubbed his eyes and let out a long sigh. He slowly got out of his car and started walking toward the motel entrance, which was just around the corner from where he was parked. The glass doors opened automatically as he approached, and he entered the lobby.

A young lady, a little heavyset, with brown hair and an easygoing smile, was standing behind the front desk.

"Hi," she said, as they made eye contact.

"Hello," Slowbe replied.

"And how are you this evening?"

"Oh, I'm doing ok...and you?"

"Just fine, thank you. How can I help you?"

"I'd like to get a room for tonight. How much are they?"

"Ninety-five dollars."

"Ok," Slowbe said.

The lady reached beneath the counter and handed Slowbe a one-page form.

"If you could just fill this out, please," she said.

Slowbe wrote down the make, model, and license plate number of his car, initialed and signed the document, and then placed his credit card on the form.

"What's the checkout time?" he asked.

"Eleven o'clock, and there's coffee and donuts down here in the morning. You're in room 213. Just go back through these doors, up the stairs, take a left and it's right there."

She handed Slowbe his room key.

"Great, thanks," Slowbe said. "Is there some sort of mini-mart nearby, within walking distance?"

"Yeah, real close. See that parking lot over there across the street?"

Slowbe nodded.

"Go on across the parking lot, and when you get to the sidewalk start walking that way," she said as she gestured to the left, "and walk down two blocks and you'll see it. It's called Grace Market."

"Thanks," Slowbe replied.

Slowbe returned to his car, pulled out his duffel bag, and proceeded up the stairs. He entered the room and dropped his bag on the floor next to the queen-sized bed. It was covered with a thick, beige-colored blanket. Across from it were a desk and a flat-screen TV that hung from the wall. Slowbe ambled toward the windows, beside which was a reading chair with a footstool. He pulled up the blinds and looked outside at his car.

All of his belongings were packed into the vehicle: an acoustic guitar; his bass guitar and amplifier; a micro thumb drive containing hundreds of his poems and recordings; microphones and recording equipment; his wardrobe; and several boxes of books and other documents, including a signed first-edition copy of Riviere's *Treatise on Singularism*. The furnishings, kitchenware, and other household items from the New York City loft he'd rented since 2033 had been donated to Goodwill. It's amazing, he thought, how much of one's life and sense of identity can be contained in such a small area, represented by so few things. Am I definable? If not, then who and what am I if I am not defined by anything? Or am I defined by so many things that ultimately it becomes impossible to categorize me? The soul is limitless. If I define myself am I limiting myself? The soul defies definition. Who am I when I am stark naked and alone in the world? When everything is stripped away the only thing that remains is pure essence. What is the essence?

Slowbe walked out into the night. It was quiet. He could see emanations from a few houses in the distance and imagined the inhabitants going about their evening routines: sitting together or in separate rooms, possibly surfing the internet, maybe reading a book or listening to music, relaxing. Or perhaps there was strife and abuse occurring, hidden from public view. He noticed the stars glistening. They seemed to be glazed over and dripping with moisture.

It took him five minutes to get to his destination. When he entered the market, the sound of a bright, high-pitched bell rang out twice in quick succession. He immediately noticed the clerk, who was a tall young woman. She wore a red-and-white University of Wisconsin T-shirt and her brown hair was tied back. She seemed a bit distant, a little preoccupied. Maybe she was just an introverted person, Slowbe thought. There was no one else in the store. He walked by the clerk on his way toward the refrigerated section, looked her in the eyes, and gave her an empathetic smile. He felt fortunate when her closed mouth spread into a slight grin, just perceptible enough for Slowbe to feel connected to her.

He approached the cold beer section, slid open the glass door, and pulled out a twelve-pack of Heineken. Slowbe walked up to the counter. The clerk smiled again, this time slightly broader.

"Is this all?" she asked in a reserved voice.

"Yes," Slowbe replied.

He gave her a twenty-dollar bill.

"How's it going tonight?" he asked.

The clerk shrugged her shoulders slightly and lowered her eyelids as she gave Slowbe his change.

"Take care," Slowbe said.

"You too," the clerk replied.

On his return to the motel he stopped for a moment beneath a streetlight. He looked down at his reflection in a puddle of water. What are you? he thought. A violet-colored spark shone for an instant in the small body of water. Slowbe looked up at the brightly lit nighttime sky. He noticed the Big Dipper, and then the North Star. He looked back toward the puddle and tapped the center of it with the front tip of his shoe. Ripples gently spread out in concentric circles. The smell of the air was clean and refreshing. He continued walking at a leisurely pace toward the motel.

The second he entered his room, he placed the twelve-pack on the ground, opened it up, and grabbed a can of beer. He pulled back the tab, put the can to his lips, and tilted his head back. Twelve seconds later he slung the empty can into the trash bin. Without pause he pulled out another beer, which was dispatched in the exact same manner. He picked up the remaining beers and walked over to the bed. Now he could slow the pace down a little bit and settle in. He felt the warm, tingling sensation of the alcohol in his body. It had already begun to subtly change his perception of the world, himself, and reality as he opened up the next beer and began to drink. He looked at the clock: 8:53 p.m.

Slowbe opened his laptop and went to the CNN website. His eyes squinted, his mouth opened slightly, and his brow grew tense. At 1:29 p.m. Eastern Standard Time the United Nations building in New York City had been completely destroyed while the General Assembly was in session. UN ambassadors from 193 nations were presumed dead. The loss of life could be over a thousand.

Amidst a hail of gunfire, a black BMW sport utility vehicle with tinted windows and Ontario license plates, driving at a high speed, had broken through the police barricade at East Forty-Fifth Street and Second Avenue and moments later had crashed into the front entrance of the nearly one-hundred-year-old building. An explosion shook the city streets for tens of blocks, producing a mind-numbing sound. Almost instantly thereafter a dark-red ball of fire engulfed the building. The explosives pulverized the structure, leaving a massive crater. As Slowbe stared at the laptop, his eyes welled up and he began to feel a slight headache. He had a terrible feeling of foreboding.

Slowbe had always had a great affinity and reverence for the United Nations. Although its power had never been great (and had even been in steady decline in the twenty-first century due to a sharp rise in nationalism), and despite the fact that it was often scoffed at and ridiculed as being ineffectual, Slowbe saw the United Nations as a tangible and down-to-earth expression of idealism, a general model for a more enlightened society, and a symbol of the prospect of peace and human cooperation. He believed a peace among nations was crucial for the future welfare and prosperity of humankind, and that a compelling international body was needed to serve as a facilitator and mechanism in order for this to come about. The United Nations could have evolved to become such an entity, he thought.

Slowbe believed in the fundamental genius of idealism. He viewed it as a tool that opened doors; allowed for potential to come to fruition; created high evolutionary standards; and set the stage for transcending mediocrity, the status quo, and apathy. No progress or positive social change; no rise of humanitarianism; no fruitful, illuminated vision had ever emerged without idealism. The United Nations, like the United States, had been born from idealism. It had been designed to be a vehicle for the creation of a better world, and if it was not the most potent institution for this purpose, it could have served as the model for a better design. Slowbe refused to accept that the human race was incapable of devising plans that ensured the general welfare of all nations and all humans. Anything less was underachievement. He continued to drink, and he mourned the strife. The problem, the behavior, was not inherent. It was learned.

Slowbe went from one website to another, watching the story unfold and listening to commentary from around the world. He was shocked by the level of suspicion, by the accusations that raged, and by the immediacy of the political fallout. A number of commentators pointed out that there were many states represented in the General Assembly and the Security Council that might privately view the occurrence as an opportunity to loosen the reins of perceived UN restrictions. In rapid succession, within hours of the event, nation after nation suspended their UN membership and activities. Slowbe was also shocked, like everyone else, by the completeness of the physical devastation.

In the years leading up to this terrible moment, the socio-political climate, like the earth's average temperature, had become hotter and hotter and more and more stress inducing. Struggles over water rights, pollution rights, energy resources, and economic inequality had citizens and nations huddled together in separate defensive postures, like herds of musk oxen, distrustful. Overpopulation; yearly crop failures; species extinction; bizarre and unsettling animal behavior (including cross-species mating, suicides among land mammals and birds, and unusual migration patterns); and increasingly deadly hurricanes, tornadoes, and typhoons had frayed society's nerves and had created a general sense of unease, and even desperation.

Slowbe sat at the edge of the bed. His mind wandered into the past, to Woodrow Wilson, the twenty-eighth president of the United States. Wilson's main political goal, and his life's ambition, had been the creation of a League of Nations and the establishment of world peace. The former had come to fruition in 1920, lasting for twenty-six years until it was replaced by the United Nations following World War II. Sometimes a human's vision is greater than the human himself, or herself, Slowbe thought, as Wilson was known to have been stricken with the spiritual and psychological disorder of racism. But, to his credit, the former president believed that world peace, as a practical matter, was possible. "We are citizens of the world... the tragedy of our times is that we do not know this," he'd once said.

Slowbe's mind continued to drift into the history of war and peace. He thought about the Kellogg-Briand Pact, also known as the Treaty for Renunciation of War. It always surprised him that he'd never met a single soul who'd heard of the accord, which was passed in the U.S. Senate by a vote of 85–1, and which, on August 27th, 1928, was ratified by sixty-two nations. Authored by Frank B. Kellogg, the U.S. secretary of state under President Herbert Hoover, and Aristide Briand, the French foreign minister of the time, the treaty had earned Kellogg the Nobel Peace Prize in 1929. The accord was ahead of its time, Slowbe thought, just like the founding documents of the United States of America were ahead of their time. Kellogg-Briand had made world peace a feature of international law, but it had a fatal weakness: there was no mechanism for its enforcement. And so it went that in 1931 Japan invaded Manchuria, in 1935 Italy invaded Ethiopia, and in 1939 Germany invaded Poland. In 1945, on the heels of World War II, the Kellogg-Briand Pact was reaffirmed under article

2, paragraph 4, of the newly created United Nations Charter. Nonetheless, the treaty slipped into the lightless, subterranean spaces of history. The fact of the matter was that it was still a binding treaty under international law and federal law in the United States under article 6 of the U.S. Constitution.

After noting in its preamble "a solemn duty to promote the welfare of mankind," the accord put forth three articles, of which Slowbe found two particularly poignant. Article 1 stated, "The High Contracting Parties solemnly declare in the names of their respective peoples that they condemn recourse to war for the solution of international controversies, and renounce it, as an instrument of national policy in their relations with one another." Article 2 stated, "The High Contracting Parties agree that the settlement or solution of all disputes or conflicts of whatever nature or of whatever origin they may be, which may arise among them, shall never be sought except by pacific means." To Slowbe, the pact was an enlightened statement for all times.

In Slowbe's view, Woodrow Wilson, the Kellogg-Briand Pact, the UN Charter, and the United Nations legitimized the idea that world peace was a reasonable objective—one that individuals who were generally sound, intelligent, and down-to-earth had proposed, and could propose. With the destruction of the United Nations, something heroic had just vanished. Even if it had not been powerful, it had at least served as a modest counterweight to the forces of aggression and as a beacon of humanitarianism. Slowbe viewed more coverage. There was a great deal of speculation regarding who might be responsible, and there were many condemnations of the act. A little after 1:00 a.m., feeling uncomfortable and uncertain, Slowbe turned off the lights in his room. He lay down on the bed, pulled the blanket over his body, and fell asleep.

The Long Dream

The poet is walking along the ocean in the early morning on a clear, warm day. He is alone. Time slows. Spiraling colors surround him. I am an expression, he thinks to himself, a brushstroke on a vast canvas. On the cliffs near the ocean, he sees a group of men and women diving off a waterfall into the inlet below. He thinks the waterfall must be two hundred feet high. After each dive the men and women swim out of the water and climb the rocks so they may dive again. Some of them wave at him, and he waves back. He wonders how it is that they don't lose their balance as they stand atop the waterfall, as the water rushes. It starts to rain, a very hard rain, but he is not getting wet. He looks up and, in amazement, sees a starry sky. As he is looking at the sky, an old man floats up to the shore in a small rowboat. The old man is strangely familiar to the poet. Somehow the poet knows his name to be Fortuno. The old man says that they must go fishing. Soon, they are out in the open sea. The poet is apprehensive. "We are going to have to go into the water," Fortuno says. The poet is reluctant, but after seeing the old man dive in he soon follows. He is underwater. I have to find peace, he thinks to himself. He emerges atop the waterfall with the men and women. One of them tells the poet that there is no future and no past, only the timeless, infinite present moment. A woman holds the poet's hand and they leap and soar above the earth.

The woman is gone and a door appears. He opens the door and walks into a nicely decorated room. There are paintings, large pillows, lit candles, and other people in the room. The people are sitting on the pillows in a circle. No one is talking, and there is music playing. He walks around the room observing the various paintings, and then turns toward the group and notices that they are all looking at him as if to say, "We know you." There is something about their eyes; they don't seem terrestrial. It seems as if their appearance as humans is a disguise. Their eyes give them away. The poet walks among them and realizes their gathering is some sort of communion. He is at ease, he feels cared for. He walks over to the window and sees a lake. He closes his eyes and when he reopens them he is sitting by the lake, quietly, with his legs crossed.

A golden eagle swoops down, grabs a fish, and is gone. The poet says aloud, "align with the sun; be the sun; it is the source." Two more golden eagles swoop down, quickly, one after the other. He looks across the lake and sees another golden eagle perched on an oak tree. He sees the eagle's eyes. It is looking back at him. It bursts into flame and is gone. The poet turns around and notices a skyscraper. I was in there, how did I get down here? he asks himself. A little girl approaches him. "There is an invisible sun," she says to the poet.

He is in a van. Angel Song is driving and Joseph Henry is in the passenger seat. The poet is trying to string his guitar, but there is a large cougar in the van that keeps getting in his way. They arrive at Larch Mountain, get out of the van, and walk into the forest. The cougar is no longer with them. A man and a woman emerge. They tell the trio that they have come into this forest to get married, and they ask if the three wanderers will marry them. The man and the woman face Angel, Joseph, and the poet. Joseph plays the flute, and the poet plays a hand drum. "Into this forest you have come, now you are one," Angel says. The man and woman rejoice. Joseph and the poet continue to play music. It is night, and they are driving down the mountain. They stop at a park along the Columbia River. They sit near the river and are looking at each other. The poet asks Angel, "Where am I?" She smiles. They begin skipping stones across the river. There are violet-colored sparks each time a stone touches the water. The poet gets into a canoe and starts paddling up the river. He is gripping the paddles tightly. He cannot let go. He hears Angel shouting from the river's edge, "Turn around, the river flows west." He turns the canoe around and resolves to release his grip on the paddles. He lets go. The paddles drop with a loud splash and then disappear into the river. "Beautiful river, I will go with you," he whispers serenely.

The poet is walking alone through a dense forest. He has a heavy backpack. It's raining, and the ground is muddy, and his feet are getting stuck. He has been in the forest for hours, he thinks. Up ahead he sees an open field, but there is a long, thick row of thornbushes between him and the field. He walks up to the wall of thornbushes. He stands there for several minutes, realizing he must push his way through. After a short time, he has made his way into the open field. There are cuts on his face and arms. He is relieved. The grassy field rolls. The tall green grasses wave. The rain has stopped.

Lillian Red Horse is standing on top of a small hill. He can't see her clearly, but he knows it's her. He walks toward her. They embrace and she tells him that the sweat lodge is nearby, that he should go to the sweat lodge. There are six heavy rocks in his backpack. "Give them to the fire keeper," she says. Two old men stand at the entrance to the lodge. The poet pulls out the six rocks from his backpack and places them in a basket that the man nearest the entrance is holding. "I will go with you into the lodge and place the rocks in the pit, then I will leave you," the old man says. The other man, whose eyes are green like a pine tree, nods in the direction of the entrance. The poet enters. It is hot and dark.

He is sitting under a willow tree with Lillian and it's a beautiful summer day. He is growing calmer. There is a full moon in the blue sky. "When I was younger, I thought I knew what a dream was, now that I'm older it's all the same," she says. The poet looks around. A scent reminds him of some place he's been before. "What did you see in the sweat lodge?" Lillian asks. "A grey wolf appeared to me," he says. "It was very large; it walked up to me and kissed me on the cheek. I began to cry. I heard a voice ask me what I knew about the six rocks I had been carrying. I said they each had a name: they were fear, resentment, conceit, greed, shame, and doubt."

He returns to the sweat lodge. He looks at the pit of burning rocks. They are moving toward him, getting larger. The lodge disappears. He is descending into a massive cave with large columns and glowing red walls. He sees himself. He has the head of a black wolf, and there are tendons and sinews hanging from his mouth. He is standing behind one of the columns and discs are being hurled at him. Although he is fearful, he moves away from the protection of the column. His head is severed by a disc. He sees a black wolf lying dead on the ground beside him.

He begins to float upward. His head and neck emerge out of the ground as if they have broken through a canvas. The rest of his body emerges. The sky is very blue and very bright. He sees a young man running wistfully along a winding stream and several others dancing in a circle beneath a tree. It is a pastoral scene. Titian or Giorgione must have painted this, he thinks to himself. It all seems familiar. It reminds him of a feeling. It is very real. He sits down on the grass listening to music. There is a festival not far in the distance. Several men dressed like scholars are walking down a pathway toward him. They are carrying books and are engaged in discussion. "The electron has a different perspective than the proton," says one. "It is not a matter of good or bad, it is simply a matter of positive and negative." "I am partial to the proton," says another. "Here, here," they all say. The poet sees a hummingbird feeding from a daylily. In the blink of an eye, the bird has left the flower and has come to within a foot of the poet. The wind is gusting and raindrops have begun to fall. He can hear the deep, swooshing buzz of the bird's wings. He feels its penetrating attention. After several long, captive moments the hummingbird flies away in a swirling dash. The wind stops and the raindrops cease. It's all connected, he thinks. He looks at the sun. He knows he must obey his conscience. He knows there is a seer who sees through his eyes.

Violet light is flashing and there is a strange oval cloud in the sky. He looks and sees dandelions on the grassy foothills and three wizened ladies admiring the foliage. "The mountain I am climbing has no summit, only ever-increasing views," he says aloud. The violet light is flashing. He hears a soft, murmuring voice from behind him, within him. It is soothing. The voice says to him, "Learn to interact with it, don't simply observe. There is nothing in Creation for you to fear."

The sky is aflame with gold and red clouds gently rolling eastward like a steady ocean current. A man on a bicycle rides by and then stops. "Have you ever seen anything like that before?" he asks the poet. "Not exactly," the poet says. "It's amazing," the man says. "And look over there, a rainbow." The poet smiles: "Yes, it really is amazing." The two strangers gaze, recognizing something remarkable. The poet says quietly to himself, "This is the world I live in. This is what I bear witness to. This is what it is my honor to behold. This is my human experience. I am fortunate." The man prepares to ride off and says, "Glad to have shared this with you." The poet is struck by the comment. It seems enlightened. "Yes," he says, as he watches the gentle man ride off. Perhaps there are no strangers, he thinks; we stand in the face of great beauty and grandeur and we are united, our human connection is made more recognizable. He bows his head and says, "To all that is greater than myself, to all that is beyond my understanding, to all that I am a part of, this is my intention: that I will not bear grudges or hold resentments against my fellow human beings, that I will embrace patience, that I will show love to myself and my fellow human beings, that I will trust and have faith in myself and in Creation, that I will let go of life as it arises and anchor myself in the eternal present moment."

He sees himself in a nighttime sky. He sees the details of his face. His arms and legs are stretched out like the Vitruvian Man. He is pulsating with light. He looks at himself. The stars are like atoms. It is now recognizable. He closes his eyes and sees the universe.

Evolutionary Thinking

On the morning of Wednesday, March 4th, 2048, Slowbe got up a little earlier than his usual 7:00 a.m. Since the January 21st release of his book *The World Within*, he'd traveled extensively in the United States doing speaking engagements and book signings. He was glad to be back in Oregon for a while and was looking forward to spending a few days at the coast. A slight breeze entered his bedroom as he got up and walked over to his east-facing windows. What a peculiar story, he thought to himself. Across the Willamette Valley, about ninety miles in the distance, Slowbe could see Mt. Hood. It was surrounded by a light-red hue. He'd been hiking near the mountain two days ago, on the Eagle Creek Trail.

Slowbe opened his windows all the way. For a moment he thought about a young girl, nine or ten years of age he guessed, and two women, who'd walked by him as he stood near Punchbowl Falls. "I don't always have to be thinking something," he heard the girl say. "Very true, Adeline," one of the women replied. Slowbe was amazed to hear a child say such a thing. How had she learned that it was possible to just be, to clear the mind, to experience inner stillness and quiet? Most of the people Slowbe had met over the years believed that the mind never ceased being in motion, or that it was simply too hard, or impossible, to make it pacific, even for a moment. Of course, many people, including Slowbe for much of his life, didn't have a sincere desire for a still or quiet mind, much preferring (consciously and/or unconsciously) distraction and unending stimulus response, if not outright mental obsession, compulsion, and hyperactivity. Over time, Slowbe had liberated himself from the fear and discomfort of being alone in an empty mind. He was no longer compelled to be in the company of even a single thought; but it had taken practice, and self-examination, and letting go, and a willingness to realign his ego. His mind had become less like rush-hour traffic through Chicago and more like Interstate 90 through Montana. He'd become oriented toward a boundless realm of silence amidst vibration, of stillness amidst flowing energy, which originated within and expanded outwardly. Perhaps the girl knew, or would know, that when the mind is uncongested and clear and untethered, like a wide-open space, like Big Sky Country, there is room for the present moment's infinitude to reveal itself in one's experience. Perhaps the girl would learn that the content of the mind determined one's experience; that the mind was an engine of creation and manifestation; and that the more spacious and unobstructed the mind, the more one was able to consciously harness and direct its power and energy.

Slowbe walked downstairs to his kitchen to make some tea and have something to eat. He'd fasted the day before, so he was particularly hungry. He took the teapot that was sitting on the beige-tiled kitchen island and held it under the faucet until there was more than enough water to fill the twenty-four-ounce glass jar that he always used for drinking water and tea. After he placed the pot back on its base and set it to boil, he filled his jar with cold water and drank it all down in one steady motion. He could feel his body being hydrated. The sensation was both calming and energizing. Slowbe opened the brown wood pantry in the corner to the left of the sink and collected two bags of green tea, a bottle of olive oil, a small loaf of Pugliese bread, and two slightly overripe bananas. Although he didn't really like the texture of bananas that had a lot of brown spots, he didn't want to throw them away; and so he planned on eating them quickly. At least, he considered for a moment, being somewhat overripe, they would be particularly high in antioxidants, like the green tea he was about to drink. He placed everything on the kitchen island and opened the tea packaging, gnawing off the string that was attached to each tea bag before dropping the bags into his jar.

Slowbe poured a large portion of olive oil onto a black plate, broke the Pugliese bread into four chunks, and sat down at the brass-framed glass-top dining table that was parallel to, and six feet from, the kitchen island. He smeared the first piece of bread in the oil and began to eat. After a couple minutes, the pot started whistling and a cloud of steam drifted upward. Slowbe began to fill the jar up with water again. While he was doing so, he glanced momentarily at the grey stone fountain that stood in the foyer adjacent to his kitchen. A gentle rippling sound emanated from it as water flowed down its three round columns. It was one of his favorite possessions—a gift from Lillian Red Horse.

Slowbe had always strongly identified with water, and some of his fondest memories from childhood and adolescence were connected to it: swimming, diving, swirling in the Scioto River, swiping his hands across the surface of the river and watching how it moved in response. "I'm very aquatic," he said to his mother one summer afternoon when he was ten years old. She raised her right eyebrow, nodded her head, and with a slight grin said, "Ok," amused and a bit surprised by his description of himself.

At some point in his early twenties, he started to think more deeply about his connection with, and reliance on, water—how his body was made mostly of water, and how it gave him, and all the flora, and all the fauna, life. In Slowbe's imaginative, poetic mind it had almost a mystical and legendary quality. And so, perhaps naturally, he eventually likened it to ambrosia, a liquid that the gods on Mt. Olympus drank. It was their primary form of sustenance. "The distance between a human and a god is not far," he once noted in his journal, "just a ripple in time and space. The soul is a god, and it takes physical form on earth and is called a human. The mind and ego can awaken to the presence of the soul, and then everything changes—perspective, identity, potential."

Soon after he got sober in 2041, Slowbe began a ritual of taking a moment to drink a large glass of water when he woke up in the morning. The idea of embracing this daily ritual came to him while he was attending a three-day workshop in Seattle entitled "Addressing Emotional, Psychological, and Spiritual Trauma at the Individual and Collective Levels: How Past and Current Trauma Affect Behavior and the Ability to Fully Self-Actualize." During one of the sessions an old Native American man stood up and spoke. He explained how every morning when he awoke he would pour himself a glass of water and step onto his deck and take several deep breaths, give thanks to his Creator, and drink his water while he admired the hills surrounding his home. The old man talked about how he was grateful for the water and how it connected him to something greater than himself, and how his morning ritual was an acknowledgment of something sacred, as well as a health-conscious act for his mind and body.

Slowbe sat at the table with his jar of tea and opened his Array. Frequently referred to as a "genius phone" and hailed as a miracle of modern technology, the Array had become a ubiquitous feature of society since it was first made available to the public in 2040. By opening the device, which was usually about 2.5 by 5 inches and 7 millimeters thick and looked like nothing more than a smooth piece of glass, one could access high-definition holographic replications with which one was able to carry out an enormous variety of tasks. In addition, one could access a three-dimensional portal within the instrument, or view information and images two-dimensionally on the face of the device. Each of these modes, and their various functions, were responsive to voice and touch command. The Array was a groundbreaking advancement that encompassed a range of disciplines, including artificial intelligence, computing, holographic and virtual reality technology, communication, and information technology. In addition, it had extraordinary capacity as a scientific instrument. For the average citizen, it was a commodity that raised their awareness and understanding of the world exponentially and even allowed them to "see" the atomic and molecular structure of physical reality.

After a brief search through an international forum portal, Slowbe stopped on a video from Jeddah, Saudi Arabia. In it a young woman spoke passionately: "Brazil, Argentina, and Paraguay fight over the damming of the Paraná River," she said. "Syria, Jordan, and Israel also fight over water resources; and the Israeli-Palestinian conflict continues. Afghanistan and Pakistan are at war over use of the Kabul River. Civil, religious, and water conflicts rage in Somalia, Niger, Cameroon, Namibia, Angola, Tanzania, Burundi, Sudan, Zambia, and the Democratic Republic of the Congo. Since 2036 close to seven million Africans have died from starvation due to drought and conflicts over water rights. Today, I am one of thousands of people in Jeddah who are gathered to demand an end to the UN Interregnum, and to demand that the Kellogg-Briand Pact be renewed." Her posting then went to a video montage of scenes from all the areas in the world affected by war and water shortages. Slowbe watched two more postings: one on solar power technology from a young lady in Chengdu, China, and another on the deforestation crisis from an elderly man in Budapest, Hungary. Slowbe closed the Array and continued drinking his tea. When he was finished, he started gathering some items for his trip. The forecast for the coast was sunny and warm.

Slowbe was waiting outside when Dara Sangree, whom he'd known since his college days, arrived at his house just after

8:00 a.m. When she saw Slowbe, her face lit up and her green eyes seemed to glisten. Slowbe, as always, was captivated by her presence. Both her beauty and her persona were striking, unusual, even otherworldly, he thought. Sangree had tan skin and straight brown hair that came down six inches past her shoulders. And although her ancestry was primarily English, Greek, and Mexican, she had a slight epicanthic fold that hinted at a distant Mongolian bloodline. She had bow-shaped lips and a soft, rounded chin. Her eyebrows were thick and dark and she had long eyelashes. She was eccentric and a bit of a loner, although very warmhearted, sincere, and playful.

During the mid-thirties, she'd gained international acclaim as a photographer, and later as an author of two works of fiction, both written in the genre of the philosophical novel; the second of these, *The Vague Mountain*, had won the Nobel Prize in Literature in 2046, the same year she moved to Portland from New York City. *The Vague Mountain* was the story of a small, isolated village and a mysterious woman named Diotima who arrives as the village is convulsing in turmoil over the disappearance of three girls following an eclipse of the sun. Sangree pulled the character Diotima from a work by Plato called *Symposium*. In Plato's tale, a small group of Athenian men, the comedian Aristophanes and the philosopher Socrates among them, sit at a banquet at the house of a man named Agathon. Instead of getting drunk (as they normally would at such gatherings), the men decide to go around the table and each give an oration in praise of love. When it is Socrates's turn, he mentions that a seer named Diotima had taught him, when he was young, about the philosophy of love. What struck Sangree when she first read the work was not that love was referred to as a god, and the oldest of gods no less, but that the men referred to it in the masculine.

With *The Vague Mountain*, Sangree explored the creative and organizing power of belief and its capacity to expand or restrict the scope of experience. She described it as being both a key to opening the door to new worlds, realities, and possibilities, and a psychological mechanism that shapes the dynamics of experience. "As the belief changes, so too does the personal and/or collective reality," Diotima says. "Examine your beliefs about yourself, your society, and the nature of reality, because your experience of yourself, society, life, and reality faithfully mirrors your beliefs. Life will be limited or expansive in accordance with the nature of the belief."

As described in *The Vague Mountain*, belief was not the same as faith. Belief was a psychic device, an internal lens that emanated a magnetic-like energy around which experience coalesced, for better or for worse, attracting either enlightenment or ignorance, self-actualization or internalized oppression, prosperity or poverty, peace or war, shaping destiny and the events of daily life. On one occasion, Diotima compares belief to the paints and brushes of the artist's workshop. Reality, she explains, is the canvas upon which the paints and brushes are applied, and experience is the picture that appears from their application; and she emphasizes that the artist is distinct from, and transcends, the paints, the brushes, and the picture. When these relationships are understood, the breadth of mental energy and the creative power of belief can be fully actualized. A human may look at their experience just as an artist may look at their painting and say, "I see myself in my art, it reflects my state of being, and it tells me something about myself; I can learn about myself from my art; and I can change my art if I use different paints, brushes, brushstrokes, and techniques."

The novel was also a meditation on the idea of love as an aggressive, permeating force; the catalyst behind all creativity and all creations; an amalgamating phenomenon analogous to the fundamental interactions that bind all things in the physical universe, namely, gravity, weak nuclear force, strong nuclear force, and electromagnetism. Love did not have an opposite; it was simply a binding, generative force. It was not restricted to emotional experience, but existed above and beyond that. It was a higher, pervasive form of energy that was fundamentally positive.

Sangree got out of her blue Tesla.

"There was a coyote that ran across the road as I was about to turn into your driveway," she said.

"Really?" Slowbe asked with mild surprise. "I've had a couple coyote sightings in the last month or so."

"I've never seen one in the city before," Sangree said.

"There's some wildlife up here. One of my neighbors told me he's seen elk, and the occasional bobcat."

"That's amazing," Sangree said, as she looked over at the collection of goods sitting at the base of Slowbe's porch. "Is that everything you're bringing?" she asked.

"Yeah," Slowbe responded.

"Great. Shall we?" Sangree said, gesturing toward the items. "Yes."

They began loading the acoustic guitar, backpack, duffel bag, and two bags of food into her trunk. Within a few minutes, they were heading down the winding road from Slowbe's home in the hills on the western edge of the city. The road led them to downtown Portland, and they soon approached the congested on-ramp at Southwest Sixth Avenue that would put them on U.S. Route 26 to the Oregon coast. Once they got on the highway, things moved smoothly. Twenty-five minutes later they were outside the Portland metropolitan area. They continued west, and the scenery gradually changed from pastoral farmland and rolling hills, to pine-laden woodlands, to coastal mountain range. An hour after leaving Portland, they connected with Highway 101 and headed south along the Pacific Ocean. They drove for another twenty-four miles until they arrived at the town of Nehalem, population 251.

It was getting close to 10:00 a.m. when they turned down Sitka Lane and pulled into the unpaved driveway leading to Slowbe's cottage. His was one of only four addresses on the secluded dead-end road. The small residence, which Slowbe had purchased in mid-February, was surrounded by shore pine, except for the open ocean view to the west. The entrance faced north, and there was a deck along the west and south walls. It was a single-story, all-wood structure with two bedrooms, a living room, a kitchen and bath, and a sliding glass door that opened to the west-facing section of the deck.

The sound of the ocean coursed in the distance. Slowbe and Sangree got out of the vehicle. They gathered a few items and entered the cottage. Sangree placed her backpack on the end table next to the front door and went to use the bathroom. Slowbe brought the two bags of food into the kitchen and then returned to the car to finish unpacking; and when it was his turn, he used the bathroom as well. After everything was settled, they loaded some water, fruit, bread, and hummus into Slowbe's backpack and got back into the car, as planned, and headed toward a favorite trail, Neahkahnie Mountain, seven miles north on 101. In the Tillamook language, which had died in the 1970s, *Neah-kah-nie* meant "the place of the supreme deity."

As Slowbe and Sangree started on the trail, they could hear seagulls calling nearby. There were no clouds in the sky and it was an unseasonably warm seventy degrees.

"I had an interesting dream last week," Sangree said.

Slowbe took his eyes off the trees and other plant life along the path and turned to look at Sangree.

"I was in a room with my parents. I don't really remember much of what was going on. My father was sitting on a chair, he was smiling, and then he said to my mother, 'We'll wait until they understand evolutionary thinking.' That's really all I remember. I think they were watching the news...but I'm really taken by this phrase 'evolutionary thinking.'"

"So, what does that mean?" Slowbe asked.

"Well, maybe it refers to thinking that engenders paradigm shifts," she said.

"Yeah," Slowbe replied, "or harmony or enlightenment..."

They approached a large fir tree that had fallen across the trail. It was covered with moss and had dark ridges and caverns where a patch of ferns were growing. Slowbe took Sangree's hand and helped her step over the lush, dead tree.

"Humans evolve on so many levels, in addition to the biological," Sangree added, "which isn't really the case with other species. We also have the capacity to consciously drive our evolution. I think that part is amazing."

"Absolutely," Slowbe said. "It is amazing that we actually have what one might call 'evolutionary agency.' There's a lot of responsibility that goes with that." He paused for a moment. "I remember I went through a phase in my late twenties, for a couple months, where I was asking people if they thought the solutions to our problems as a society were primarily political, social, or, quote unquote, spiritual, or in which area was change or growth most crucial for society. I only recall one person ever saying 'political'; it was always one of the latter two."

"I guess, at some point, the answer has to be all three," Sangree said. "We need to evolve on all three of those levels, and we have the creative license and authority to do so."

"I agree," Slowbe said.

"If I had to pick one, though, I would say the spiritual because I think it speaks most completely to who and what we are, in the big picture. It could be argued that the spiritual encompasses, or at least influences, every possible dimension of human evolution...even biological, technological, and scientific."

Sangree didn't avoid using the term "spiritual," as Slowbe had become inclined to do. Although he felt the word was poetic in a way, and by and large had positive connotations, he generally thought it was clichéd and archaic. In his thinking on the nature of reality, the idea of spirituality seemed too compartmentalized, not pragmatic or existential enough. Nevertheless, he did occasionally rely on the term, simply because it was part of the common vernacular and there was a general, if vague, understanding of what it referred to. He knew people, Lillian Red Horse, for example, who asserted that "everything is spiritual." He'd never asked her what exactly she meant by this, or what she felt was implied in the statement, but he had a sense that, to her, "spiritual" encompassed a set of interrelated ideas—specifically, that existence was a process of growth and learning and creation and discovery; that love was a founding principle; that the underlying nature of reality was non-corporeal and infinite; that there was meaning in all things; that peace, harmony, and balance were of the essence; and that consciousness was pervasive and immortal. For Slowbe, all of this was true; but there was no need for a label, one that invariably had religious overtones. He simply thought in terms of truth, potential, and the nature of things—and his basic assumption was that these matters were associated with infinitude.

A red-and-green hummingbird suddenly appeared on the trail, hovering about seven feet above the ground and a few feet directly in front of Sangree and Slowbe, close enough for them to hear the furious woosh of its flapping wings. They both stopped and stood motionless. The creature zipped up, down, and to the left as it inspected, or attempted to relay a message to, the pair of hikers. After a few moments, it moved into a spot almost perfectly centered between Slowbe and Sangree, a little over two feet in front of them and eye level with Sangree, who stood five feet, nine inches tall. It hovered for close to fifteen seconds. Then, in an instant, it spirited off and disappeared into the forest.

"Amazing," Slowbe said.

"That was really close," Sangree replied.

"The humming sound of its wings was incredible," Slowbe said, "intense."

"That was a good sign," Sangree said.

"Absolutely," Slowbe said.

The two resumed walking along the trail and the wind picked up.

"I would say evolutionary thinking is thinking that challenges paradigms and the status quo," Sangree said, "and seeks to expand the depth, scope, and range of human experience—thinking that describes a vision of human potential, and of true human nature. I think it must have an element of the universal, and I would say it's necessarily idealistic, necessarily optimistic. Maybe an evolutionary thinker is someone who brings the future into the present, or someone who communicates about transcendence."

After a half hour on the winding and ascending trail, in the shade of the canopy cover, Slowbe and Sangree finally came to an opening. They could now really feel the ocean air swirling about as they stood atop the 1,680-foot mountain, and they could see the ocean waves rushing in concert toward the shoreline that stretched for miles until it was interrupted by jutting capes. A group of seagulls soared close by, and in the distance cormorants dashed across the glistening water. A half-moon tilted upward in the east, surrounded by blue sky. It was a serene, yet furious, spectacle. Slowbe and Sangree sat down.

"Literally nothing in this world is as it appears," Sangree said. "It never ceases to amaze me that, relatively speaking, there's as much space between the atoms of my body as there is between the stars in the sky, and that my body is more than 99.9 percent empty space. What a beautiful illusion. Where is my conscious self if my body is so much empty space?" she said lightheartedly and somewhat rhetorically.

"In the now, and certainly not defined by, or limited to, a physical body," Slowbe said matter-of-factly. "I guess we can say that much."

"Indeed," Sangree replied. "Did you know that if you took all the atoms that form all of humanity and removed the empty space from the atoms, you could fit what's left into the volume of a sugar cube?"

Slowbe shook his head no.

"I just read that the other day."

Sangree took a deep breath and held her arms out with the palms of her hands facing upward. "Whenever I'm at the ocean," she said, "I always feel so tuned into the largeness and grandeur of everything, the earth as a huge sphere...I really sense that I'm on a planet in the cosmos. I feel the universe right here...it doesn't seem distant."

"The universe not feeling distant...I like that. There's definitely an intimacy between all things in the universe. Everything is made of the same stuff: atoms, dark matter, dark energy, molecules, et cetera, and there's this constant intermingling. The atoms that form my body now are the same atoms that were once supernovae. On one level we're of this universe, part of the whole, the single system; so there's that intimacy. But the universe is also, in a way, like a figment of our imagination, like a hologram; so, I would say that on another level the universe is of us—an outward projection of something within."

"Didn't Emerson say that 'the whole of nature is a metaphor of the human mind'?"

"He did. Perhaps he shared the view that reality is a product of consciousness. He certainly felt that the mind and the universe were akin. There are infinite ways to perceive, but without a perceiver...atoms respond to consciousness and mind. It's all very intimate," Slowbe said in a reflective tone. "The vast outer landscape rises from a remarkably more vast inner landscape."

"But if form is a projection of consciousness, and intuitively I agree with you on that, how do you respond to the observation that form appears to have existed long before human consciousness arrived?"

"Well, I'd just say that there was certainly consciousness in this universe before there was physical consciousness...and... obviously I'm not referring to any mythologies or religious fairy tales...and, of course, not all consciousness is human consciousness," Slowbe replied.

"On the one hand, we're intimate with the universe because the universe is a projection of creative consciousness, soul, or mind. And then on the other hand, we are intimate with the universe because we're from the universe and made of the physical stuff of the universe. That's a nice little contradiction."

"Both are true. Reality, like truth, is always paradoxical," Slowbe said.

"We should form a salon, Edward," Sangree said unexpectedly.

"That's an interesting idea," Slowbe replied.

"The discussions could revolve around themes or ideas found in the artworks of the participants, but maybe having a general focus on topics like idealism, creativity, human nature and potential...the nature of reality, paradigms, an exercise in evolutionary thinking. I'd also like to possibly use the salon as a focal point for some sort of social marketing campaign, or other form of social action."

"Sounds like you've been thinking about this a bit."

"I have, actually, ever since my dream."

"We should do that," Slowbe said. "I'd love to participate. Several people come to mind that might be interested: Lillian Red Horse, Angel Song, Joseph Henry, Seven."

"Definitely. We'd want to make some news."

"Of course," Slowbe said.

Sangree and Slowbe both turned their attention to the ocean below and the successive groups of waves approaching the coastline. They reminded Sangree of herds of horses running in unison. It occurred to her that a section of the Pacific Ring of Fire called the Cascadia Subduction Zone, where the Juan de Fuca tectonic plate moved east beneath the North American plate, was just fifty miles offshore. From her vantage point she estimated that the horizon was about sixty miles away. The area of the subduction zone was within her range of vision.

Sangree's memories of seismic activity were never too far

removed. She had survived the magnitude 8.0 earthquake that struck along the Ventura–Pitas Point Fault at 6:13 p.m. on June 24th, 2043. Scores of buildings collapsed in the Los Angeles metropolitan area before the arrival of the tsunami, which killed nearly one million people. She had been saved by rescue workers who airlifted her and three others from the roof of a three-story apartment building. Her friend, Arla, whom she was visiting, had not made it to safety. In the six months prior to the Los Angeles earthquake, tsunamis had also devastated Juneau, Alaska, and Tokyo, Japan, killing seventy thousand in Juneau and 2.5 million in Tokyo. The following year, Santiago, Chile, was struck by a magnitude 8.5 earthquake, which killed almost 2 million people and leveled most of the city. Another 1.5 million perished between 2045 and 2047 due to earthquakes and volcanoes along the Pacific Ring of Fire, with major events occurring near Manila, Seattle, and Jakarta.

Just past 3:00 a.m. the morning after the catastrophe in Los Angeles, Slowbe was surprised, as he lay alone in bed, by a soft, ethereal voice that said, "Don't give them money, give them power." It was a beautiful voice, unearthly, with a slight feminine quality to it, and it came from within. He had never heard voices before, although over the years he had at times longed to hear an inner guiding voice, as Socrates supposedly had. Slowbe pulled back his blanket and sat up on the side of his bed. He put his hands on his face and rubbed his forehead with the tips of his fingers. He'd been lying in his bed for several hours but had been unable to sleep. There was no cell service to Los Angeles.

Slowbe became preoccupied with the voice that had just rippled through his mind and body. He felt a relative calm—the same type of calm he felt when he looked out across the ocean and listened to the tide come in. His bedroom was almost pitch black. He sat silently, staring directly ahead. An undulating body of electromagnetic energy emerged through the blackness. It hovered like a pool of violet-colored water on a large swath of the wall before him. Heightened activity, he thought to himself. Even though his body felt largely relaxed, as he sat with his feet firmly planted on the floor and his back somewhat erect, he could still sense a thin, persistent layer of tension in his abdomen, shoulders, and neck. It was a baseline tension, always present to some degree, more often subtle than sharp. He knew its origin was psychological, and he'd been working on eliminating it from his system. Slowbe took several long, deep breaths. He clasped his hands and stretched his arms above his head, toward the ceiling.

It'd been eighteen days since he'd celebrated two years of sobriety. All the negative internal dialogues, narratives, and labels that had previously distorted his self-concept, and which had oppressed him and confined him, were beginning to get properly examined. He felt his dilemma had been fittingly depicted in a vision he once had when he was twenty-three. It was of a lion contained within a small, rectangular cage. The cage was so small that the lion's mane pressed up against the bars, and it was unable to move. The image had stuck with Slowbe. It was clear to him that it represented his own lack of psychological freedom and self-actualization. Year after year he would ask, When will I be free? How will I become free? He recognized that there was a significant portion of himself that was afraid of the power and vastness within, afraid to let go of the tension and constriction and limitations. Why is it so hard for me to acquiesce? he wondered. More and more he began to realize that the cage was self-imposed, albeit originating in childhood trauma.

Slowbe sat on his bed in his dark room. He was still in between the world of internalized oppression and the world of personal liberation. The moniker he had privately used to describe himself in prior years, "the drunk mystic," no longer applied because the drink had been removed from the equation. This revolutionary act changed the fundamental context of his life. But there was still the gnawing pang of self-doubt and the lingering addiction to negative mental and emotional states. An array of thoughts passed through Slowbe's mind as he sat in the darkness: Why am I not more than I am? Why am I not more evolved by now? he asked. There is a difference between knowing and realizing: knowing is cognitive and intellectual, realization is visceral and fully integrated awareness, he opined. I know things, but I do not realize them, he thought. Be what you know, he said to himself encouragingly, thinking that if he fully realized what he knew to be true then he would have the sense that he had found himself and was aligned with something transcendent. I am still a slave to impulse, and the foibles of my ego, he wistfully reflected.

Unbeknownst to Slowbe at the time, the Los Angeles earthquake had struck on the twentieth anniversary of Aaron Beck's death, to the very minute. Beck, renowned as the father of cognitive therapy, had lived to 102. According to the model he developed and popularized, the quality of an individual's personal experience was largely dictated by the core beliefs they held about themselves—about their worth, their efficacy, their personality traits, et cetera. These core beliefs, affirming or detrimental, were like a set of assumptions that influenced the basic character of the individual's thought patterns. One's thought patterns, then, triggered certain emotional states and behaviors, all of which reinforced the individual's core beliefs, for better or for worse, like a feedback loop. Beck's original treatment manual stated that "the philosophical origins of cognitive therapy can be traced back to the Stoic philosophers."

On a balmy afternoon in mid-May 276 BC, while speaking to a group of thirty or so individuals at the Stoa Poikile—Painted Porch—on the north side of the Agora of Athens, Zeno of Citium, the founder of Stoicism, had declared: "All things are parts of one single system, which is called Nature; the individual life is good when it is in harmony with Nature."

Slowbe was familiar with the quote. It had been printed on a pamphlet he'd picked up at an Earth Day rally in 2040 in

Lagos, Nigeria. He'd kept the pamphlet as a souvenir and it was tucked away somewhere.

Zeno's quote entered Slowbe's mind for the first time in almost three years. He began to feel an even deeper calm settle into his body, and he crossed his legs and positioned himself in the center of his bed. The violet, pulsating light had become increasingly vibrant and now covered the entire wall before him, as well as much of his peripheral view of the room. He stared directly ahead and took deep, measured breaths.

"Nature," he quietly said to himself. His conception of the word's meaning not only included the trees, the rivers, the mountains, and the fields, but also encompassed mind, body, soul, universe, and infinity. Oneness, he thought. Slowbe closed his eyes and concentrated intensely on his psychic body. Eventually, he was able to induce a deep meditative state, akin to a trance or a dream. Slowbe followed a river within himself, deeper and deeper, until he came to a spot where he saw fallen trees and all sorts of debris obstructing the flow of energy. He stood amidst the debris. He had observed it before; at times by himself, at times with the aid of Lillian Red Horse, at times with the aid of Joseph Henry. Layers of negativity had been peeled back over the past two years, beginning with an experience in a sweat lodge.

Slowbe pulled at the debris. He threw twigs and branches to the riverbank. He let go. Finally, beneath the tangled mass of fear, greed, resentment, conceit, shame, and self-doubt, he uncovered, in plain view, the core belief from which his hindrances originated: I am not worthy. It looked like a ball of thick tar. Somehow, the belief would have to be removed and replaced. Slowbe opened his eyes. He recognized that harmony had eluded him because of a negative and false, belief that had infiltrated his system long ago.

But it wasn't just the deleterious belief he held about himself that was at issue; there were also deep-seated beliefs about the nature of reality and the realm of possibility that demanded a more rigorous examination and reckoning. There is cognitive theory and, for all intents and purposes, there is "existential cognitive theory," he thought. In other words, one's core beliefs about the nature of reality and the realm of possibility will determine how, and to what depth, reality and possibility are experienced. Depending on the belief, the level of awareness will be transcendent, purely physical, or somewhere in between. Even though Slowbe had lived with the inescapable fact of the violet realm for twenty years, over half of his life, he felt that he had not yet moved past the stage of observation to the stage of full integration, full realization, and agency. There remained a nagging inability, or reluctance, to allow himself to be immersed in, and subsumed by, the energy, light, and expanse of the violet realm, despite the fact that this had long been his stated objective, even the most important mission of his life. The internal narrative that he'd repeated over the years was that there was something he was afraid of that stopped him from completely letting go and diving into what he felt was limitlessness. It was as if he walked along the edge of an endless ocean, squeezing the wet sand with his toes, gazing across the waves, occasionally letting the tide come up to his ankles, sometimes his knees, but no further. Periodically, water splashed in his face, but the fact remained that a big part of him feared that he would lose himself and that his identity would be lost if he went underwater, so to speak, and acquiesced to the world within, although he had once heard that in order to find oneself one must lose oneself. On a certain intuitive level he understood that, and believed it to be true. There was simply a gap between the idea and the experience that had yet to be traversed.

Slowbe's experience of the violet realm had persisted despite his alcoholism, as his encounters with it would occur whether he was intoxicated or not. Over the years, with regularity, it had filled his mind's eye as he lay down at night to sleep, or when he sat to meditate; and it even, on occasion, pervaded the walls of his bedroom as he watched with open eyes. At times, he experienced it as something that was extremely luminescent and spacious; at other times, it was prominent but less scintillating; and, somewhat frequently, its presence was evidenced by a spark of violet light that flashed before his line of vision while his eyes were open. Most often, it was subdued and blended in with the blackness that he generally saw when his eyes were closed. To some degree, even if only slightly, it was always discernible. With concentration he could induce greater illumination, but there were also times when the violet realm was unexpectedly radiant and pulsated vigorously without any apparent effort on the part of Slowbe to bring about such a state. Invariably, it was just behind the curtain, shimmering, glowing. He had come to suspect that when the human exists in a higher state of consciousness, psychically liberated, there is continuous and vivid illumination, and the absence of darkness, throughout the inner plane. This, he felt, was characteristic of the natural state.

All is one; there is no separation anywhere, ever, he said to himself. But, at the same time, he experienced dissonance. He found it difficult to fully accept the violet realm. It somehow seemed mythical or unreal, or too sensational to be true, even, somehow, after so many years. On a core level, he could not fully believe what he was actually seeing, even as he bore witness. He struggled to reconcile and amalgamate the reality of his ego and his five senses with the pervasive non-physical reality he beheld with his "own eyes." It was like two beliefs, belief in the corporeal and belief in the transcendent, rushing up against one another, as if they were conflicting and mutually exclusive, although he knew they were not. Indeed, the ego does not easily relinquish its orientation or its grip. It is a jealous and covetous ruler, and the five senses, though unreliable, are extraordinarily powerful hypnotists. Nonetheless, Slowbe's yearning and calling had allowed him to crack open the door to another plane of existence, to a different orientation. He had, without doubt, found a chink in the armor of the deeply rooted corporeal paradigm. But his exploration of, and acceptance of, the new paradigm was restricted by fear and a negative belief.

It was as if he stood on a great scaffold astride a tremendous, monumental cement dam, which symbolized his ego. He had chipped away a small section, enough to create a slight passage for the lucent, violet water to pass through. He watched it trickle down the cement wall. He touched the water and knew that it was transcendent, but he was reluctant to create larger fissures in the cement, or to deconstruct the dam altogether, for fear of a deluge, for fear that he would be overwhelmed, for fear of plummeting into the unknown. The reluctance of the ego to abdicate its throne in favor of something greater than itself is tremendous, even if it has evidence that to acquiesce would reveal untold wonders and freedom. Ultimately, it clings to very strict and predictable frameworks, bound by physical reality, and it desperately wants existence to be defined solely by such frameworks, even though it has the capacity to move seamlessly between the corporeal and the immaterial. Slowbe knew there were realities and experiences beyond the five senses that were accessible to all humans. He presumed that if awareness of these became second nature for humanity, thus making human experience multidimensional, it would completely redefine what it meant to be a human—a new paradigm would be cast, and new talents, insights, and powers would be unleashed. He had to let go. He had to de-hypnotize himself.

"Power," Slowbe uttered beneath his breath. "Me in relation to...intersecting with...a field of power, effortlessly and fearlessly." He continued to gaze ahead at the violet, nebula-like, amorphous light. An image of a sphere covered with pulsating colored circles then appeared before him. I am a system, and, I am part of a system, he thought. He imagined that he was one of the circles and that the sphere was a greater entity of which he was a part. "Why am I afraid?" he asked with great emotional intensity. He closed his eyes.

Power, he thought, is not only having direct access to resources, but also having the willingness and wherewithal to accept and utilize them. Power is also the resource itself. All resources are a form of energy. The most potent resource is inherent: the Self. How deep and wide are the waters of the Self? They are virtually infinite. Am I willing to accept and utilize this resource? Acceptance is the igniter of personal agency. I am a universe unto myself, abounding with vital, dynamic resources. I create. I am unique. Can I use love to access all of my inner resources? Love disintegrates barriers and falsehoods. Believe in limitlessness. I will use love. The droplet need not fear the ocean; it is the ocean. Look within and have no fear for what is there. Be in the universe as a child playing in the grass. Accept no belief that is antithetical to love and the integrity of Self.

Slowbe opened his eyes and turned on the small reading lamp near his bed. He looked at the shadowy reflection of himself in the mirror across the room. His eyes were red and glassy and his eyelids hung low. His mouth was slightly open and his dark, curly hair was matted. He walked over to a sketchbook that was sitting on a small table near the bedroom door. He turned the room light on, sat down, and began flipping through the pages. The sketchbook was almost entirely full, mostly of landscapes, geometric figures, faces, eyes, and a few phrases that had come to him. The last page of the book was blank, except for a passage at the top that he'd written a few days earlier, which read "The fundamental trait of reality is its infinitude; ultimately, this is where all things dwell: amidst the infinite." The idea that each individual is a system, and part of a system, settled in his mind. Slowbe picked up a pen, wrote "MACRO SELF" in all capital letters, and began to sketch a diagram.

First, he drew three small, interlocking circles. Then, surrounding the three interlocking circles, he drew another circle, and then one more. The two outer circles were drawn with dashed lines in order to indicate an open system. He then drew two perpendicular lines that intersected at the center of the diagram and extended past the outer circle, and two additional lines that intersected at forty-five-degree angles with the first set of lines, and which also extended past the outer circle. On each of the lines, he intermittently added arrows that pointed inward and outward, to indicate the interaction and linkage between the various levels, or dimensions, of the Macro Self, and to imply an absence of boundaries.

He began to add labels to the diagram. Next to the three interlocking circles, he wrote the words "ego," "body," and "mind," respectively. Above the first circle, just to the right of the vertical line, he wrote the phrase "inner self," and above the second circle, to the right of the vertical line, he wrote the word "soul."

Slowbe entered his study, which was adjacent to his bedroom. He sat down at his desk and opened a new journal in his Array and began to take notes. "This life is simultaneously a training ground (a sometimes painfully rigorous obstacle course) and a playground," he wrote. "We are engaged in a story line, with billions of individual narratives, thousands of group narratives, and a single universal narrative within which all the plots and subplots coalesce," he wrote. Then he added, "My book is about idealism and creation. It is about navigating the realms of the psyche; experiencing reality behind the veil, beneath the surface appearances; and accessing the resources, power, and information therein. Life is about expression, learning, exploration, evolution, and relationship."

Slowbe wrote that physical reality was a symbolic reality, and in many ways like a mental construct. Into this framework the soul projects itself and sustains an image of itself in human form. Slowbe noted that the soul materializes into the earth-based, corporeal construct not only with a vast multidimensional context and "history" (and "history" of human form), but also with a general blueprint of particular challenges it wishes to undertake in its present human manifestation; certain relationships it wishes to have; and certain skills, abilities, lessons, and experiences it wishes to focus on. Experiencing reality through the human lens, with its hyperfocus on the physical, the earth, and the universe, was an invaluable and unique process. The soul peers through human eyes. There is an experiencer experiencing the experiencer. So, Slowbe wrote, it wasn't just the ego, the body, and the conscious mind that were engaged in the precious experience of "the human condition amidst an ever-expanding universe," but also deeper levels of the Self.

At the top of another page Slowbe wrote, "The purpose of the entity dawning physical clothes," and underlined the phrase. He noted that "the context of physical reality offers a unique stage for the soul to expand and enhance its experiential range, or empirical knowledge base, in areas like identity and relationship, creating personal reality, creative expression, channeling and directing energy, emotional experience, belief, and 'return,' among numerous other areas. Certain perspectives, lessons, and understandings can only be gained through corporeality. The human construct and physical reality are essentially pedagogies for the sentient being. They are distinctive ways of understanding reality and experience. The same lessons, or similar lessons, could be gained within different dimensional contexts, but the skill sets and types of understanding would be different in subtle or overt ways." Slowbe underlined the phrase "experiential range" and continued with his train of thought: ". . . as the ego and conscious mind navigate this curriculum through their perspective, the soul is engaged from its own orientation. The learning experience of the soul, with respect to the human condition, is in large part about observing/experiencing how the ego and conscious mind interact with the inherent challenges and dynamics of physicality, thought, emotion, belief, and relationship; and about observing/experiencing how the individual develops in relation to creativity, self-actualization, and ability to manifest ideas. But, the soul is not just an observer of the ego and its interpretation of physical reality; the soul is engaged in the construction of physical reality and in supporting the structure of the ego and the structure of the ego's experience."

By "return," Slowbe was referring to what he believed to be the greatest of all human challenges: the problem of the ego not knowing of its origin within a Macro Self system, or of its connection to, and relationship with, larger systems—of its existence within soul. Slowbe wrote in his notes that as a part of the "arrangement," the ego and the conscious mind are given free rein and free will, but, out of necessity, are designed to be somewhat hypnotized by corporeality. Without a measure, or at least a modicum, of hypnosis, a human experience of physical reality could not occur, as the experience required, to a certain degree, that a particular frame of reference be upheld. With the idea of "return" Slowbe implied that the ego is able, if it so chooses, to freely reorient itself with its source within the deeper levels of the Macro Self. The ego does not generally realize that this "return" is the road to its own liberation and transcendence. Slowbe mentioned two other particularly daunting challenges that "come with the territory" of the human condition: experiencing oneness when by all outward appearances everything seems divergent, linear, disseminated, or dualistic; and coming to the realization of love and immortality.

Encompassing and pervading this world and any world, he thought, was the act of creation. "Everything," he wrote, "from the swirling of the electron to the drifting leaf and the single blade of grass, from the flow of blood to the flow of words, from the joyous to the horrendous, from the formation and expansion of universes to the ebb and flow of history, is invariably a creative act." Further down the page he wrote, and underlined, a phrase that Riviere had used several times in their conversations: "Divine responsibility." Now more than ever the urgency and gravity, but also the joy, of this idea pressed upon Slowbe. "Humans, consciously and unconsciously, individually and collectively, wittingly and unwittingly, create their experience, their reality, and the events of their lives, through their thoughts, their emotions, their beliefs, their expectations, and through the projection of mental energy. It may sometimes seem counterintuitive, but on every level, down to the last iota, we create the reality that we experience. We are responsible."

Pope Leo sat in his study as Slowbe was taking his notes. Leo's brow was furrowed and his eyes peered penetratingly through the windows at the heavy dark-grey clouds that filled the sky.

"Piero," he said in a somewhat stern voice to the assistant who was making his way out of the room after having brought the Pope some tea, "I will not be taking my walk."

"Yes, Your Holiness," Piero said.

Salon

"When are you going to be back in the States?" Slowbe asked.

"Late July," Seven answered. "I'll be in Europe for a month; six weeks in Africa; then a month touring Indonesia, the Philippines, New Zealand, Australia, and Japan; then some dates in South America. I'm planning on spending a little time in the Andes after the tour, around Mt. Aconcagua, in Argentina. Then back to the city."

It was 5:43 a.m. in Portland, and from his kitchen Slowbe could hear a cacophony of calls and whistles. His property, flush with trees and bushes, and stocked with eight bird feeders, was a popular gathering spot for a wide variety of winged creatures. There was only one species whose call Slowbe didn't particularly care for: the blue jay, with its loud screeching. They were beautiful to look at, he thought, but not easy on the ears. They were welcome nonetheless. Slowbe stepped onto his deck.

"I just got back from the coast last night; spent a few days out there with Dara."

"In Nehalem?" Seven asked.

"Yeah."

"That sounds nice. I love the Oregon coast."

"We had a good time, very relaxing."

A breeze moved across the patio of the London penthouse Seven was renting, causing his white silk robe to flutter against his skin. As he looked out over the old city, scattered groups of high-altitude cumulonimbus clouds and low-lying altostratus clouds passed east to west. Large swaths of blue completed the skyscape. It was a comfortable nineteen degrees Celsius.

"So, what time is it in Portland? It's almost two in the afternoon here."

"It's about six in the morning."

"Up early."

"Got up with the birds."

"Have you read the blog Lillian posted yesterday?"

"No," Slowbe replied. "What's it about?"

"The idea that the persistence of war in human history speaks to a sort of collective borderline personality disorder; and, as kind of a thought experiment, she suggests that humanity in general, as a whole, would benefit from cognitive therapy because we carry so much angst and trauma. It's a satirical piece, but also empathetic in a way."

"War is a romanticized disorder," Slowbe subtly interjected.

Seven reclined into an armchair before continuing.

"She says that if one could mold a single, representative human from all of humanity, the representative human would be creative, ingenious, and resilient, but also disoriented, insecure, and prone to self-destructive behavior, and that world peace is probably one of the bars by which we should be measuring the health and progress of our species, just like inner peace should be for the individual."

"Many people, though, maybe even most, tend to think that war and violence is our nature—of course, this belief just perpetuates, or even justifies, the behavior," Slowbe pointed out. "I like what Riviere said, that the 'higher nature is the truer nature.' He would probably say that the baser actions and impulses are indicative of the psychological disorder, or of a distortion, or a disturbance in the system."

"That's a good quote," Seven said. "The higher nature is the truer nature."

"To realize the soul is to realize the true nature of our being.

Part of the human dilemma is that the ego picks up all sorts of negative and limiting beliefs along its way, and eventually, in many cases, begins to mistakenly view the negative and limiting beliefs, and the resultant behaviors, as human nature. We find ourselves enmeshed in the residue and distortions of mistaken identity and false beliefs, and we don't even know it. But, the deeper one goes into the Macro Self, or the greater Self, the more the residue and distortions fall off like dead skin."

"So, are you talking about human perfection, or saying that humans can be perfect?" Seven asked.

"Yes and no. We should strive for what we're capable of, the best of what we're capable of, that is, and for what's available within us, within our nature. We have extraordinary potential, on so many levels, and that's an understatement; but no matter how far we evolve, there will always be room for error and miscalculation, growth, mistake, and unknowing. Since the point always has been and always will be about process, I'm not sure if the idea of perfection is a useful concept applied to humans. It might not be dynamic enough."

"I heard someone once say that there are two...states of being, I guess...that speak to what might be considered human perfection: the attainment of inner love and the attainment of inner peace," Seven said, as he looked down at the River Thames twenty-one stories below.

"I'd agree with that," Slowbe said. "Maybe authentic, abiding self-affirmation and self-esteem could be said to be a form of human perfection, although I guess they would be implied in the attainment of inner love and inner peace."

"Self-affirmation and self-esteem sans any egoism and arrogance."

"Exactly...kind of rare."

"True," Seven replied.

There was a slight pause in the conversation.

"I saw your BBC interview last week," Slowbe said.

Seven was constantly in the news, as much for his outspoken

views, and occasional lack of tact, as for his immense creative output and frequent touring. His candor got him in hot water in late 2035 when, during an interview with *Rolling Stone* magazine, he went on an anti-religion rant, criticizing the Hindu caste system, ridiculing the idea of Jews as being chosen ones, and blasting Christians for living in an irrational biblical fantasy land. But the portion of the interview that caused a particular row was his comments on Mohammed. He stated that the prophet Mohammed had blood on his hands because he had led men into battle and had presumably killed men on the battlefield. Mohammed was not only a religious and political leader, but a military leader as well, he said. None of the other founders of major religions had ever killed, he went on to say. Seven had to stop touring for over a year because of the threats on his life after the Iranian cleric Uday Talebi put a fatwa on his head, although his album sales benefited greatly from the highly publicized ordeal.

Almost immediately after the fatwa was issued, Seven made a live public apology on the Al Jazeera website. In March of 2037, noticing that the zeal for his demise was not abating, he went to Iran to speak with the cleric at the U.S. embassy in Tehran; but the night before their meeting Talebi keeled over and died. After the inconclusive trip to Tehran, amidst tight security, Seven resumed his normal schedule, which was to tour for about four or five months and then return to New York City for seven or eight months to write, produce, record songs, and relax, and then resume touring again.

"Pretty uneventful interview," Seven said.

"Well, I guess that's a good thing sometimes," Slowbe replied.

"Sure, sometimes."

"You mentioned that you and Lillian have talked about working on another album."

"Yeah, that's something I'm looking forward to."

"That's interesting news."

Red Horse and Seven had known each other since July of 2038, when they met at a "healing gathering" in northern Washington State. About two hundred people had convened for the three-day event in the hilly, isolated region south of Oroville, near the Canadian border. There were several teepees set up, a few horses roaming the grounds, and a large tent that served as a communal kitchen. Tucked away in the trees that surrounded an open field, the gatherers set up their tents. Most of the participants were from Seattle, Portland, or Vancouver, British Columbia. A slight majority were Native American. On the first day, there was a rain-making ceremony, which, to Seven's amazement, induced raindrops from a sky that was predominately blue with only sparsely scattered patches of thin, white, waif-like clouds. He could hardly believe it. That's mind over matter, he thought.

In the morning of the second day, Seven was sitting alone on a patch of grass admiring the nearby hills and trees when Red Horse came over and sat next to him, as if she already knew him. He recognized her immediately and, not knowing that she would be at the gathering (she had arrived late the prior evening), was a little surprised, and a bit awestruck. She looked quite young, but at the same time there was something about her that made Seven feel like she was much older than him. She was thirty. She had deep brown eyes, high cheeks, light-brown skin, and black hair that ran to the bottom of her spine. Seven was struck by her enigmatic beauty. And there was something about her presence. It was as if gale-force winds resided within her. He'd heard people say similar things about her. By the time of the gathering, Red Horse was a spiritual voice and healer not only for the Nez Perce, but for many non-Native admirers around the world as well. She was also a musical genius and an acclaimed poet and was known to be startlingly clairvoyant.

Red Horse was a direct descendent of Chief Joseph, the nineteenth-century leader of the Wallowa band of the Nez Perce tribe who'd once famously declared that "the earth and myself are of one mind." His birth name, Hinmaton-Yalaktit, meant "thunder rolling down the mountain." Red Horse's maternal grandfather had also been a chief, and her maternal grandmother a medicine woman. From the time she was a small child, her grandmother had taught her about spirits called *wyakins* that served as personal guardians and provided a link to the invisible realm of spiritual power and to the world of Nature. She was told that when she was fourteen years old she would spend a night alone along the Snake River to seek out her *wyakin*, which might appear as an animal; as a natural phenomenon, like lightning; or as a vision. In the days leading up to this, she would have to fast and pray and meditate. It would be a very personal, sacred experience, she was told, one that she must never share with another human being.

Shortly after her fourteenth birthday, she drove with her grandmother to a remote location on traditional Nez Perce land. They arrived in the mid-afternoon, and her grandmother helped her set up a place to sleep. Her grandmother said that she would return at the same time the next day and that Red Horse should begin singing when she left. As her grandmother walked away, the young girl began to sing, and a feeling of calm fell upon her. She sang for almost two hours before drifting off into a deep sleep. When she awoke the sun had just dropped below the horizon. She got up and walked toward a spot along the Snake River where there was a large rock on the bank. She climbed atop it and stood, looking across the river at the high cliff faces on the other side. Behind her, Venus was rising brightly on the horizon. A few other celestial bodies were also beginning to appear. Far off to the northeast, large, pale-grey clouds had amassed. Red Horse sat down and continued looking to the east as the river rushed behind her. To her absolute delight, a lightning storm began to rage in the distance, while overhead the sky was perfectly clear. Eventually, the sky became illuminated with stars. She climbed off the rock and walked toward her sleeping area, which was set up about thirty feet from the river. It was a warm evening. She opened up her small backpack and drank some water. Above, she could see all of her favorite constellations: Ursa Major, Ursa Minor, Orion, Cassiopeia, Aquila, Cygnus, Lyra, and Aquarius.

The eerie sound of elk calls began to ring out loudly through the night air. Red Horse could tell they were coming from close by. She sat calmly, with heightened alertness. She closed her eyes and in her mind started to entreat her *wyakin* with great emotional and mental intensity. The sound of the elk calls grew closer and closer and seemed to surround her. Red Horse continued to implore her *wyakin* to make itself known to her. She had assumed that it would appear as a vision, and not as a physical manifestation. For nearly an hour she engaged in this seeking activity, her eyes remaining closed the entire time. All she saw was blackness, but she remained in a state of anticipation. Finally, an image emerged from the darkness. It appeared to move toward her, and as it did, she could see that it was an elk. There was something about its eyes that seemed both unusual and somehow strangely familiar. They had a shimmering brown color and there appeared to be sparks and particles of light swirling around within them, and they were disarmingly penetrating. Red Horse's breathing slowed as she watched the figure that stood silently before her. A gradual metamorphosis began to transpire. The body of the elk faded away, but the eyes remained. Red Horse was transfixed by them for what seemed like a timeless moment. The eyes then disappeared, and she began having the sensation that she was falling backward, descending deep into something. She felt like she was looking up at a starless nighttime sky. It was black, but it seemed to have depth, and in a way it seemed to be subtly infused with light. Red Horse opened her eyes. She heard the elk calls again. They were coming from a greater distance than before.

Years later, when asked if she felt culture framed or colored one's experience of inner reality, she replied, "Yes, to a degree, of course, each individual will have a unique experience of inner dimensions, inner realities, of their own soul; but first and foremost we are all one hundred percent human, and there will always be certain common threads in our experience of our transcendent nature."

Seven and Red Horse talked for hours on the second and third days of the gathering. Before they parted ways she gave Seven a card. She told him that she traveled frequently but made her residence in Portland. She would love to hear from him, she said, and potentially collaborate artistically. Seven made a point to follow up, and from May to August of 2039 they wrote and recorded music, primarily at Seven's studio in New York City, for a fifteen-song project they called *Psychic Motherboard*. It became Seven's eighth multi-platinum recording and Red Horse's first.

"We've talked about starting work on some music when I return from Argentina," Seven said.

"Have you spoken to her recently?" Slowbe asked.

"I actually saw her last week. She was in London."

"Oh, wow. Well, I wanted to mention that there's an idea for a salon."

"A salon?"

"Dara and I have been talking about it."

"Ok," Seven said in a tone suggesting his curiosity.

"We want to link it with some sort of program of action, some sort of activism around raising consciousness, possibly a social marketing component, but we really just want to have fun and enjoy art and conversation."

"Who's involved?"

"That's kind of open right now—myself, Dara. I'm planning on talking to Lillian soon. There are some others we're going to contact: Joan Monarch, Joseph Henry, Angel Song, Mia Sabin. I hope you might be interested in being a part of it."

"Absolutely."

"Everyone we've thought of so far is based in the Pacific

Northwest, except for you, so I imagine we'll usually meet in Portland, but if we can't all meet here, we can use Virtual Reality Imaging on the Array to bring us together."

"Please keep me in the loop on that."

"I will."

"So, there's a truth of consciousness rally starting at 3:00 p.m. over in Hyde Park. They're expecting close to eighty thousand."

"I heard about that."

"It's the fourth one in London this year."

"Amazing."

"I'm gonna get going and make my way over there."

"Sounds good. Talk to you later."

"Ok."

They both closed their Arrays. Slowbe walked downstairs to a dark, windowless room in his basement and closed the door.

Fifteen minutes later Seven was meandering alongside the River Thames, quite incognito, in a pair of loose black jeans; a black turtleneck; a beige coat (with the collar turned upward) that covered his slender five-eight frame from shoulder to foot; a dark-brown Stetson cowboy hat, tilted forward across his brow; and large black sunglasses. When he reached Vauxhall Bridge Road, he crossed over to the north bank of the river. Thanks to his shades, he was free to stare at, and carefully observe, the many pedestrians who crossed his line of vision. He was curious about their unique facial features, the distinctive shapes of their bodies, their manner of walking. Would they look at him? What was their story? After a leisurely two-mile walk, Seven approached Park Lane and could see the large crowd that was gathered in Hyde Park. His pace quickened and there was a slight pulsing sensation in his torso. When he came to the edge of the crowd, he stopped for a moment, then proceeded into the sea of humanity.

The truth of consciousness rallies had always been intended as a response to the discord, trauma, and disequilibrium on the planet—an effort to concentrate love and positive energy, to heighten humanity's sense of responsibility, to raise standards and expectations for society. And from the beginning they'd been inspired by a set of premises espoused by Toussaint Riviere, who, along with a network of idealistic nonprofits, organized the first rally in Detroit, Michigan, in 2025. According to Riviere, consciousness was the most powerful force in the universe. He was passionate about this idea, and at the rally in Detroit he'd distributed thousands of copies of a little pamphlet called *The Laws of Consciousness*, which put forth four premises: 1) consciousness is never destroyed; 2) consciousness constantly changes form; 3) consciousness exists independently of form; and 4) all realities and manifestations emerge from, or are projections of, consciousness. Speaking at a rally in Philadelphia in 2027, Riviere told the crowd, "To create is the greatest of all powers. Consciousness creates. Be mindful. All humans bear responsibility for the state of the world and for the future of the world because individually and collectively, on the most intimate level, and down to the most minute detail, humans create their experience and their reality through the power of their own consciousness. Consciousness isn't just a perceiver of experience and reality, it is the active agent that creates the experience and the reality. And where human beings are concerned, the immediate epicenter of consciousness is the soul. From there the energy of consciousness flows and filters through the guidance systems of mind, ego, belief, thought, emotion, and action—a process by which consciousness is essentially transformed, and manifested, into events and experiences, and reality itself. Life can be very dysfunctional or destructive when consciousness is used irresponsibly, or when there is no awareness of how it correlates directly to experience and the manifestation of events."

The truth of consciousness rallies were universally viewed as a phenomenon. They had a self-sustaining, spontaneous energy that only increased over the years. This consistent, organic growth reinforced a belief among the participants that humanity's future could be bright and prosperous. Unwavering faith in humanity emerged as a guiding value within the movement. In 2036, following the UN bombing, the rallies started to become more issue-oriented; namely, they began to focus on peace between nations, and on peace, or equilibrium, between society and earth.

For all the diversity and sheer numbers present at the London rally and others, there was an impressive degree of unity around the idea that these gatherings were not "anti" anything, they were only "pro" something; and in keeping with this credo, they were remarkably free of political, moral, and religious criticism. As Seven ambled through the crowd he reflected on this, and upon his past and present relationship with causticity and judgment. He thought about the "high road," that elegant, refined, and supremely civilized avenue that winds through the narrow, high mountain passes. The individual is free to traverse this golden road, Seven thought, and even to maintain a permanent address along these ways; but certain all-encompassing alignments must be made within one's internal systems.

At 4:10 p.m. the mass of people began to move like a huge body of water. The procession began at the intersection of Park Lane and Bayswater Road.

"Do you know the route?" Seven asked an elderly lady who was wearing white-rimmed glasses and whose hair was dyed purple. She seemed at least eighty years old. Seven hoped he might be able to strike up a conversation. He tilted his cowboy hat back slightly, revealing more of his face.

"Yes, dear," she replied, "up Bayswater Road past the Mayfair and Soho districts. We turn on Millbank Road and then again on Piccadilly, which will bring us around the other end of Mayfair and Soho and back to Hyde Park." She was American. He noticed as soon as the words left her mouth.

"Thank you. Where in the States are you from?"

"Taos, New Mexico. Yourself?" The lady asked. Seven could tell that she was a talker by the way her face lit up when he asked her the first question, and he suspected he would be able to spend a little time with her.

"I'm from New York City."

"Are you on vacation?"

"I'm here for work. I'll be here another week. Really enjoying my stay here."

"Oh, what do you do?"

"I'm a musician."

"Wonderful. Is this your first time in London?"

"No. I've been here quite a few times; still getting to know the city, though," Seven said.

"Yes, it's quite big. I'm vacationing." After a short pause, she asked, "What's your name, by the way?"

"Seven."

"Nice to meet you, Seven. I'm Dorothy."

"Nice to meet you, too." A look of curiosity came over Dorothy's face, and she leaned in to get a closer look at Seven. Seven took off his sunglasses and looked her in the eye.

"I know who you are. Oh my goodness," Dorothy said.

Seven smiled and then put his sunglasses back on.

"So, have you been to truth of consciousness rallies before?" he asked as they made their way out of the park and onto Bayswater Road, which, like the rest of the march route, had been closed off to traffic. The expressive white clouds that had been delicately hovering overhead not long ago had all moved north of the city, toward the countryside.

"Oh yes, many, many; since they began in 2025. I've attended them in cities all over the world."

"Quite the modern marvel."

"Indeed. Especially since 2036. The size and frequency of them is just astounding."

"I guess you've seen a lot in your day," Seven said, curious about the historical context of her life.

"Oh yes."

"What year were you born in?" Seven asked.

Because he felt slightly uncomfortable asking an elderly person their age, he commonly used the backdoor method of asking what year they were born in, so as to be a little less direct with his inquiry.

"1960," Dorothy replied.

"So, you're eighty-eight?"

"I'll be eighty-eight tomorrow, as a matter of fact."

Seven smiled widely. "That's great," he said, "happy birthday."

"Thank you."

"That was an intense decade, the '60s. Very dramatic: social movements, war, an outpouring of musical genius, great idealism."

"Oh yes, a truly remarkable decade; inspiring, but also tragic in many ways."

"In your life what historical events have stood out to you the most?"

"Oh," Dorothy said in a surprised voice.

"I know that's a pretty heavy question."

"Well, the twenty-first century strikes me as a defining epoch for humanity, like a crossroads. I can definitely say that the things I observed in the first half of my life, including the fall of the Soviet Union, pale by comparison to what I've seen since the turn of the millennium. The UN bombing and subsequent dissolution is just stunning beyond words, hard to fathom, but the truth of consciousness rallies also stand out as among the strangest and most dramatic occurrences I've ever seen. I remember after 9/11 when the United States was leading up to war there were peace marches all over the globe, the largest and most widespread peace marches that had ever been held. I remember being so disappointed when they died down. I felt that these were things that needed to continue in force indefinitely, to promote the principle. Somehow, that's what's happened with the truth of consciousness rallies.

"The Arab Summer of 2039 was shocking to me. It's incredible how suddenly historical upheaval can occur, like a volcano that explodes with no warning. With the Arab nations, I thought that many of them would have remained governed by authoritarian regimes for many more decades than was actually the case; and now there are democracies in almost everyone, and even women presidents in Egypt, Saudi Arabia, Morocco, and Iran, all because of the uprisings that swept through the Middle East and North Africa in 2039. That seems to be the story of the twenty-first century: repeated earthquakes, conflagrations, tsunamis, and volcanoes, literally and figuratively. Speaking literally, the effects of global warming, and also pollution and habitat destruction, are quite profound and unsettling. This century is unique in human history in that never before has humanity been confronted with threats to the viability of its own existence on the planet—and the threats have arisen as a result of our own behavior, no less. Maybe the overall theme of humanity in relationship to earth, and the current crisis with regard to this matter, is what stands out the most. You really got me going now."

"Please, continue."

"Another thing that has amazed me about this century in particular is the popularity of these, I guess, metaphysical and philosophical ideas, and these new philosophers, starting with Riviere, the father of the truth of consciousness rallies; and Sarah Goulle; Char Ron; Joseph Henry; Lillian Red Horse; and Edward Slowbe, with his book *The World Within*; and quite a few others. Like I said, you never know when some deep chord is going to be struck across a large swath of humanity. I suppose the reason your question is so difficult for me to answer in a nutshell is because I'm entirely enthralled by this era, including the scientific and technological advances, the Array, the telescopes, solar power; and there seems to be a consensus that we live in an artistic renaissance. Strangely,

9/11 feels like the moment we entered this new age. For me, it's when the unreal became the real."

"What do you mean by the unreal becoming the real?"

"Well, to many during that time, probably everyone, it was very difficult to imagine that something like that could happen. It was really hard to believe. There was a real cognitive dissonance. We could see that it actually happened, but it seemed like something that would occur in a movie, a fictional tale, not in real life. The word 'surreal' was mentioned a lot. Since then, there have been so many events, episodes, and developments that have affected me, and others, I believe, in a similar way."

"I think we're living in a renaissance, although it's a painful rebirth—a hard labor."

"I agree," Dorothy said. "I think of this century as being the ultimate transition period for humanity."

"Transition to what?" Seven asked.

"Reconciliation, maturity, healing, awakening."

A small, blond-haired girl, blowing a kazoo, skipped past Seven and Dorothy. The crowd moved steadily through the Mayfair district. Although he could tell that a fair amount of people recognized him, despite his attempt at concealing himself, no one approached him.

"So, do you have children?" Seven asked.

"I do. I have three children, eight grandchildren, and two great-grandchildren."

"Wow," Seven said. "You're a real matriarch."

Dorothy smiled. For a brief moment Seven wondered where her husband might be.

"My eldest son lives here in London. I'm staying with him through next month."

"I see. What does he do?"

"He's the Bishop of Salford."

"Really?"

"Yes, his father was English, and Ralph has lived here since he was a teenager."

"So, he decided not to come with you today?" Seven said lightheartedly.

"Well," Dorothy said, as she chuckled, "the Church of England doesn't exactly endorse the truth of consciousness rallies. I guess one thing we can say for certain is that the Christian, Jewish, Hindu, and Muslim leadership are uneasy about this movement, because of its tone of independent spirituality and the trans-religious sentiment. Ralph and I just don't talk about it."

The Happening

Slowbe and Sangree checked into the Empire Hotel in upper Manhattan shortly after 2:00 p.m. on Friday, June 5th. They took the elevator to the twenty-seventh floor and made their way down a long hallway elaborately adorned with gold, spiral-patterned wallpaper; regal busts; and delicate chandeliers, until they reached suite 2776. Slowbe turned the brass door lever. Upon entering the room, he set his roller luggage in a resting position, then walked intently toward the finely embroidered curtains that covered much of the east-facing wall. He opened them as wide as they would go and stood with his arms crossed, looking out over Central Park.

"I'm not particularly interested in going back into that heat. We have our little sanctuary up here," Sangree said.

"I agree, let's spend the rest of the day inside. Maybe tonight we can go do something if we want," Slowbe said. He turned toward Sangree and added, "It's good to be back in the city."

"When was the last time you were here?" she asked.

"2036," Slowbe replied. "Amazing that it's been so long, but I feel the timing is perfect. Now's the time."

"Yes, definitely," Sangree said with a warm expression on her face.

Slowbe opened a bottle of water and took a quick drink before reclining into the reading chair to the left of the glass balcony doors. Sangree lay down on the king-sized bed, propped her head on a couple pillows, and stretched her arms and legs. The two enjoyed a silent half hour as the city swirled about. After having almost fallen asleep, Slowbe got up and began to dig around in his luggage. He pulled out the pair of binoculars he'd brought for bird-watching in Central Park and stepped onto the balcony. He unscrewed the lens caps and aimed the binoculars toward a fairly large bird soaring in the distance. Once the lenses were properly focused, he immediately recognized it as a red-tailed hawk.

Slowbe watched it glide above the tall oak, elm, and cypress trees, against the backdrop of skyscrapers and a cloudless sky, its reddish-orange tail flaring out dramatically like a fan painted in bold brushstrokes. He traced the raptor's movements for about forty seconds as it angled about, playing off the air currents and flying in a broad circle, until it suddenly dove into a mass of foliage. Slowbe turned his binoculars to the street directly below. He slowly looked up and down the block, zeroing in on people and places of business. After a few minutes, he was overcome by surprise.

"There's a store called Grace Market down there," he said.

"Yeah, I've been there. They specialize in imported wines. They also serve great vegetarian dishes and have incredible desserts," Sangree replied.

"How interesting."

"What?"

"I was just...wow...huh."

"What?"

"I just had a bit of a flashback."

"Really?"

"When I was driving cross-country from New York to Portland, I spent the night at a motel in Janesville, Wisconsin," Slowbe said as he took another drink from his bottle of water. "There was a Grace Market near the motel and I bought some beer there. I remember the lady at the counter."

"That's an interesting coincidence," Sangree said.

"You know, Sunday is my sobriety date: June 7th, 2041, seven years."

"Congratulations, that's great," Sangree said.

"It really is."

"There's some grace for you."

"Indeed."

"Take a look at this," Sangree said. "NASA released some of the latest photographs from the Stephen Hawking Space Telescope."

Slowbe moved onto the bed and sat next to Sangree. Their legs and shoulders pressed against each other as they looked into Sangree's Array. There were 124 new photographs of galaxies, supernovae, star clusters, planets, and nebulae. Slowbe and Sangree perused the collection.

"They say there are over 300 billion galaxies," Slowbe said, "each with anywhere from one hundred billion to a trillion stars or more. Galaxies the size of IC 1101 are thought to have around one hundred trillion stars. Which would be more incredible to you—if we are the only intelligent life in the universe, or if there are other intelligent civilizations out there?"

"The odds of either scenario being true seem so astronomical...excuse the pun," Sangree replied. "Perhaps it would be slightly more incredible to me if we were the only ones in such a vast realm, with the universe all to ourselves. Part of me suspects that the universe is at least sprinkled with societies, biological organisms, ecosystems, and intelligent beings. How could it not be, given the fact that it's basically incomprehensibly immense? On the other hand, it seems that the biological emerging from the non-biological would be an extraordinary anomaly in the universe, because it utterly defies logic or any laws that we know of. It seems impossible, like something emerging from nothing, life emerging from non-life."

"I tend to lean toward the opinion that life is scattered around the universe, if not abounding," Slowbe said. "I think scientists will make the discovery of how that's possible, how life emerges from non-life. Before they do, though, I think they'll have to figure out what consciousness is, and that will lead them to solving the mystery of life's genesis in the universe. But yes, I agree, on the surface it does seem counterintuitive that something animate could ever be born from something inanimate."

As of June 2048, over forty thousand planets had been discovered within "habitable zones" in the Milky Way galaxy, close to two thousand in the previous eighteen months. These findings lifted the idea of human colonization of other planets to the forefront of global consciousness.

A recent poll had shown that three out of four people in the United States thought that humans would begin colonizing other planets en masse within two hundred years. A slightly higher percentage, as well as a majority of scientists, felt that first contact with extraterrestrial intelligence was imminent.

For the remainder of the afternoon and evening Slowbe and Sangree lounged in the spacious suite. Around 6:30 p.m. they had room service delivered, and later they watched a news program. Seventy-nine Palestinians and a dozen Israelis had been killed in clashes in the Gaza Strip. As the sky outside turned pitch black, Slowbe began working on a poem, and Sangree read from her copy of Friedrich Nietzsche's *Thus Spoke Zarathustra*. At 11:00 p.m. Sangree fell asleep. Slowbe continued writing. An hour later, he put his pen down and opened his Array to check for messages. There was a video email from Joan Monarch entitled "Paradigms," which she had sent from her campsite inside Utah's Natural Bridges National Monument, an International Dark Sky Park and one of the best places in the United States for observing celestial objects and extraterrestrial events. She mentioned that she was very interested in the salon, which brought the total to eight who would be meeting on July 15th. Six individuals—Dara Sangree; Slowbe; the writer and philosopher Joseph Henry; Lillian Red

Horse; the painter Angel Song; and the art historian, classicist, and poet Mia Sabin—had already met for dinner at Slowbe's house in late April to discuss current art projects and ideas for the salon (the gatherings, it was determined, would remain small for the time being and gradually expand in participation).

After he finished watching Monarch's video email, Slowbe spent a few moments looking at the image of her face that remained on the display. She was the only person he'd ever met that had heterochromia iridum, a condition in which one iris is a different color than the other. She had a sapphire-blue eye and a jade-green eye, and they stood out dramatically against her black hair, brown skin, and full eyebrows.

Monarch was a child of the Badlands and of the big city. She'd been born on the Pine Ridge Reservation in South Dakota in 2012. At the age of two, she'd moved with her mother to New York City, where she lived for ten years before moving back to the reservation. The plan had always been to return. As it turned out, soon after completing a PhD in sociology at Columbia University, her mother was offered a position at the world-renowned Society of Care Research and Policy Institute at Pine Ridge. A week before they moved back, in an effort to build excitement about the relocation, Monarch's mother bought her a telescope. The clerk who'd assisted them with the purchase told them that it was powerful enough to see galaxies five billion light-years away. "More than a third of the way to the beginning of time," she said.

Monarch and her mother arrived at Pine Ridge on a warm summer evening just after 11:00 p.m. The sky was a vast, intricate mosaic of stars and clusters, pulsing, unlike anything Monarch had ever remembered seeing. She was awestruck. By chance, every time she'd been to the reservation to visit relatives she'd either been to bed too early to see the fullness of the night sky, or there'd been cloud cover.

"See the long, wide strip," Monarch's mother said, as she pointed across the sky at the astronomical object that stretched from horizon to horizon. "That's the Milky Way, that's the galaxy we live in. Less than one in ten humans ever gets a chance to see it, mainly because city lights make it hard for us to see the stars, and most people live in the cities. Before the invention of the light bulb, it was normal for people around the world to see this many stars, and the Milky Way, on every clear night."

In the months and years to come, Monarch and her mother would take frequent nighttime excursions into the Badlands and the Black Hills to explore the Milky Way, Andromeda, Triangulum, Sextans A, Wolf-Lundmark-Melotte, and other galaxies. They would talk about the Big Bang, and the worlds that existed beyond the edge of the universe, and all the worlds that existed within the universe. And they would talk about eagles, and horses, and foxes, and the tall grasses, and the hills, and the trees, and balance and harmony, and how everything is connected in a great circle. Her mother told her that everything that can be imagined exists somewhere in this universe or in other universes, and that there are things that exist in faraway places that we can't even imagine. She told her that there were worlds that we could not see with our eyes, but only with "second sight," as she put it.

The morning after her first night back at Pine Ridge, Monarch's grandmother mentioned that a white buffalo had been born on the reservation two days prior and that Monarch and the calf had something special in common. So, they went to visit the newborn after breakfast. Monarch was astonished when she noticed that she and the young buffalo had the same heterochromia iridum, left eye sapphire-blue, right eye jade-green. Following the encounter, Monarch became obsessed with drawing and coloring pairs of eyes—only eyes, not faces, eyebrows, or lashes. She would draw irises of amazing detail. There were murmurs around the reservation. Eventually, she began doing oil paintings on a variety of subjects. By age twenty-one she was universally recognized as an artistic genius and had become an international sensation. She was twenty-six when she and Slowbe were introduced to one another by Mia Sabin at the 2038 Hedge Club Art Exhibition in Cambridge, Massachusetts, which featured the works of Monarch, Angel Song, Sam Glowston, Bridge Mayfall, and Caroline Abadie— all of whom were being referred to as geniuses, and all of whom were part of a school of art called Singularism, whose major themes of connectedness, oneness, and consciousness were influenced by Riviere's philosophy of the same name.

Slowbe and Sangree arrived at Printed Word Copy Outlet, the largest bookstore in the United States, at 11:00 a.m. on Sunday. Fifty-Seventh Street between Eighth and Ninth Avenues was blocked off and thousands filled the streets, spilling into nearby Central Park. Since it was going to be impossible for everyone to get their copy of *The World Within* signed, the store manager, Slowbe, and Slowbe's literary agent, Jazz McKinley, decided that Slowbe would sign until 6:00 p.m. and then address whatever crowd remained. They would announce the plan at 12:00 p.m., ask people for patience and cooperation, and then begin allowing folks into the bookstore in small groups. Amidst the electrified atmosphere, everyone hoped for the best. It was a hot, muggy day, and the din of the crowd reverberated. The employees at Printed Word Copy Outlet were upbeat. It felt as if the store were hosting a celebration of some sort. A small film crew was present to record the atmosphere and some of the interactions.

At 12:08 people began filing into the bookstore, and as each person approached Slowbe at the book-signing table, he was very intentional about making eye contact—and about paying attention to the color, dynamics, and uniqueness of these windows to the soul. The interactions were brief. People were polite. No one hoarded time or tried to engage in conversation beyond a few comments. The many "hi, how are you"s were genuine and heartfelt; the "thank you"s were warm and meaningful; the "good to see you"s were true. Phrases such as "lifting the black veil," "inner illumination," "vast new dimensions," "the source," "new vantage point," and "field of energy" were mentioned to Slowbe numerous times.

After three hours Slowbe took a twenty-minute break, then resumed for almost another three hours. The last book was signed at 6:09 p.m., and shortly thereafter Slowbe excused himself to a back room for a few moments to himself. By then, a small stage and PA system had been assembled on Fifty-Seventh Street at Eighth Avenue. A huge crowd was assembled. When Slowbe returned he spoke briefly with Sangree, then went outside to the stage, which had a microphone stand placed front and center. The film crew was poised. As he began to address the crowd, an enormous front of dark-grey storm clouds could be seen overhead to the east, rolling like a tidal wave with unmistakable majesty and power.

"This has been a wonderful experience for me today, and I thank you so much for being here. I feel very connected to all of you. I hope we all feel connected."

Slowbe paused and looked out across the crowd.

"When I was a young boy growing up in Chillicothe, Ohio, in addition to being given to catching fireflies, grasshoppers, caterpillars, bumblebees, and the occasional praying mantis, I never passed on an opportunity to grab—and, if necessary, chase down—the floating cottonwood seeds that would drift about in the spring and summer. I know there aren't cottonwood trees here in the city, but their seeds are soft, puffy little things that kind of look like very thin cotton balls. Somewhere along the way, I'd picked up the notion that they had the same magical properties as shooting stars and birthday candles. If I caught one, I believed, I could make a wish, provided I gave the seed back to the wind. I'm not sure if I was pushing the limits of wish-making etiquette, but I always made two wishes per every seed I caught. I thought I was within my rights to do so because one of the two wishes was always for peace in the world; and then the other would generally be for some materially oriented thing, something just for me. With such a valuable thing as a wish, I couldn't find it in myself to keep it solely for my own purposes. Now, I must confess, maybe there was a slight sense that someone or something was watching over me, interested in seeing what I would do with a wish, and maybe I wanted to be agreeable to the 'It' that I thought might be observing my wish-making selections. But I always thought, and felt, that peace in the world was the best altruistic wish I could make.

"To this day, it remains my wish for our society: a peace among nations. Some say it will never happen, that humankind is too violent and aggressive. No doubt we have been, and continue to be, violent and aggressive, although, thankfully, we are significantly less so than we once were. Great progress has been made. As conspicuous as these baser tendencies are, the fact remains that we are also ingenious, creative, and resilient, and perhaps most importantly, we are endowed with a power, an essence, that is fundamentally positive and transcendent. The power we have within can lead us away from violence and excessive aggression and help us to dissipate these things. Of course, not all aggression is bad, but violence against another is always a fear-based reaction, and it is indicative of an absence of true power. Violence and war don't exist independently of fear. Now, we can deal with fear; we can address it, overcome it, rise above it, leave it behind. I am saying that we don't have to be afraid of anything.

"The skeptics and the cynics remind us that the human race has always been at war, and from this fact they draw their defeatist conclusion: that there will always be war and open discord. But, is it wise to say that the patterns of the past always become the patterns of the future? If this were so, then I would still be drunk, and would never have been able to summon the strength and wherewithal to write my book, or stand before you today, or discover my true self. I came to embrace newness, light, and power—and every last iota of my life changed. Have hope and faith in the regenerative abilities of the human species. Don't concede a dark future because we see that the past has been tumultuous. Life is a self-fulfilling prophecy. We have the power of creation at our fingertips. Do we not see how miraculous we are? Born of stardust. We must take time to look around at the incredible progress, spurred by idealism at every step, that we have made as a species. Let us focus on our accomplishments for a while, and the progress we've made. We have come far in the last two thousand years, we've come further in the last two hundred, and we continue forward, despite hardship and misunderstanding. We just need to relax. We just need to relax; release our tension. All of us. We all need to become"—Slowbe paused and a smile spread across his face—"relaxists."

There was applause and shouting. The impressive, daunting clouds had now enveloped the sky directly above, and the air had become cooler and more moist.

"So, I have an even greater wish," Slowbe continued, "and that is for the peace of the individual. This is inextricably connected to the peace of nations because a general peace in the environment, setting, or context supports the development of peace within the person. Conversely, the peace of the individual increases the likelihood of peace in the society. Ultimately, my hope now is for the fulfillment of each person, each precious person. I understand that finding true peace within can be almost as challenging as finding a peace between nations. But I embrace idealism, and I hold it dear, because from the broadest, most illustrious vision comes the broadest, most illustrious experience. When Ralph Waldo Emerson, one of my heroes, said 'hitch your wagon to a star,' he was most certainly suggesting that we set great goals for ourselves and pursue them fearlessly. But I also think he was telling us that we must allow our minds to entertain and pursue unrestricted, perhaps even unconventional, views of human potential and human nature. He didn't say hitch your wagon, meaning yourself, to the tallest tree or the highest mountain, or to the moon, he said hitch it to a star. In other words, hitch it to something in the heavens, whose light spreads out in all directions across countless millions of miles. What could the star symbolize? Peace? The soul? Creation?"

Slowbe looked up at the cloud cover. Many in the crowd also took note, curious, before Slowbe began to speak again.

"The peace of the individual is sturdiest when the human being is immersed within a place that is positive, affirmative, and transcendent. It is a place that can be sought out in creative and unique ways. Each person must find their own path using their keenest, most discriminating, and most explorative faculties. The peace of the individual is not a place of brevity, or distraction, or convention, or tension, or fluttering in the wind. It is motionless even amidst energetic action. It is silent even amidst the din.

"We must relax into this place, like the musician relaxes into the playing of the instrument and, because of her relaxed state, is able to play with mastery and wizardry. To be relaxed in mind, body, emotion, and spirit is to be in a place of peace. Deep relaxation is the place of peace. Now, many will think of resting by the poolside, taking a nap, looking into an Array, or many other passive experiences, when they imagine relaxation. It is these things, but it's more. Deep relaxation dissipates the layers of doubt, fear, anger, negativity, and separation; and this is an intentional and energetic process on many levels. We can relax our way to fearlessness. We can relax our way to second sight and the third eye. We can relax our way to creative brilliance. We can relax our way to joy and long life. In deep relaxation we become, in a manner of speaking, free from heaviness; we become light, as in carrying less mental and emotional weight; we become light, as in illuminated energy; and we can change the world. Relax, and observe, carefully, as you settle into the deep core of your being, like sand settling to the riverbed. It will help you, and it will help others.

"Make the twofold wish; embrace it, and endeavor to fulfill it within yourself. Create world peace within yourself.

Enjoy yourself and live so that your experience simultaneously benefits you as well as others. Life is the great artwork, as is your very being. Wield the paintbrush of your life, and your being, with creative abandon, and together we will rise to the occasion; we will surpass our wildest expectations . . ."

Slowbe then raised his right hand and looked to the sky. Suddenly, a bolt of lightning struck right where he stood, appearing to touch his outstretched hand as if it were a lightning rod. The PA system screeched loudly. To the crowd, who let out an unearthly gasp, it looked as if he had pulled the beam right out of the sky. Slowbe lowered his arm and stood, unscathed and expressionless, as the crowd reeled with disbelief, awe, and fear. He then turned around and walked off the stage. There was a rapt silence. The video swept across the planet almost immediately, making headlines at virtually every news outlet and spurring frenzied speculation.

The Pope Returns

Leo rested his elbow on the arm of the burgundy leather reading chair he was seated in and leaned his cheek against his loosely clenched hand, his eyes focused on several landscape paintings that hung from the walls of the stately guest room at St. Joseph's Seminary in Yonkers. As a young man, he'd studied theology on this campus, which, since 1896, had been the principal seminary of the Archdiocese of New York. Now, he'd returned as the most important guest the seminary had ever hosted, having arrived the previous morning, June 14th, with plans to stay until the 20th. His visit to New York City would include an address at Yankees Stadium, a meeting with President Eagle Staff, lunch with Mayor Otero, mass at St. Patrick's Cathedral, and the three-day Religious Reconciliation Assembly.

Leo looked over at the small bronze clock on the table directly to his right. It was 5:36 a.m. Outside, the sky was mostly cloudy, but faint morning light filtered through the diamond-grid windows on the east wall of the room, as did the sound of birdsong. Through the windows Leo could see a picturesque courtyard with rhododendron bushes; bird baths and feeders; gardens of amethyst, begonia, hydrangea, lilac, and aster; and a pond with a fountain sculpted in the form of a cherub. He reached down to his left and pulled a copy of *The World Within* from his briefcase, which was leaning against the reading chair. He held the book in his lap for several minutes before placing it facedown on the table without having opened the cover. The lines of his forehead deepened and he brought his left hand to his lips. His piercing dark-blue eyes, surrounded by dull, brownish rings, and resting squarely in the middle of his distinctly round face, began to scan the room.

In the corner to the right of the doorway Leo noticed the slight movements of a spider in its web. He lifted his imposing, slightly hunched-over six-foot-six frame from the burgundy chair, grabbed a tissue, and proceeded across the room with his long, deliberate gait. When he got to the corner, he slowly got down on his hands and knees and leaned toward the spider and its interwoven concentric circles until his head was less than a foot away. He peered closely at the creature, which was now motionless, and then quickly swept it, and the entire web, into the tissue and squeezed his hand tightly. He got up and threw the tissue into a trash bin. As he returned to the reading chair, he picked up his Array, which was on a desk next to what had been the spider's corner.

Leo sat down, opened his Array, and said "Edward Slowbe" into Google. News portals and YouTube videos filled the entire first sphere, except for an Amazon portal and two Wikipedia portals (for *The World Within* and Edward Slowbe, respectively). The Pope clicked on a June 12th *New York Times* article. The unusual occurrence at Printed Word Copy Outlet was already being referred to as "the happening." Slowbe had not commented on the matter, and speculation had quickly run rampant around the world. Some were convinced Slowbe was some sort of illusionist or had collaborated with others to set up an elaborate hoax, but no evidence of holographic imagery had yet been uncovered. Others thought it was a miraculous act. And some believed it was an extraordinary coincidence, noting that lightning strikes had been seen in Brooklyn and Queens prior to his speech. Amidst the conjecture, international sales of his book took a sudden and steep upswing over what had already been remarkable figures.

Leo played the video of Slowbe's address and the lightning strike that appeared to touch his outstretched hand. He'd watched the video more than a dozen times over the course of the previous six hours. He glanced again at Slowbe's book, and an uncomfortable tingling sensation overcame him. The pace and depth of his breathing increased and he felt a slight tightening in his neck and shoulders. Leo grabbed the book and placed it back into his briefcase. After a few minutes, his body relaxed and a great heaviness overcame his eyes. He'd not slept well over the course of the night. He made his way to the queen-sized upholstered sleigh bed situated along the south wall, a dozen feet behind the burgundy chair, and soon he was sound asleep. Leo dreamt he was at sea on a large boat filled with passengers. A storm blew over the vessel. His papal tiara, a violet stole, and a gold crosier were swept overboard and lost. When the tempest subsided no one on the boat recognized him. A knock at the door awoke Leo. It was 8:17 a.m.

"Come in," the pontiff said in his gravelly baritone voice. The tall wooden doors of the guest room opened gradually and the Pope's assistant, Piero della Francesca, entered.

"Your Holiness," he said, bowing, "would you like breakfast?"

"No, thank you, but please bring me some coffee."

"Of course, Your Holiness." Piero left the room, closing the doors behind him.

Less than ten minutes later, he returned carrying a silver tray containing a delicate blue china cup; a silver coffeepot, creamer, and sugar set; a silver spoon; and a small beige napkin. He placed the tray on the table next to the burgundy chair where the Pope was now seated.

"The press conference will begin at 11:00 a.m. in the main hall, Your Holiness. It's scheduled to last forty-five minutes. Just as a reminder, a one-hour lunch with the mayor will follow, and then your afternoon is free until the 6:00 p.m. commencement dinner for the assembly talks at St. Patrick's Cathedral."

"Thank you, Piero," the Pope replied. Piero bowed his head and left the room again.

Religious Reconciliation was a program initiated by Leo in 2024 for the purposes of fostering greater dialogue and cooperation between religions and improving public perception of religious institutions. The first assembly convened in Avignon, France, in August 2024, with 137 leaders and representatives from the Christian, Hindu, Buddhist, Jewish, and Islamic faiths in attendance. At the Avignon assembly, it was decided that subsequent convocations would occur every four years and would last three days. The assembly had, since then, met in Moscow (2028), Baghdad (2032), Jerusalem (2036), New Delhi (2040), and Bangkok (2044). As was the case in 2024, the focal point of the 2048 assembly was the elimination of all violence in the name of God or religion.

The most controversial assembly to date was the 2032 meeting in Baghdad. The roots of the controversy could be traced back to 1999, when Pakistan presented a resolution to the United Nations Commission on Human Rights that became known as "Defamation of Religions." The resolution exhorted all nations "within their national legal framework, in conformity with international human rights instruments, to take all appropriate measures to combat hatred, discrimination, intolerance and acts of violence, intimidation and coercion motivated by religious intolerance, including attacks on religious places, and to encourage understanding, tolerance and respect in matters relating to freedom of religion or belief." The resolution was easily adopted without a vote being required.

Several similar resolutions were brought to the Commission on Human Rights between 2000 and 2011, all of which passed, but by shrinking margins due to the growing concern that they were devolving into international blasphemy laws. In 2031, at the urging of Leo and a prominent Pakistani cleric named Muhammad Al-Al Abid, Pakistan, Brazil, and the Philippines presented a new "Defamation of Religions" resolution to the

UN Commission on Human Rights, the first since 2011. In what was widely viewed as an embarrassment for both the Pope and Al-Al Abid, the Commission voted lopsidedly against the resolution, arguing that it sought to stifle criticism of religious institutions and traditions. The vote received intense media attention. The 2032 Religious Reconciliation Assembly became, in effect, a platform for many of the attendees to unleash their criticism of the United Nations.

Leo entered the main hall of St. Joseph's Seminary almost fifteen minutes late for the scheduled press conference. Eight photographers and twenty-one journalists were in attendance, only a few of which had ever seen Leo in person. His reputation preceded him, though, and he was widely regarded as both a reformer and a strong-willed, extremely learned, if not dogmatic and egoistic, pontiff. The journalists were taken by his imposing presence.

"His Holiness will now take questions," Piero stated through a small microphone. "When I point to you please present your question."

Piero gestured to the reporter immediately to his left.

"Your Holiness, what do you think happened in front of Printed Word Copy Outlet last week?" the reporter asked.

Leo leaned forward and clasped his hands.

"Clearly, some sort of hoax, a great deception," the Pope replied.

"But many who were present, and many others around the world, believe something supernatural—"

"Thank you for your question," Piero interjected. He then pointed to the next journalist.

"Good morning, Your Holiness. Internationally, the number of individuals identifying as irreligious, or as having no religion, has now surpassed the number of individuals who identify as Christian. How can the church regain its former prominence and influence?"

"The church is very strong right now, perhaps as strong as

it's ever been. Our membership is growing and there are many young people entering the priesthood, particularly since the door has been opened for women to serve in this manner. The church is preparing the way for Christ's return in very powerful ways—for example, by using social media to reach young people, by increasing the number of missions we are sending out around the world, by building new schools and speaking out against injustice, and by working to promote compatibility between religion and science. The church continues to exercise tremendous influence, but we do not draw comparisons."

Piero pointed to the reporter seated directly in front of Leo.

"Your Holiness," the reporter said, "thank you for gracing us with your presence this morning. My question is: Have you read Edward Slowbe's book, and do you feel it's at odds with, or undermines, religious tradition?"

"I have not read the book," Leo said in a slightly agitated tone, "and I don't intend to. My metaphysics is based solely on the Bible."

"Next, you, sir," Piero said as he pointed to another reporter.

"Your Holiness, how do you feel about the extraordinary popularity of Slowbe's book?"

"Not another question about this charlatan Slowbe!" the Pope yelled, as he banged his fist on the table before him. The hall went silent.

Singularism and the Socratic Method

Slowbe's Array began to vibrate. He reached over to the glass table next to the hammock he was lying in and felt around until he grasped the device. It was a call from Lillian Red Horse.

"Lillian," he said enthusiastically.

"Hi Edward. Have you looked at the *New York Times* portal this morning?"

"I haven't," Slowbe replied.

"A couple very interesting things in there today."

"Really?"

"Yes. First, *The World Within* is now the number one best seller in 117 different countries. And that's a record. There's a brief write-up about this in the Books section. There's also a great feature article by John Washburn, called 'Are We Experiencing a Paradigm Shift?'"

"He actually contacted me in early May," Slowbe said. "We had a nice little conversation. He said he was working on something about the truth of consciousness movement, and he asked me a few questions about my book and about my friendship with Toussaint; but he didn't say much else regarding the article or when it would be finished. I mentioned the salon."

"It's an interesting piece," Red Horse said. "He discusses how observance of the world's major religions, particularly Islam and Christianity, has declined sharply in recent decades; and he draws a correlation between the move away from these old hierarchical and dogmatic systems and the rise in popularity of a more 'direct, and realistic experience of the transmundane,' as he put it. The article also talks about the truth of consciousness rallies that have taken place this year in London, Peking, Rome, Cairo, Singapore, Buenos Aires, New York, and Portland, and how the size of the rallies has increased from previous years.

"And he makes a few comments on *The World Within*. He notes how the content, and even the writing style, of your book has struck a deep psychological, and a seemingly psychic, chord in the global community, similar to the response to *Treatise on Singularism* when it came out in '27, but to an even greater degree. He also discusses some of the ways in which contemporary art, science, technology, and recent historical events have begun to alter how we view ourselves and our world, and mentions that the timing of your book seemed remarkably propitious.

"Let's see, he touched on Pope Leo's response to you and the book, and Leo's comment at his press conference just a couple days ago that his 'children should beware of false prophets who talk of mystical powers and inner realities accessible to the average man and woman.' He mentions how what took place in New York has been such a major topic in the public discourse. He was present at your book-signing speech, but doesn't offer any personal opinion about what transpired. Oh, and he does mention the salon, and refers to the group as 'Relaxists.' It appears he was adding content up until shortly before the story went to print."

"Relaxists. Interesting. Am I quoted in the article?" Slowbe asked.

"No," Red Horse replied.

"I'll have to take a look at that later," Slowbe said.

"Well, the other reason I was calling is I was wondering if you'd like to go out to Mt. Hood tomorrow for a hike."

"I'm actually heading to the coast tomorrow," Slowbe replied. "I'll probably be out there for a couple weeks. Thanks for the invitation, though."

"Sure. I'm planning on heading up to Cooper Spur."

"We'll have to do a hike together soon. It's been a while."

"Maybe when you get back from the coast."

"Yeah, let's plan on that. And you're welcome to come out to the cottage if you have time. Just let me know."

"I might take you up on that. I'll have to see what the calendar looks like, but I'll get back to you."

"Did you know it's Toussaint's birthday today?" Slowbe asked.

"Yes. June 17th is a special day."

"Talk to ya soon. Thanks for calling."

"Sure. Bye, Edward."

Like many of the mid-twenty-first century, Slowbe and the other salon members had been deeply influenced by the philosophy of Toussaint Riviere. Singularism, as it was called, was a philosophy of the one, or oneness; of connectedness; of no separation; of a single, illimitable present moment; of non-duality; of an animated, all-encompassing field of energy. And while implicitly collectivist and universalist in nature, Singularism also espoused a "one human, one soul, one God" principle that placed each person squarely at the center of a limitless universe. Furthermore, Singularism embraced the idea that reality was always an emanation and a reflection, never distinct from, separate from, or independent of what Riviere, in his treatise, referred to as "the entity."

Riviere was, by his own account, a mystic, and claimed that his personal experience had provided him with evidence that direct knowledge of God, soul, universal truths, and other dimensions could be gained subjectively. But, at the same time, he was an enthusiastic proponent of the sciences and of the scientific method. He agreed that scientists had a moral obligation to come to conclusions scientifically, to be skeptical, and, moreover, to theorize courageously and imaginatively. Personally, he held to the assumption that the known universe, and any system of multiverses, existed within larger dimensional contexts—larger dimensional contexts in which time and space didn't necessarily exist but in which phenomena that human beings generally thought of as falling under the category of "science" (like energy, for example) continued to play out. "There is science before and beyond the Big Bang," he once said. He believed wholeheartedly that the arc of scientific discovery was unending. He also believed that in order for humanity to move toward its potential it was important that individuals challenge their own beliefs and understanding about the nature of consciousness, the nature of the universe, the nature of reality, about what exists and what is possible—and that they be explorers, because the current paradigm is always, eventually, transcended by new discoveries and new awareness.

Slowbe, Sangree, and Sabin first saw Riviere speak at a truth of consciousness rally in New York City on July 2nd, 2029, shortly after their graduation. He was fifty-three at the time. Riviere was short and had a slight limp. He was dark complected, had a sonorous speaking voice, and bore a striking resemblance to the nineteenth-century abolitionist Fredrick Douglass. His comments that day, as was often the case with his speaking engagements, were delivered in a somewhat nonlinear, stream-of-consciousness manner:

"There is no separation, anywhere, ever. Everything is connected. Everything is part of an infinite continuum, or oneness, comprised of information, intelligence, consciousness, energy, creativity, and love. These confluent traits, as I like to call them, are present within all states of being and all states of becoming, in all systems and in all manifestations, physical and non-physical. This oneness can be imagined as ongoing, interconnected, concentric circles. It can also be imagined as an all-encompassing sphere that has no perimeter, if you can bend your mind to intuit that. Ultimately, the essence of oneness is infiniteness, and the essence of infiniteness is oneness.

"The idea of infinity is crucial because this universe, physical reality, and we ourselves do not exist in isolation, or in a vacuum. To hold an exclusively physicality-time-space worldview, cosmology, or paradigm necessarily limits our potential, our understanding of reality, and our understanding of our own nature. It is to put oneself within a box, or to erect walls where none truly exist. This boxed-in perspective keeps the individual from experiencing connection to a greater oneness, or even a lesser oneness, and from accessing certain types of insight, information, liberation, and power.

"Inside the box exist time, space, brevity, physicality, separateness, duality, birth, and death; outside of the box exists limitlessness. The box resides within the limitlessness. The box can be opened. Physicality-time-space is a construct that emerges from, or out of, a deeper reality; and it exists part and parcel of this deeper reality, not removed from this deeper reality in any respect but for the superficial boundary building of the ego and the conscious mind. Embracing an exclusively physicality-time-space paradigm is like embracing the paradigm that there is only one galaxy. And yes, such a paradigm was dismissed in 1924, by the great Edwin Hubble, when empirical evidence proved it to be insufficient and inaccurate. Hubble's discovery that there were, in fact, numerous galaxies was made possible by experimentation, exploration, open-mindedness, courage, imagination, resolve, and vision. Historically, these are the tools that have been used to expand our understanding, and our experience, of reality. And they consistently bring about paradigm shifts. Learn to embody them. Explore your consciousness and see what you find. The truth of the universe is inextricably linked to the truth of consciousness.

"The basic yearning of all sentience, wittingly or unwittingly, spoken or unspoken, is to be a part of, connected, whole, at one. The basic fact of science is that all things are interconnected.

The basic truth of reality, I will say, is that it is an infinite oneness. There are many aspects of oneness. For example, the individual may think in terms of being at one with Nature, themselves, the universe, or another human. The quantum physicist may refer to oneness as a theory of everything; or they may speak in terms of a field of infinite possibility; or they may look to the fact that all things in the material universe are made of the same stuff, atoms. Philosophers like Schelling and Hegel, for example, might speak in terms of the oneness of mind, and of the unified nature of consciousness. In the search for oneness, some among our species look to the idea of all ideas: God. Ultimately, there is nothing but one, nothing but oneness. This is the sublime, simple truth. And no doubt, the physicality-time-space construct is a valid, meaningful, and rich experience, and a manifestation of infinite reality, but it must be placed in perspective, in its proper context: a part of, not the be-all and end-all. Oneness is simultaneously a uniform, harmonic singularity and a dissonant, paradoxical contradiction, within which is found diversity, distinction, difference, and uniqueness. This is an inherent paradox that is also reflected in our own existence as beings.

"Each person is an epicenter. Each person is an eternal universe. Each person is unprecedented and exquisitely unique, a category unto him or herself. There is no goal more worthy than that of finding oneness within, and of finding one's connection to limitlessness. I often think of this inner oneness as the 'singular alignment of the individual.' Imagine a single, vibrant beam of light that rushes through the body, leaving the body through the top of the head and ascending to no end, and also leaving the body through the bottom of the feet and descending to no end. Imagine being surrounded by, and infused with, this dynamic beam of light. This is an exercise you can try. It is important to note that as a result of aligning with oneness within, the individual will instinctively become attuned to the interconnectedness of all things.

"We are always within something. For example, we are within the universe; it surrounds us. And not only this, but it pervades us because, physically speaking, we are composed of the materials of the universe. Literally, our bodies are composed of materials released from supernovae. We are actually stardust. And the atoms that currently make up our bodies have been moving about the universe for countless eons, taking this form and that form. They will leave our bodies and, in short order, others will take their place. So, we can say that we are surrounded by the universe and at the same time it is inside us in the form of atoms, molecules, energy, et cetera. As Neil deGrasse Tyson said, 'the molecules in the body are traceable to phenomena across the cosmos.' And he points out, in a fashion almost celebratory, that 'we are in the universe and the universe is in us.' There is an inseparability. What would it mean to go within the universe? On one level it means nothing more than to step outside, look up at the nighttime sky, and recognize that, at least by appearances, we are engulfed by it and utterly surrounded by it. It also has something to do with recognizing that the nature of the universe is actually quite different from what is apparent to the naked eye, and understanding that the universe is mostly void of physical form and consists primarily of non-physical phenomena such as dark energy, which makes up almost seventy percent of its entirety. Lifting the veil off the world as it appears, then consciously intersecting and interacting with what is revealed, is to go within. This can be done scientifically and psychically. It involves using high-powered instruments—the mind included—to observe consciousness, energy, and the subatomic, i.e., the otherwise invisible aspects of the universe. We can think of that which is within in terms of that which is beneath the surface, so to speak.

"As we exist within the universe, we also exist within something infinitely greater. Our relationship to the universe is analogous to our relationship with this infinite reality in that we are surrounded by it and it pervades us. And just as we are made of the stuff of the universe, we are also made of the stuff of infinity. We don't have good language to describe this level of reality, but for now, for simplicity's sake, we can call it a primary, or greater, reality. Now, what does it mean to be within or go within the infinite? It means to be present with, and to orient oneself toward, the primary reality, or greater reality. This can be done through various forms of meditation and/or through a personal paradigm shift: a fundamental shift in how reality is conceptualized and understood. Explore consciousness in natural ways and your intuition, and your awareness of a greater reality, will develop. You simply need to seek it out. The pathways of energy and consciousness are intertwined and connected, linking all realms, planes of existence, dimensions, probable realities, and continuums. All systems are open and interconnected. So, if one delves deep enough into the physical universe, one will eventually find oneself in other dimensions, or in the world of the infinite and the immaterial.

"The individual might think that going within, or being within, is the opposite of observing the external world around them, but this is not the case. One can go within with their eyes closed and with their eyes open. That which is recognized with the five senses and that which is understood with the intuition, the psyche, and the mind's eye exist in one 'place.' Ultimately, all is within. Everything originates from within, from beneath the surface. To go within is to focus on, and perhaps even see, the convergence of infinity, consciousness, and the present moment. This is generally an empirical and subjective proposition—as is life itself. To say that life is internal is to say that the seen emerges from the unseen and that formlessness precedes form. The New Testament proposal that the 'kingdom of God' is within you is, perhaps, a useful metaphor. The present moment is the access point. It is the point where all power and energy resides. It is the place where oneness is found. And while the present moment is always motionless and unchanging, it is also always in a dynamic state of vicissitude and becoming. This is part of the paradox of oneness. May peace be with you."

In 2036, as Slowbe drove across the United States on his way to Portland, part of him secretly hoped that Riviere would become the father figure he'd never had. He arrived at Riviere's property on October 27th just after 6:00 p.m. It was a cloudless day and Slowbe felt a great sense of calm and relief as he cruised down the long, narrow driveway to Riviere's home. Despite being only twenty minutes away from downtown Portland, the property felt remote and isolated and was thick with ferns, rhododendron bushes, Douglas fir trees, and other flora. The sun was beginning to set and its rays dashed through the tapestry of foliage, highlighting and contrasting the various shades of green.

Slowbe made his way to the end of the driveway and parked his car in front of the house. He turned off the engine and sat for a while taking in the sight before him. So this is where the old sage lives, Slowbe thought to himself. For a moment he reflected on the fact that his relationship with alcohol had never been brought up in any of the numerous conversations he'd had with Riviere over the last few years. He hoped Riviere would never know this side of him. Now was the time to quit drinking; this was the perfect opportunity. Before leaving New York City, he'd told himself that his journey across the country would be his last six days of drinking. The day he arrived in Portland would be his sobriety date. Slowbe opened the door and stepped out of his car. He inhaled deeply. The air was clean and fragrant. As he walked toward the large grey stone house he heard the sound of a northern flicker, the most common of the six species of woodpecker found in the Portland metro area, furiously plying away high up in one of the Douglas firs.

Riviere and his wife, Natalia Rhia, had lived on the three-acre, densely wooded parcel of land for almost thirty years. In 2007, shortly after he finished his master's degree in divinity from Harvard University and became a member of the Unitarian

Universalist Society, he inherited the property from his aunt, the actress Sharifa Riviere. This development coincided with him taking a position as pastor at the First Unitarian Church, located at the corner of Thirteenth and Main in downtown Portland—a position he held for sixteen years, until January of 2023, when he decided to leave the church. Instead of a final sermon, he offered the parishioners a brief account of how and why he had come to his decision.

He began by explaining that although he had benefited greatly from Christianity, he'd come to view Christian doctrine as a rung on the ladder of his personal evolution, and no longer the alpha and omega. Religion, he said, now felt more like a set of blinders that limited the scope of his vision. He described a somewhat recent experience he'd had while camping alone on Steens Mountain in the remote southeastern corner of Oregon. He told the congregation that on the third night, as he was gazing up at the Milky Way and the countless stars, he was struck by an analogy. The ego is like the city lights, he said, beautiful in its own right and of great value, while the soul is like the nighttime sky in the remote parts of the planet when the Milky Way and all the constellations are visible to the naked eye and the sky seems filled to the brim with sparkling points of light. The countless stars are always present, but when one is amidst the city lights, or consumed by them, the view of the heavens is obstructed.

He told the congregation that later into the evening, after he'd been in meditation for close to an hour, he'd had "an awakening experience," one that suddenly and dramatically changed his sense of who and what he was. He didn't go into detail about the specifics of the whole experience, but he told them that he'd heard a voice: "You have your seven jewels, there is no religion," it said. Riviere explained that the statement immediately resonated with him because just days before, on the first day of his camping trip, while writing in his journal, he'd spontaneously started drawing artistic renderings of seven words, values-based words, that for him, taken as a whole, represented the essentials of being a good person, of being his best self, of leading a good life, of being whole and well and powerful. When he'd finished his drawings he decided to call them the "seven jewels": love, patience, self-affirmation, forgiveness, positivity, presence, and acquiescence (by "acquiescence" he meant letting go and allowing his ego to acquiesce to his soul and to a Creator). "To align with them as much as possible in daily life," he'd written beneath the picture of his values. He mentioned to the congregation that when he'd heard the voice say "there is no religion," he interpreted it as meaning that allegiance to the institution was not a necessary part of aligning with his seven jewels, or of discovering truth, for that matter, and could even be a hindrance. Divine truth comes directly from within, he said; it is subjective and personal.

Riviere went on to say that, for him, religion, with all its pageantry, dogma, hierarchies, rigidity, and judgment, had become like the city lights of the ego that kept him from viewing the unobstructed nighttime sky of the soul. He was being called, he said, to deconstruct himself and his belief system, as he sought to see and experience the starkest, most essential, and most natural state of his spiritual Self. He was no longer a Christian, he said, although it would be appropriate to refer to him as a Christ-ian. In other words, he was still drawn to the mystery of Jesus Christ, and the reality of Jesus Christ. He was still a follower of Jesus Christ, but he was walking away from the church, away from religion. He had taken his relationship with, and his understanding of, the Christ entity entirely out of the context of religion and had placed it, unembellished, in the realms of the cosmos, multidimensionality, and the infinite consciousness.

Riviere added that while his trip to Steens Mountain had been a pivotal and transformative episode, his distancing from church tradition and church doctrine had been underway for some time. He explained that over the years he had edited and revised the Jesus story to his own liking and had taken full creative license in interpreting the Gospels: dismissing certain sections and statements and ideas, inserting alternative narratives, all to such a degree that he could no longer be said to be supporting the accepted faith. Then he announced that he did not believe that the virgin birth, the crucifixion, or the resurrection had actually occurred, and stated that, in his view, "there is no Trinity, there is only one thing." The congregation gasped loudly and there were rumblings and whispers. And no longer, he said, did he accept the idea of original sin, nor would he lend the power of his beliefs to the constructs of a heaven or hell. He also noted that he didn't believe Jesus of Nazareth ever intended to establish an institution.

Riviere went on to say that he adored Jesus the man and believed that he had most certainly done things that astounded and frightened his contemporaries. Jesus was a human being whose ego and mind were fully actualized within the soul, which was why he had direct and uninhibited access to certain powers and insights, such as the freedom of mind over matter, Riviere claimed. In the person of Jesus, there was no undue compartmentalization or separation between mind, ego, and soul. Jesus was soul incarnate like the rest of us, he said, the difference being that he was fully aware of his nature. Riviere explained that he was starting to see fewer and fewer distinctions between the idea of "Christ" and the idea of "soul." They were becoming one and the same. So, for him, another way to think of the moniker Jesus "Christ" would be to say Jesus "the human being who was fully cognizant of soul, who was completely in unison with it, and who understood it as his nature." Jesus of Nazareth knew there was a truth that transcended religion, Riviere assumed, but intentionally spoke in terms that could be understood by the people of the time. A "Christ" figure in the twenty-first or twenty-second century, he stated, would frame the message quite differently and would most likely not use religious language or references. Riviere concluded by saying that he would always be guided by the truth of love.

Slowbe approached the front door of Riviere's home and rang the doorbell. Three long choral chimes reverberated in succession. Shortly after the fourth chime, Slowbe could hear someone approaching. The door soon flung open.

"Edward," Riviere said joyously in his rich baritone voice, "so good to see you." He reached out and embraced Slowbe affectionately.

"Toussaint," Slowbe replied, smiling broadly.

"Come in, come in. How was your drive across the country?"

"It was beautiful. It's a beautiful country, so many incredible landscapes."

"Wonderful," Riviere replied. "Let's sit down, Edward, and relax for a while."

Riviere led Slowbe into a large room to the left of the front entrance. The beige-colored walls were covered with artwork and pictures of what Slowbe assumed to be family members. At the front and back of the room were large windows. The west-facing windows, in the back of the room, looked out onto a lawn that was surrounded by ash and Douglas fir trees. A fireplace adorned the south wall. There were two couches, one of which was dark brown and located in the center of the room where there was also a coffee table. The other, which was floral patterned, was located along the west wall. In the corner of the room, near the east-facing windows, was a black grand piano with the lid propped open. The room smelled slightly of rosemary. Riviere gestured for Slowbe to make himself comfortable on the dark-brown couch as Riviere sat down in the club chair to its right.

"My favorite sights were the Badlands and the Black Hills in South Dakota, and Yellowstone and the Grand Tetons in Wyoming. Although, I actually got caught in a brief snowstorm crossing Teton Pass, which I think has an elevation of around eight thousand feet. There was snow everywhere, and a few cars veered off the road. It was a bit harrowing."

"I'm glad you made it safely," Riviere replied.

"You have a wonderful art collection here," Slowbe said.

"Thank you," Riviere replied, "most of them were left to me by my aunt when she passed away, but my wife and I purchased a few of the pieces."

"Is your wife here?" Slowbe asked.

"She's in Taiwan visiting a friend of hers, but she'll be returning to Portland in a couple days. She's looking forward to seeing you. Are you hungry, Edward?"

"I am, actually."

"Good," Riviere said, "does smoked salmon and cheese sound ok for a snack?"

"Absolutely, that sounds great," Slowbe replied.

"You stay here and I'll be right back," Riviere said.

"Ok."

Several minutes later Riviere returned with a silver tray that had several plates on it: one with large portions of smoked salmon, another with cheese and crackers, and a third with bundles of Thompson seedless grapes. In addition, the tray contained a teapot, two small cups, and a small bowl with various types of tea bags.

"Oh this looks great," Slowbe said.

The two began eating.

On the lamp table that stood between the couch and the club chair was a framed photo that caught Slowbe's attention. "Who are these two?" he asked, always curious to glean what he could about family dynamics and family histories.

"Those are my parents, Geo and Lucinda," Riviere replied.

Riviere had hundreds of family photographs in his house, most of which were collected in albums, although many were framed. For those who inquired, he was always happy to discuss some of the details and historical contexts of his lineage. More often than not, he found himself recounting stories of his father's side rather than his mother's side, as a result of people being curious about his name; but his mother's family, the Peabodys, were originally from England and had immigrated to the American colonies in the 1760s, settling in Concord, Massachusetts. In 1859, two Peabody brothers, George and Fredric, and their families made their way to Oregon via the Oregon Trail and put down roots in the eastern part of the state, eventually becoming ranchers—a family enterprise that continued until 2001, when a decision was made to sell the property. George Peabody was Riviere's great-great-great-great-grandfather.

Riviere's paternal great-grandfather, Umi Riviere, was born in 1897 in Saint-Louis, Senegal, a former slave-trading post established by the French in the seventeenth century. From 1673 until 1902 it had been the capital of the French colony in Senegal, and from 1895 to 1902 it was the capital of the colonial territory called French West Africa, which incorporated the entire region of Senegal and seven other African nations. Umi's ancestors on his mother's side were of the Serer ethnic group and had lived in and around the area of Saint-Louis for generations. His father was a French soldier who'd arrived in 1881. Both were deeply religious, and they imparted their Roman Catholic faith to their son.

When Umi was twenty-seven years old, he and his wife, Mura, heard news that there was an abundance of employment opportunities in the Holy Land. As a result of a League of Nations decree called the British Mandate for Palestine, established to administer the region following World War I and the breakup of the Ottoman/Turkish Empire, the British government was employing large numbers of general laborers to aid in infrastructure projects, such as road building and dam construction. Administrative control of Palestine, whose population of 750,000 was approximately 80 percent Arab-speaking Muslim, 10 percent Jewish, and 10 percent Christian, was officially transferred to Britain in 1923. An explanation for the Mandate had been outlined in article 22 of the Covenant of the League of Nations, stating that "certain communities formerly belonging to the Turkish Empire have reached a stage of development where their existence as independent nations can be provisionally recognized subject to the rendering of administrative advice and assistance by a Mandatory until such time as they are able to stand alone." In 1924, drawn by the lure of an economic windfall, as well as by religious zeal, Umi and Mura traveled to Jerusalem with their six-year-old boy, Sengee, to start a new life, unaware that the seeds of future geopolitical strife in the region had already been sown.

Seven years prior to their arrival in Palestine, a letter had been written by British foreign secretary Arthur James Balfour to Walter Rothschild and the Zionist Federation of Great Britain and Ireland, which would eventually become incorporated into the British Mandate for Palestine. It stated that "His Majesty's government view with favour the establishment in Palestine of a national home for the Jewish people, and will use their best endeavours to facilitate the achievement of this object, it being clearly understood that nothing shall be done which may prejudice the civil and religious rights of existing non-Jewish communities in Palestine, or the rights and political status enjoyed by Jews in any other country." The correspondence was leaked to the press and would later be known as the Balfour Declaration.

Not long after Sengee himself was betrothed, to a young woman named Fatima whose family was among the ten percent of Palestinian Arabs who were Christian, the Arab revolt in Palestine first erupted. Sengee was eighteen. These uprisings, which occurred between 1936 and 1939, grew out of a desire for independence from British rule and resentment over the growing number of Jewish immigrants arriving in Palestine. Between 1929 and 1939, 250,000 Jews, primarily from Eastern Europe, had immigrated to Palestine in what became known as the Fifth Aliyah. Concerned that the huge influx would destabilize the region, the British government attempted to slow immigration by creating strict quotas on Jewish arrivals, making it illegal for any Jewish immigration to occur beyond these quotas. The wave of 110,000 Jews that were smuggled into Palestine between 1936 and 1948 in violation of the quotas was called the Aliyah Bet, or "secondary immigration." In his early adolescence, Sengee had once asked his father what the word "aliyah" meant, and why so many Jewish people were moving to Palestine.

"Aliyah is when Jewish people from different parts of the world migrate, or return, to the region they call the 'land of Israel,' and to the city of Jerusalem," Umi told his son.

"Jerusalem is in Palestine," Sengee said.

"True, but the Jewish people call this land Israel. It's been their ancestral land for thousands of years."

Umi, an avid student of history, particularly of the ancient world and the Near East, explained to his son that "aliyah" was a Biblical term and that there was a long history of the Jewish people wanting to return to Israel. He mentioned how the Babylonian king Nebuchadnezzar had exiled the Jews from Israel in the sixth century BC and had destroyed Jerusalem. He told Sengee that the Persian King Cyrus the Great later allowed the Jews to return after he conquered the Babylonian Empire in 539 BC, but that in many subsequent periods of history they had been forced to live outside of their homeland. He mentioned that Jews living outside of Israel were called the Jewish Diaspora, and that many different empires and peoples had controlled the land of Israel, including the ancient Greeks, the Romans, the Byzantine Empire, the Fatimid Caliphate, the Crusaders, the Ayyubids, the Mamluks, the Mongols, the Ottomans, and the British.

"In the year 70," Umi said, "the Roman Empire crushed a Jewish rebellion that had risen up against Roman authority. Jerusalem was again destroyed. That was the last time the Jewish people had their own homeland. After this, many Jews fled to Persia, Iraq, Arabia, and other more distant places. Eventually, many moved to Europe, Russia, and North Africa. Aliyah has been the goal and wish of Jewish people for a long time. Between the years 200 and 1800 there were a few minor instances of Jewish migration back to Israel, but in 1882 this began to greatly increase because that's when many Jews started a new fight to re-establish a nation of Israel. The different stages of Jewish immigration to Israel since 1882 have been called the First Aliyah, from 1882 to 1903; the Second Aliyah, from 1904 to 1914; the Third Aliyah, from 1919 to 1923; and the Fourth Aliyah, from 1924 to 1928. They say the Fifth Aliyah began in 1929 and is still underway. Each one of these aliyahs was spurred on not only by a desire to re-establish a nation of Israel, but also because Jews were fleeing violence perpetrated upon them in other countries."

"What's the ancestral land of the Palestinians?" Sengee asked.

"That's a good question. Many Palestinians believe they can trace their history in this land back to the year 640 when Muslims conquered the region. So, that's almost fourteen hundred years ago, but this part of the world has been called Palestine since ancient times. Many Arabs moved here after 691 when the Dome of the Rock was built. And by the ninth century, most of the population was Arab Muslim. Palestinians have wanted their own nation, just like the Jewish people. There was even an uprising in 1834 against the Ottoman conquerors that, in the end, proved unsuccessful."

Sengee was astounded by this information, and he remembered the conversation in the spring of 1936 when he was asked by friends to join the revolt against the British and the Jews. He declined to participate, telling his friends that his father would not allow him to take sides, even though Umi had made no such prohibition. Many of Sengee's friends turned their backs on him because of his refusal to take up arms. During the revolt numerous Palestinian villages, including thousands of homes, as well as crops, were completely destroyed, and hundreds of Palestinians were held without trial in unsanitary and crowded prison camps. By the time the British army, with support from the Jewish paramilitary group called Haganah, finally suppressed the insurrection, five thousand Palestinians had been killed and fifteen thousand wounded. Three hundred Jews and 262 English were also dead. Six of Sengee's childhood friends were killed. For the Palestinians, the strength of their military and administrative leadership was significantly diminished, although there remained a sense of national identity.

In December of 1948, three generations of Rivieres, including Toussaint's father and aunt, Geo and Sharifa, born in 1938 and 1944, respectively, moved to Oregon to escape the war-torn Holy Land. A new wave of conflict had emerged following the 1947 United Nations Partition Plan. Adopted by the UN General Assembly, Resolution 181(II) had called for dividing Palestine into "independent Arab and Jewish states and the Special International Regime for the city of Jerusalem." While the Jewish community accepted the plan, Palestinian Arabs were staunchly opposed, primarily because it allotted Jews fifty-six percent of the territory, even though they comprised just thirty-two percent of the population. Palestinian Arabs also questioned the authority of the United Nations to partition the land in the first place, arguing that it contravened United Nations principles regarding national self-determination.

Although the resolution was cause for joyous celebration among the Jewish residents, who had achieved the long sought-after state recognition, it fomented intense consternation among Palestinian Arabs. Once again violence broke out. The Civil War in Mandatory Palestine, fought between Israeli and Palestinian forces, erupted almost immediately after the adoption of UN Resolution 181(II) and lasted from November of 1947 to May of 1948. The conflict ended in defeat of the Arab Palestinians and marked the beginning of a number of significant developments, including the breakdown of Arab society in Palestine and a massive exodus of Jews from Muslim nations. On the last day of the British Mandate for Palestine, May 14th, 1948, Israel declared itself an independent state. In the morning of May 15th an invasion force of Egyptian, Jordanian, and Syrian militaries entered Palestine, commencing another conflict, the Arab-Israeli War, which lasted until March of 1949. Israeli forces were victorious over the armies of the Arab League, and at the war's conclusion nearly seven hundred thousand Palestinian Arabs became refugees.

"Your parents are quite a handsome couple," Slowbe said.

Riviere smiled and gave Slowbe a look of understanding. "Would you like to take a walk around the property?" he asked.

"Yes, absolutely," Slowbe responded.

On their way to the front entrance, Slowbe mentioned that he'd done a DNA test a few years prior and found that his ancestry was fifty-four percent West African, mainly from the region of Nigeria and Ghana; forty percent European, mostly Italian, but also some English; and six percent Native American.

"There are some old pictures and a few heirlooms that have been passed down," Slowbe said, "and some old family Bibles that have birth dates written in them, but I don't really know much about my family history. I'd like to do some research at some point."

"I'm sure that would be an interesting project," Riviere replied.

The two stepped outside into the cool fall evening. The sun had just dropped below the horizon. Riviere reached into the right pocket of his loose-fitting brown corduroy pants and pulled out a small amethyst and a little bundle of sage that was tied together with a piece of red string.

"These are for you, Edward," Riviere said. He handed Slowbe the two items.

"Thank you...very much," Slowbe said.

Slowbe held the sage and the amethyst in his hand, admiring

them, and then clenched the two objects as if to absorb their energy.

"Consider them housewarming gifts," Riviere said.

Slowbe and Riviere headed along a trail that meandered amidst tall trees and shrubs, eventually coming to a small meadow, and then to a pond, where they decided to sit for a while. On the west side of the pond was the cabin where Slowbe would live for an indefinite period of time.

"So, Edward, tell me about the new poetry you're working on."

"There will be seventy to seventy-five poems in this volume, and I think it'll be finished by early next year. I love writing about Nature, so that's always a topic, but a number of the poems I've been working on recently have been exploring the meaning of death, our relationship with it, and how we cope with and respond to it. I would say some of the other major themes in the collection are...I'm writing about the intersection of idealism and realism...also the ego and identity. Human relationships, primarily family dynamics and healing, healing from family trauma, childhood trauma, and the individual's relationship with themselves. Life is messy, and why is that? What are the sources of the messiness?"

"Life doesn't fit into a tidy little box, does it?" Riviere replied.

Slowbe nodded his head in agreement. "I'm intrigued by the messiness," he said. "Sometimes it's beautiful because it's about an authentic struggle to grow and change and find a way to survive, and about navigating a life that is often hard and confusing, and even disorienting; and sometimes the messiness is unnecessary, horrible, or just plain ridiculous. So often there's a contradiction between our ideals and our actual behavior, on a personal level and as a species or society. I struggle with this... and how compulsions and fear, and other factors, create great discrepancies in daily life, and in society, between ideals—or maybe not even something so lofty as an ideal, maybe just the personal good or the common good—and actual experience. I'm interested in how fear impacts the individual and the society. There are so many levels of fear. Some are subtle and others more overt, and I think it manifests itself in ways that one wouldn't even, on the surface, necessarily suspect. For example, arrogance, and often anger, are basic fear responses, in my opinion, that don't look like fear on the surface. It's counterintuitive, but fear can even become a comfort zone, or it can become so normalized and embedded that it's hard to detect and uproot. I think it's the scourge of humanity. I suspect that all our negative behavior is in some way linked to it. Above all, I'm interested in how fear denies one the ability to let go. What is the individual controlled by?"

"Well, I am very excited about reading anything you may have ready."

"Definitely, I have about fifty poems that I think are finished or very close to being finished. I'd love to share them with you and get your feedback."

"Certainly. So, Edward, have you ever considered writing any prose, taking the themes from your poetry and expanding upon them in essays, a novel, or some type of philosophical work?"

Slowbe raised his right eyebrow and pursed his lips slightly. "I've had a couple ideas cross my mind," he said. "I do enjoy writing prose. In school I was always most comfortable in the classes where the major assignments were essays or research papers."

"Just a thought that occurred to me."

"I'm sure I'll get to work on a novel, or some type of longer prose work, at some point."

"Yes...so, you've been thinking about death lately?"

"I think about death a lot," Slowbe said, somewhat light-heartedly. "I've always thought about it a lot, and the afterlife, even when I was a kid."

"I'm fascinated by it as well. It reminds me that we're always surrounded by, and immersed in, the unknown. What happens next is probably the greatest mystery of all."

"Do you think most people fear death?"

"Oh yes, on one level or another."

"Sometimes I've wondered...if an individual is able to entirely eliminate the fear of death, on every level, have they effectively eliminated all fear?"

"Perhaps. What do you think?" Riviere asked.

"Well, fear in general is usually related to the prospect of losing something, experiencing physical or emotional pain or duress, or confronting the unknown; and I think these are the main reasons people fear death. I suppose I do feel that if one has truly and completely overcome the fear of death—which is often specifically about a fear of losing one's identity or existence and being thrust into the unknown—one of the by-products is that there is no longer fear of loss, emotional and physical pain, or the unknown. One is able to fully accept the present moment."

"That may be."

"Humans are quite conflicted about death."

"Yes, we are."

"There are many ideas about what a good death is and what a bad death is, and what's an acceptable death. I'm not sure if the manner of death is consequential to the soul; perhaps it is in some way. We have some interesting notions. We say things like 'she died before her time' or 'she died too young.' There's a part of us that seems to think that death should only come to the elderly, or soldiers. In any case, on the one hand we're very used to death and understand it as a part of life, and sometimes regard it in a very noble light, and on the other hand we're deeply repulsed and unnerved and frightened by it. Death can traumatize the living, and often does, even though it's one of the most common, basic experiences that we know of."

"Well, we can certainly say that birth implies death, and I would say that the opposite is true as well."

"Are there good deaths and bad deaths?"

"I think the only truly bad death is when one is killed by another. There is a sanctity of life that has to be preserved, on principle, as a higher law, and when an individual takes the life of another who has been born into this world it's a terrible loss for humanity. Society shares blame. Society is culpable."

"Do you consider death on the battlefield to be murder?"

"I do," Riviere replied.

"What about death by suicide?"

"That's very complicated. I'd just say that it's tragic, except in the case of euthanasia."

"Deaths that occur by natural catastrophe, accident, and disease can be very sad, but isn't it the way of the world, of Nature, for these things to happen? Oftentimes people look at these types of deaths and point at God in anger, or they'll say things like 'if God exists, how could It let these things happen?' Or, they'll simply stop believing in a God altogether. I feel this is a misplaced reaction."

"Death is a mystifying aspect of reality, a very profound and emotional experience for the living. But I do think individual consciousness and collective consciousness have much to do with determining, even preordaining, the causes and circumstances of death in our society, in our world."

"Can we have a concept in which there is no such thing as death, where there is only life and rebirth?"

"In the big picture, definitely. When I think of death," Riviere said, "I often think of timeless dimensions that the consciousness, or personality, returns to after the physical body has expired. I don't believe there is any such thing as death as an ultimate end, but rather I see it as an ultimate rebirth. It's a framework of change, growth, or transition. There aren't any real bookends in capital-L Life, in my view. I think once we complete the cycle of our lives in this physical plane the consciousness enters non-physical planes. It's kind of hard to imagine given our current orientation, but we're very capable of intuiting it. I imagine a place without limit, of heightened awareness, profound freedom; a place, so to speak, where there is room, so to speak, for ineffable expression and discovery. Perhaps one might consider it a godlike realm. I think when one emerges, or re-emerges, into this place they are more alive than they were in physical form. Our world, our physical universe, exists as a part of this limitless place, like one blade of grass in a boundless field. We can't escape the limitless place, it's everywhere, whether we're attuned to it or not. People speak of eternal life after death, but we may as well begin to speak of eternal life before death; in other words, dwelling within the eternal and the temporal simultaneously. There is no innate separation. We can, if we are so inclined, peek our heads through the firmament of physical reality and into the realm of immortality."

Over the course of the next two months, Slowbe settled into a comfortable routine. He awoke early, around 6:00 a.m., and would work on poetry for a couple hours, after which time he would have a small breakfast and then take a short walk that usually ended with him sitting for a while on a certain fallen tree next to the pond. He would return to his poetry until around 12:00 p.m., when he and Riviere would usually meet for lunch and a couple hours of conversation. Following his afternoon meeting with Riviere, he would take an hour-long nap and then continue working. He rarely ate much in the evening, often just fruit or salad, and he would drink tea. Between about 7:00 p.m. and 8:00 p.m., he checked national and international news. The rest of his evening hours were spent reading, meditating, journaling, and playing or listening to music. Occasionally, he would go on outings around Portland, to a poetry reading, an art gallery, or a musical performance. He was also exploring Oregon. He'd been to the coast six times, had traveled to Crater Lake, had gone on two hikes in the Mt. Hood National Forest, and had been on several hikes in the Columbia River Gorge.

In the morning of December 27th, as he sat next to the

pond, Slowbe noticed a splash out of the corner of his eye. He turned his head and kept his sight focused on the spot where the commotion had occurred. Forty seconds later, about a hundred feet to the left of where he had fixed his gaze, a common loon emerged from beneath the water. Slowbe recognized the species immediately, and he was particularly surprised because he knew that sightings were rare in Oregon, except near the coast. He'd never seen one before, outside of pictures and videos. He'd first become intrigued by loons after having read about them in *Walden* when he was sixteen. They'd taken on a special, mystical place in his imagination ever since. In the chapter called "Brute Neighbors," Thoreau had described an experience where he was observing a loon repeatedly dive and resurface in Walden Pond and, referring to the loon's call, which he'd heard numerous times while living in his cabin in the woods, wrote that it was "a long drawn unearthly howl... perhaps the wildest sound that is ever heard, making the woods ring far and wide."

The sky was overcast and it began to drizzle slightly. Slowbe watched the loon dive and re-emerge several times over the next fifteen minutes. Once more it dove into the deep, placid waters. Slowbe waited and scanned the pond, anticipating its reappearance somewhere. He waited for about ten minutes, but the bird seemed to have mysteriously disappeared. Unbeknownst to Slowbe, it had come up in a far corner of the pond behind some fallen branches that hung over the water.

Slowbe stood up and began walking back to his cabin. After he took a few steps toward the trail, he experienced a clenching pulse that passed through his body like a flash of electricity. It came and went in a millisecond, and Slowbe immediately sensed something was wrong. He began to walk at a hurried pace toward the main house. Moments later, when he heard a horrifying scream penetrate the forest, he began to run as fast as he could. Slowbe arrived at the house and saw Natalia hunched over Riviere, who was lying motionless on the ground. He'd been cleaning leaves from the gutters and had slipped and fallen awkwardly off the ladder from a height of over twenty feet. A sharp piece of bone protruded from the side of his neck. Natalia was holding her hands over the wound in a vain attempt to stop the blood flow as she wailed hysterically. Slowbe called for paramedics, who arrived twelve minutes later, but Riviere had died almost immediately. The rest of the day and night were blurry and chaotic.

The next morning Slowbe drove to the liquor store on Barbur Boulevard. His heavy, sullen look stood out to the store clerk, who watched Slowbe meander around the store in a daze. Slowbe approached the checkout counter with a bottle of Jim Beam. The clerk greeted him, but Slowbe gave only a muted response. He drove back to the property and retreated into the cabin and began to drink, after having been sober since the day he arrived in Portland. Riviere's funeral took place in Portland on January 3rd, 2037. Two days later there was a public memorial, also in Portland, which was attended by sixty thousand people and viewed by millions on the internet. On the sixth, Natalia flew to Brazil to be with family. During the next few weeks, Slowbe spent hours next to the pond looking for the loon. He never saw it again, but he heard its call several times late at night. On February 1st, he moved into an apartment in southeast Portland near Mt. Tabor Park.

*

Slowbe continued resting in his hammock after the call with Red Horse. The warm sun and light breeze seeped into his body and he felt like he might drift off at any moment. He thought about Riviere for a while longer. Then his mind wandered further. Life, as he now understood it, had begun with poetry, he thought, and he was overcome by a deep sense of gratitude for the hundreds of poems he'd written over nearly three decades, many of which had been published in three widely read collections: *Follow Me to Your Favorite Colors*, in 2033; *Where is My Ego?*, in 2037; and *I Was Running Away*, in 2043. Slowbe thought of how poetry was like a spirit that had guided his life. It was something beyond words. It had inspired him to seek. It had been a sacred pool within which he could explore and beckon the mysterious, connect with the unseen, and commune with Nature, history, mythology, and the cosmos. He'd discovered it one long, dream-like day while walking through a dark-green forest, while daydreaming of intergalactic travel, while gazing at the spirits of another world, while wishing for world peace; and in his very first poem, when he was twelve years old, he wrote, "If I was king of the universe, I would share all that was mine."

His earliest poems were as much spontaneous writing as anything else, with only a semiconscious sense of style and structure; although, on occasion, he would try to rhyme. He followed impulses and internal rhythms, and he would look for the meaning in what he'd written only after the words were on paper, as if the poem was delivered to him on some sort of metaphysical conveyer belt up from the regions of his soul to the regions of his conscious mind. As months and years unfolded, he began to delve into the works of others, Romantic poets like Shelley and Byron, and twentieth-century American poets like Cummings and Frost and St. Vincent Millay. And even as he began to style his verse more consciously, he continued to embrace the notion that poetry was a bearer of ancient truth, and that it was woven into the fabric of the universe, telling and retelling the story of birth, emotion, beauty, virtue, death, and eternity. Eventually, he came to believe that the Muse and his soul were one and the same.

Poetry had not only guided him toward the seeker's path in the first place, but it had also provided light along the way. It had offered a measure of balance amidst the turbulence he carried; had served as a vehicle for creative expression; had given him an identity, "the poet," that he valued; and had helped him to develop an inward focus that would lead to the most important discoveries of his life. Poetry had even played a role in fostering relationships that would become important catalysts for his growth and healing, most notable among these being his relationships with Riviere and Red Horse.

It all led to the writing of *The World Within*, a process that, for him, was like crossing a final threshold, like crossing a sacred river into another life—a crossing that, all told, took four years to complete, from 2043 to 2047. The process had left him with no doubt whatsoever that the solutions to all his problems, and the answers to all his questions, lay within, and had conditioned him, once and for all, to embrace the power and limitlessness within, and to be relaxed amidst the great current, the great wave, the great wind, amidst the deep sea and the vast spaces, amidst the unknown and the mysterious, amidst the most profound realities and experiences, and to love himself and trust himself unequivocally, and to discard all limiting beliefs.

Red Horse had helped him approach the banks of the river. In 2041 she invited him to spend the summer at her home in northeastern Oregon, near Wallowa, to work on clearing the entanglements and disruptions within his system, and to begin a process of redirection. The invitation followed some forthright comments she made as the two shared dinner at her Portland residence one evening.

"I love your poetry, Edward, and so many people benefit from this gift you share. There is so much beauty and wisdom in your heart. But your drinking, your addiction, just adds chaos and negativity to the world, not to mention to your own life," she said to him. "Do yourself and the world a favor and remove the drink from your life once and for all, and replace it with peace, and sobriety. Forgive your mother and your father. Forgive yourself. Come to know your tears, and accept them. Put down your sword and surrender to something greater than yourself. You can't afford to live narcissistically; you can't afford to live for pleasure and pain, or with any semblance of shame or resentment. There is no more time for procrastination. It's time to stop running. Stand in the here and now. You know what's waiting for you, and you have a responsibility."

Red Horse questioned Slowbe on the principles he held in his mind, and how they conflicted with his manner of living; she questioned him about the state of his character and integrity; she inquired about what he claimed to truly want from life; she asked about his experience of the violet realm and if he fully honored it and fully embraced it, and what he thought it would take for him to truly understand, utilize, and be in relationship with it; she questioned him about what he claimed to believe in and to what degree he lived in accordance with those beliefs. "Who are you?" she asked him.

Slowbe was stunned by Red Horse's candor, and by the solemnity with which she delivered it. When she proposed a retreat, and indicated that she would support him with it, he felt he had somehow crossed a point of no return, that a cycle had come to its conclusion, and that the prophecy he'd held about his inevitable sobriety was unfolding before his very eyes. He could only acquiesce.

They made their way east on June 7th. During the next three and a half months, Slowbe would go into the sweat lodge, spend time alone in the wilderness, meditate by the Wallowa River, participate in healing ceremonies with Red Horse, and engage in a therapeutic practice with her called Motivational Interviewing. MI, as it was also called, was a behavior-modification method developed by psychologists William Miller and Stephen Rollnick, who introduced the technique in 1991 with their book *Motivational Interviewing: Preparing People for Change*. Derived from the Socratic method, MI used a process of pointed questioning to help the individual develop greater clarity around potential discrepancies between their behavior and their own best interest and, most importantly, to help them align themselves with internal truth. Slowbe began to settle into the change that was underway. He knew he could no longer lie, or run away, or play hide-and-seek with himself, or suppress his emotions, or be separated from his own experience.

"This is just the beginning, Edward," Red Horse said on the drive back to Portland on September 23rd. "There are many layers of negativity that need to be peeled back, a lot of healing, but sobriety makes this work possible. Be patient, but be diligent and rigorous." When they entered Mt. Hood National Forest, they decided to do the short hike to Tamanawas Falls. It was a sunny day and there were no clouds in the sky.

Transitions

At 12:00 a.m., the alarm on Slowbe's Array began to ring. A few hours earlier, he'd fallen asleep on the couch at his cottage in Nehalem. In his right hand, resting on his chest, was a copy of Ernest Hemingway's *The Old Man and the Sea*. Slowbe's thumb was inserted between pages seventy-six and seventy-seven. He opened the book for a moment and scanned the section where he'd left off: as a mako shark has caught the scent of the marlin the old man has killed and tied to the side of his boat. Slowbe made a small fold at the top corner of page seventy-seven and then placed the book on the floor next to the couch. The steady "shhhhhh" sound of the ocean waves drifted into the living room through the open sliding glass doors.

During the eleven days that he'd been at the coast, he'd adjusted his sleeping schedule to allow for a couple hours each night, between midnight and about 2:00 a.m., for astronomical observation. The Ophiuchid meteor shower had reached its peak during the first three nights of his stay, on June 18th, 19th, and 20th, and he'd seen dozens of "shooting stars" on those evenings. The frequency then tapered off, but there were other celestial occurrences that were of interest to him. On the 23rd the moon and Mars were in conjunction, on the 25th there was a full moon, on the 26th the moon and Saturn were in conjunction, and on the 27th Jupiter and Mercury were in conjunction. And while his retreat had been primarily solitary, he had received a few guests, all of whom were motivated to travel to the coast in large part by a desire to escape the heat wave that was bearing down on Portland. Red Horse and Sangree came out on the 20th, which was the summer solstice. The three combed the beach and watched the sunset together. Red Horse left that evening, and Sangree stayed until the morning of the 22nd. Angel Song had arrived on the 28th and was planning on returning to Portland on the 30th.

Slowbe glanced toward the glass doors and could see that a thick fog had rolled in—not promising for stargazing, but he decided to go for a little adventure nonetheless. He grabbed the coat that was dangling from a chair in the kitchen, put on his sandals, and headed outdoors. In a couple minutes, he was at the edge of the beach. As he continued toward the shoreline, the dry, loose sand made his movements slightly laborious; but the farther he walked, the wetter and more congealed the sand became and the easier it was to walk on. Eventually, the ocean started coming into view, and Slowbe stopped and took in the sound and energy of the force before him. The ocean seems especially intense on a foggy night, he thought, even slightly ominous, almost as if were one to get too close they might never be seen again. Slowbe looked up and began checking the sky for breaks in the fog. While he was doing so, the tide snuck up on him and submerged his feet and ankles. His feet sank into the sand. Through the din of the surging waves, which sounded like a great wind roaring through a deciduous forest, he heard a seagull cry out. He turned his head to the left, where the sound had come from. He paused and listened carefully.

Slowbe took a few more gradual steps into the ocean. The fog and clouds were moving south and a clearing had opened up. He could now plainly see the vast procession of waves in front of him crash and curl in perfect rhythmic unison. He continued forward, slowly, step by step, until he was in up to his calves. Then he stopped and bent over to put his hands in the water. He heard the seagull cry out again, this time much closer.

Slowbe looked around but couldn't see the bird. Suddenly, it swooped down and passed less than six feet from his face. Slowbe felt a gust of air and heard the swooshing sound from the bird's wings. His eyes opened wide and his head and torso jerked back as the bird veered off and disappeared. He turned around and started heading back toward dry land, to a spot where he could sit down well out of reach of the encroaching water and make himself comfortable. Soon, he was settled into the cool, loose sand. Thirty minutes later the entire nighttime sky was visible above him. Down the coast, in the distance, the silent herd of cloud and fog continued on its ghostly way.

Slowbe scanned the Milky Way for patterns and clusters. Some of his favorites were commonly known: Orion's Belt, the Pleiades, and the Big Dipper. The latter often made him think of Seven. One summer evening, following their ninth-grade year, he and Seven were sitting on a park bench playing their guitars.

"Do you know how to find the North Star?" Seven asked.

"No," Slowbe replied. "Do you?"

Slowbe had first heard of the North Star in elementary school during the lessons about Harriet Tubman and the Underground Railroad—how runaway slaves had followed it to the free states. The woman, the death-defying journeys to escape slavery, and the star, had captivated his imagination.

"Yeah," Seven replied. "Look at the Big Dipper. See the last two stars of the bowl? The one at the tip of the bowl is called Dubhe and the one beneath it is called Merak. Follow the line from Merak to Dubhe and it points to the North Star."

Seven traced the line with his finger and extended it out to the North Star, noting that the distance from Dubhe to the North Star was about five times the distance between Merak and Dubhe.

"Do you see it?"

"Yeah," Slowbe said, very impressed with Seven's knowledge and quite pleased to have gained this information for himself.

The ocean waves rolled steadily and continuously to shore, as they had for hundreds of millions of years.

"Edward."

Slowbe turned around.

"Hi Angel," he said just loud enough to be heard across the twenty yards between them.

Song approached Slowbe, sat down beside him, and took her sandals off. She crossed her legs and pressed her feet into the sand.

"I was working on some sketches in bed and heard your alarm go off," Song said. "I figured you'd be out here. I thought I'd come and join you for a little while before I go to sleep."

"It's a beautiful night," Slowbe said.

Slowbe and Song had known each other since the fall of 2038, when they were introduced by Mia Sabin at the Hedge Club Art Exhibition. Song was twenty-nine years old. A natural, easygoing rapport was quickly evident, and a deep affection eventually developed—one that remained platonic. Song had already been an international celebrity for years when they met, and two books had been written about her and her work, one of them by Sabin. Many art critics and experts considered her one of the greatest painters in the history of Western art. And though she'd grown accustomed to being showered with accolades, she was completely without pretension, and this was something that stood out to Slowbe when they first became acquainted. She had a calm demeanor and was soft-spoken, but at the same time she exuded an unmistakable self-confidence. Her ancestry was Chinese, African American, and Dutch. She was of modest stature and had a tan complexion and dark hair. Her eyes were a deep, penetrating hazel color with prominent limbal rings. As the only child of Robert Song, a media mogul and philanthropist, and the film writer and director Lea Banes, she had been born into great wealth. From her father she had inherited not only a fortune, but also a great love of astronomy. She'd grown up with telescopes, and sky maps, and family trips to Dark Sky Parks to stargaze. In January of 2036, her father had made headlines around the world when he gave twelve billion dollars, almost a third of his fortune, to NASA for the construction of what became known as the Robert Song Electromagnetic Spectrum Array, which was launched on October 4th, 2044.

"I remember when I first found out that the universe wasn't infinite," Slowbe said, breaking a momentary silence. "I was fourteen. I remember I was up late one night searching the internet and came across a documentary on Stephen Hawking. It was my first real introduction to the Big Bang theory and this idea that once upon a time an infinitesimally small particle exploded, and from this explosion the entire universe emerged—a continually expanding universe, no less. That's when I realized that this universe had a beginning, and therefore must have actual boundaries, and thus couldn't truly be infinite. It came as quite a shock, although I'm not exactly sure why I thought the universe was infinite in the first place. Of course, the first question that came to my mind was, 'What came before, or what exists before, the Big Bang?' I remember Hawking addressing this in the documentary and saying that it was a meaningless question because the Big Bang was, essentially, a moment at which all the laws of physics break down, that there was no concept of time available to use as a reference, and that it was like asking what's south of the South Pole. The idea that the infinitesimally small particle came from nothing seemed supremely counterintuitive to me. I started wondering how the particle came into existence and what it was made of. And what caused it to explode? And what is, or was, the particle exploding into? I also wanted to know if there were other such particles, or if it was one of a kind. All the particles I'd learned about in school, like quarks, electrons, atoms, molecules, and even sand, existed in massive quantities. Was it the same with the Big Bang particle? It's funny, though—not long before I came across the documentary, I'd told my friend Bruce about a notion I had: that if the universe was infinite then everything imaginable must exist somewhere in the universe. It would be impossible for something not to exist in an infinite universe, I said. I remember telling him that there must be a planet where there is a real Batman. I viewed the universe as a realm of infinite imagination."

"So, what happened when you had your idea of an infinite universe upended?" Song asked.

"Well, eventually I guess I began looking elsewhere for infinity," Slowbe said with a wry look on his face.

"I see," Song said. She paused for a moment and then continued, "A few years ago, I watched an interview that Hawking did back in 2010. He said he thought there was intelligent life on other planets, and that if they were to come our way it wouldn't be a good thing for our species, kind of like Columbus making contact with the Indigenous peoples of America, a disaster for the natives."

"It's hard to say what the result of first contact would be," Slowbe said. "The prevailing view of our collective consciousness seems to suggest we think it would be negative. If you look at the history of film, for example, most of the time when aliens come to earth from outer space they're not friendly. It's always a threat, something to be feared. And then, of course, there's Orson Welles's radio broadcast of 1938. Do you know what I'm referring to?"

"No."

"In 1938 Orson Welles had a radio program, and during one of his broadcasts he did a fake news announcement that the earth was being attacked by Martians. Thousands of his listeners believed him and panicked, and many were literally out running in the streets. It was quite a controversy after the truth came out. But it speaks to the fear of the unknown, and of what's out there. Personally, I feel that if there are civilizations sophisticated enough to travel all the way here, then they have probably evolved past issues of war and violence."

"I don't know. I'm not sure we can assume that high technological sophistication always coincides with high social sophistication."

"I suppose you're right. There are a lot of variables."

"So, what are your thoughts on those questions about the Big Bang?" Song asked.

"Well, I feel that where I come from speaks to who and what I am. I assume the universe didn't come from nothingness, or nothing. I don't believe there is such a thing as nothingness or nothing. On one level, I come from this universe. I am of this universe. There is a direct line from the Big Bang to me. I also think there's a direct line from me to the realm that the Big Bang particle emerged from and dwelled in prior to its explosion. In the big picture, I'd say I come from that place as well; and it's obviously not a realm bound by time and space and the laws of physics. So, whatever realm the universe emerged from and is exploding into, which would essentially be the same, has something to do with who and what I am. I would also say that the place from which the Big Bang emerges, and which surrounds and envelops the expanding universe, also pervades the universe. It exists in the now. Maybe it's always existed. In any case, there's overlap and infusion. To me, the universe is like a circle expanding within a much larger circle. The boundaries between the inner circle and the outer circle are superficial. They come together like overlapping, interwoven dimensions. I think consciousness and energy are always central issues in all of this. What caused the particle to explode? I don't know, maybe a thought. Are there countless Big Bang particles? I think so."

"Georges Lemaître, the Belgian priest who conceived of the idea of the Big Bang, called the infinitesimally small particle the 'primeval atom,'" Song noted.

"That sounds like a good name for the thing. I'm sure we'll eventually, by scientific means, learn more about the particle; but on a metaphysical level, the thing that exploded, and continues to expand, is an idea—an idea that originally took the form of a primeval atom and then proceeded as a dynamic expression to become what we call the physical universe, exploring the possibilities of its own existence within a framework of logic, order, chaos, and creative abandon."

For a moment, Song wondered if there was a connection between dark energy and the realm beyond the universe that Slowbe was conjecturing about, or if the inner dimensions and realities discussed in *The World Within* were in some way related to these things.

"My father was always so fascinated by the universe," she said. "Have you heard of Keck Observatory?"

"I think I've heard of that."

"It was built during the '80s and '90s. The site actually consists of two telescopes: Keck I and Keck II. At the time they were the largest telescopes in the world. I was there with my father shortly before he died, and we were given a special tour of the facility. It's fantastic: almost fourteen thousand feet above sea level, at the summit of Mauna Kea on the island of Hawaii. It was dusk when we arrived, and all you could see were a few peaks in the distance surrounded by an endless blanket of clouds that lay motionless like rolling sand dunes. It felt like being on a cloud planet. I had flown above the clouds before but had never felt like I was walking on them. The horizon was orange, pink, and yellow, and the sky above was blue with a few stars and planets scattered about. A couple hours later when it turned black, it was a mosaic like no other. That night I looked through the observatory's telescopes at seven different galaxies: the Milky Way, Andromeda, Triangulum, IC 10, Phoenix Dwarf, Leo A, and Sextans B. I looked across almost ten billion light-years in one night."

"That is amazing. How beautiful," Slowbe said.

Tears began to well up in Song's eyes. She tried to hold them back, but soon drops began rolling down her cheeks. She pressed her fingers against her eyes.

"I've been having nightmares," she said, "recurring night-mares of my father. In each one he appears to me as a terribly deformed version of himself, and I'm always trying to run away from him, but I'm unable to move, and I'm horrified. I loved my father, Edward. I miss him so much, and I can't understand why I would be having these dreams. I wake up and I'm full of anxiety. It's been bothering me a lot, and I feel guilty that I'm having such awful dreams about someone I love so much."

"Maybe they're not really about your father at all," Slowbe said. "When did they start?"

Song was silent for a while as she thought. It'd been less than a year since her father passed away in his sleep at age seventy-two. The cause of death disclosed to the public was natural causes, although the more specific cause had been heart disease. He'd died at his home near Hāna, on the island of Maui, surrounded by family.

"In February," she said.

"I wonder what was going on in your life around that time."

"I was in Tel Aviv painting. I'd been in Israel for a few weeks. I can't think of anything all that unusual that was going on. There was a cease-fire." Song turned to Slowbe. "They started shortly after I began reading *The World Within*," she said.

"Maybe the dreams are more about your concept of death, or some sort of fear of death, or something related. *The World Within* is designed to elicit a tangible, subjective experience of the awesome power and depth of our being, our psychic structure, the larger Self. For most people, exploring these depths, or even considering them, is as unsettling, at least initially, as the idea of death itself. And if one fears death, then they will fear the depths of their own soul, and vice-versa. When the ego's preeminence is made even slightly precarious, people cringe, for fear of the unknown, for fear of losing themselves. The images of your father might represent a fear of death, or some sort of fear of your deep inner self or soul—or trepidation around getting too close to such depths."

The waves rolled ashore ceaselessly. Song took long, gradual breaths as she focused on the sound of the ocean. She began to feel a deep centeredness and calm. A seagull called out in the distance.

"Did you hear that?" she asked.

"Yes," Slowbe replied.

*

Seven stepped out of the shower of his presidential suite at the Duxton Hotel in Perth, Australia. It was 4:00 p.m. and almost time to leave for Optus Stadium to do a sound check for his 8:00 p.m. show. During his short stay in Australia, he'd been scheduled to perform two concerts; the first one, in Sydney, had occurred two nights before, on June 27th. He pulled one of the towels off the towel rack and pressed it against his face, and then his chest. It was soft and thick and felt good on his skin, and it absorbed the moisture quickly. When he was completely dry, he walked over to his luggage, which was lined up against one of the walls in the bedroom. He opened his beige suitcase and pulled out a pair of blue jeans and a dark-violet T-shirt that said "don't hate me" in bold white letters. For a few seconds, he entertained the idea of giving Slowbe a quick call. Perth was fifteen hours ahead of Pacific Standard Time, so it was about 1:00 a.m. in Nehalem, and he knew Slowbe would be up late watching the stars on the Oregon coast. He decided he'd call after the concert.

Seven settled into the plush couch situated in the center of the main living quarters of the suite. He opened up his Array and entered the CNN portal. The headline read "Pope Leo refers to Edward Slowbe as 'diabolical.'" In the article that followed, the Pope was quoted as saying that he didn't believe anything supernatural or unexplainable had happened in New York City; that it was obviously an elaborate hoax; and that the mere fact that Slowbe would undertake such a deception was evidence of his sinister nature. Seven read half the article and then closed the Array. He leaned his head back on the couch and his eyes slowly followed the contours of the ceiling as he cleared his mind. After twenty minutes he got up and stretched his arms. He stood in front of the west-facing balcony overlooking the Swan River and continued stretching. From his viewpoint the river seemed motionless, but he could see sparkling particles of light bouncing off the water. His Array began to vibrate. It was his manager, Heart Stevens.

"Seven, how are you?" Stevens asked.

"Doing great, yourself?"

"Fantastic," Stevens replied. "Your limo is here. Are you ready to roll?"

"I am."

"Excellent, I'm down in the lobby, see ya in a few."

"I'm on my way."

Seven strapped on a pair of sandals for the limo ride to the stadium and headed out the door. A little ways down the hallway, he passed a portly, cheerful-looking cleaning lady who greeted him with a warm smile. Seven smiled back and said hello. When he arrived at the elevator, he pressed the down arrow and almost immediately there was a pleasant chiming sound and the doors slid open. It was empty. Seven entered and pushed the button that had an "L" on it. The doors closed and the elevator glided all the way to lobby, fourteen floors, without any stops. When the doors opened again, he walked into a flurry of sound and activity.

"Seven," Stevens called out.

Seven smiled and walked over to the revolving doors where Stevens was standing with several others. There was a familiar excitement in the air. Stevens put his arm around Seven's shoulder and followed him through the doors.

"Perfect weather for the show," Stevens said, as they stepped outside.

"Indeed," Seven replied, "very nice day."

The limo was parked about thirty feet from the hotel entrance. Seven looked up and saw a half-moon in the blue sky. Then he heard shots fire. In what seemed like an instant, he was looking down at his wounded body lying on the ground in a pool of blood. He watched the chaotic scene. I'm here, now, he thought to himself. After observing more of the scene unfold, he soon turned his attention elsewhere. Everything was expanding, and he was overcome by an indescribable sense of awe. I'm here, now, he thought to himself again. The physical scenery began to fade. Something was familiar. He left the earth-realm behind.

Two days later it was revealed that the murderer was a man named Ali Abiz-Assur, an Australian citizen with a history of violence and religious fanaticism, who'd harbored a desire for revenge ever since Seven's comments about Mohammed.

Heavy Weather

The United Nations Research Institute for Social Development report came out on July 8th, 2048, one week before Joan Monarch, Edward Slowbe, Joseph Henry, Lillian Red Horse, Angel Song, Mia Sabin, and Dara Sangree gathered for the second salon. Begun in 2046, it was the largest qualitative research study ever conducted. It spanned all 195 countries and surveyed close to 3.3 billion individuals. Entitled *Reflective Survey on the Human Condition*, the study was funded by an endowment made up of UN dollars and private contributions, which all the salon members had donated to. Its purpose was to examine humanity's concept of, and beliefs about, itself. The effort, it was hoped, would provide insight into how to approach humanity's most persistent problems and challenges related to the social, political, and psychological dimensions of the human condition.

For some observers the survey brought to mind the three questions posed in the title of French painter Paul Gauguin's most famous work, *Where Do We Come From? What Are We? Where Are We Going?* The phrases, sans question marks, were inscribed in the top left corner of his canvas in such a way as to resemble a three-line stanza. Gauguin's painting then depicted three groups of women, all islanders, that represented birth, youth, and old age, respectively. A strange blue statue, placed left of center, symbolized what he referred to as "the beyond."

Various flora and fauna were also portrayed in the picture, and hints of the sky and the ocean were nestled into the background. Gauguin considered the work, composed in 1897 when he was forty-eight years old and living in Tahiti, to be a masterpiece and his ultimate artistic statement. The painting's name was derived from a catechism written by his boyhood teacher, the bishop of Orléans, Félix-Antoine-Philibert Dupanloup, which posed the questions: "Where does humanity come from?" "Where is it going to?" and "How does humanity proceed?" With these questions the bishop had hoped to impress upon his students a proper course for spiritual reflection on the meaning of life. Well into Gauguin's adulthood, even after he had distanced himself from the church and had become an adherent of theosophy, the questions remained in the forefront of his mind.

*

After forty straight days of sunny, hot weather in Portland, the temperature on July 15th hovered in the low sixties. By 5:00 p.m. the full, dream-like clouds, which had been white as snow in the morning and early afternoon, had turned dark grey and were moving east with winds approaching twenty-five miles per hour. A rare clap of thunder was heard throughout the city, followed by several bursts of lightning. Soon, it was raining torrentially. Within an hour leaves and small branches were scattered across the streets and lawns of many neighborhoods around town. Larger branches also buckled and crashed to the ground in some areas. By 6:00 p.m., electricity had gone out in a large section of Portland east of the Willamette River. Sangree began suspecting that her fellow salon members would soon be calling to say that they wouldn't be able to make the drive to her house, ten miles northwest of downtown off U.S. Route 30. The calls never came. One by one, starting at 7:36 p.m. and ending at 8:01 p.m., the attendees pulled into Sangree's driveway, parked their cars, and made a mad dash through the pouring rain, up the steps to her porch, and to her front door.

Sangree lived on Sauvie Island, one of the largest river islands in the United States, almost thirty-three square miles, situated between the Columbia River to the east, the Multnomah Channel to the west, and the Willamette River to the south. Her 144-year-old house was painted yellow with black trim on the windows and had white railings that framed the wraparound porch. The landscape from different vantage points around the house included fruit orchards, wetlands, and groves of cottonwood and white oak; lush, rolling hills to the west; and on a clear day, views of Mt. Hood and Mt. St. Helens to the east and northeast. Adding to the bucolic imagery were the hundreds of bird species that gathered on the island either year-round, during autumn migrations, or for overwintering (between December and February the number of visiting ducks, geese, and swans sometimes exceeded two hundred thousand). Even amidst the present storm, there was a certain serenity about the place. One could sense why it had been considered sacred by its original inhabitants, the Multnomah band of the Chinook people. It was still sacred. And the prayers that the Multnomah had said and sung and danced and lived remained animated, and continued to give new meaning to the place, long after all but a few had fallen to smallpox and malaria in the 1830s.

The smell of candles, sage, and tea filled the living room as Slowbe and Henry helped move some furniture. When they were done, Sangree quickly arranged a collection of large, intricately embroidered pillows into a circle in the center of the space. Countless raindrops paraded on the roof and clamored against the face of every window. They seemed to want in.

A few moments after everyone was seated, a sharp cracking sound came from outside. The lights went out.

"I think that was a tree. I'm going to go take a look," Henry said.

"I'm gonna take a look too," Sangree said.

They both got up and walked toward the front door while the rest of the group stayed seated. Flickering, oblong shapes danced on the walls, mimicking the flames from the various candles. Curiosity soon began to fill the circle, and before long the porch was filled with onlookers.

"Right over there," Henry said, pointing to a giant oak tree whose severed branch lay across a group of power lines.

The group stood on the porch peering through the wind and the rain and the darkness. Unusual sound frequencies; strange, bellowing harmonics; and bizarre overtones swirled around them.

"You're all more than welcome to spend the night here if you like," Sangree said, noticing that the weather had intensified since their arrival.

They each responded with subtle, ambiguous, yet approving facial expressions. Red Horse raised her right eyebrow, as if to say, "that's a possibility."

"Let's go inside," Sangree suggested. "I'll get some more candles."

The group ambled through the front door and into the shadowy abode, toward the circle of pillows and the dancing, oblong reflections. Sangree turned on the flashlight in her Array and headed toward the basement. A couple minutes later, she returned to the living room with four more candles to add to the three that were already lit. She placed them strategically, set them aflame, and then sat down with the others in the circle. Light fluttered and pulsated throughout the room, climbing the walls, encroaching on the darkness. The natural chiaroscuro effect illuminated the eyes of everyone in the room. The seven pairs, each with their own startling presence, seemed to radiate. Slowbe, in particular, took note of this.

"I've been thinking of Seven a lot, as I know we all have," Sabin said. "I brought some poems that I've written recently that I'd like to share, and recite in his honor."

"Wonderful," Sangree said.

"They're all untitled," Sabin said as she pulled the typed poems out of her bag and prepared to read. "There are five of them."

Sabin began to recite:

"I remove my feet from the earth,
Open the floodgates and swim
Over the tops of trees,
And into a patch of blue.
The early evening seeps through my bedroom walls.
I am a windswept heartbeat,
Collecting stardust beneath the streetlights.
In the fireplace snow is melting,
While mother weaves her tale,
With yarn of veins and coiled branches,
And drumbeats that stand still,
Like a quiet city where tigers appear at night.
The thoughts become the dream,
And the dream the thought,
Of passing days of dusk and dawn,
Upon the hills that wonder why,
Remembering the wishing well."

There was silence, and then the sound of paper being moved as Sabin began to read the second poem.

"All that is left is pure essence,
And the image of the sun
Setting upon the western hills.
The future is gone now,
The moon, tilting, drips
With milky light
Upon the visibly surprised and gracious valley.
Dark green clouds

Stare into the sky;
Old man opens his eyes,
And softly utters,
'It's beautiful isn't it?'
He sees nothing but
The stars in his mind.
All that is left is pure essence,
No longer waiting for the goddess
Who is meditating on that snowy mountain.
The past disappears,
One faint pebble
On black sand beaches,
Falling off the edge of the earth
Into a still pool.
The Fates have taken leave,
But for an occasional wry glance;
They sit on a grassy slope facing east,
With their watercolors,
Their pastries and warm tea,
Indifferent, content, distant."

She placed the poem to her side and prepared to continue reading. As she was about to utter the first line of her next poem, Sangree's cat, Venus, strolled nonchalantly into the room and started to move delicately across several pillows. Her movements were watched carefully. She stood in the center of the circle momentarily, considering where to take her place, and then drifted over to Sabin's lap and settled in.

Sabin scratched the top of Venus's head. "Do you like my poetry?" she asked.

"Full moon over the whispering iris,
Quiet riverbed
Submerged beneath the dreams
Of cosmic travelers

Who see the dawn.
Distant bluff peering over the ages of infinity,
Opening the hidden door
To the land of art and light,
Come and rain on my parade.
Ancient book of rhyme,
Pale violet orchid,
Making love to the wind on a summer day
With cries of joy
For the morning star.
Faint heartbeat on the edge of fantasy,
Calling me to the nearby pond;
Make the day turn to night,
And the night to day.
Fire engulfs this living space,
Carelessly taking flight;
The sunflower awakes,
I fall silent.
Come again with me Isis,
I have come to shore, with the eagle,
And the brewing storm."

"Two more," Sabin said.

"There is a sun inside the moon,
A gold marble that glances outwardly
Upon these meadows;
Perhaps at a peculiar plane,
Or a strange place,
Perhaps to an idea of interest,
Always getting deeper.
The universe is obliging,
It comes to us,
As a reflection in the river,
As an eclipse, or the equator;

It appears presently
In the immediate environment,
Reflecting our immediate mind;
We come to it in our landscape.
The pictures of the past,
From the telescope
That sails the twilight sea,
Reveal a further environment
That the denizens of the universe,
As the tree, and the mineral, and the atom,
And the human,
Are intertwined with
In a web
Of psychic projections
And dissipated supernovae.
We are not earthbound.
The cosmic system dwells in the palm of my hand,
It floats in the wind and in every drifting leaf,
And is heard at the ocean's shore,
An echo, a reflection,
From beyond the Big Bang."

Sabin held the last poem and began to read.

"I am the person in the middle,
Unbridled white flame, burning.
The lake and mountain surround me,
Birds soar: bald eagle, great egret,
And upon concentric circles
I sit in silence,
Like a weathered rock,
And peer inward
At my body, my mind, my ego, my soul.
They are my environment, my ecological system,
And I seek to thrive.

I am the person in the middle.
I dive into the cold, blue abyss,
The purifying crater deep within the earth
And I weep
Because my trauma and my sadness and my pain
Are assuaged
By something beautiful and tender,
Something great and mysterious,
That enters into my environment, silently.
I am the person in the middle,
Slow breath, dust settling
Like music.
I come to the open spaces,
Sublimely still,
As I release the tension from my body
And focus my mind on the present moment.
I am born and die, day and night,
I awake and dream,
But I am alive at all times.
There is a sun-like eye within me.
I am the person in the middle.
Beaten by the storm,
Made of minerals and dust
And childhood memories
Of ghosts and unready fathers,
Seashells and spaceships.
I drink from the well of my emotions,
And digest them entirely
While flutes and drums
Resonate in my room."

"Thank you so much, Mia," Slowbe said.

"How about if we dedicate this evening's salon to Seven by listening to a few of his recordings?" Henry suggested. "Unless anyone else had something they really wanted to share."

"I was going to show you all some new photography, but the light isn't really optimal," Sangree said. "I'd love to spend some time listening to Seven."

"I think that's a great idea," Song added. The other salon members expressed their approval.

Before long the room was resonating with Seven's soaring vocals, smooth instrumentation, and breathtaking melodic wizardry. The group sat and listened to Seven's first album with hardly a word being spoken. They listened for every minute detail, soaking up the dynamic vocalization; the rich compositional styling; the interaction of sound production and arrangement; the shifts in effects; the masterfully ordered rising, falling, and swirling of emotion. Each note and harmony rang out with new clarity. The group listened to three albums in total over the course of two and a half hours. After the last note of the third album faded out, Slowbe spoke up.

"When Seven and I were in high school our favorite band was Led Zeppelin, and on a few occasions we conducted what we called 'Zeppelin séances,' where we would listen to four or five Led Zeppelin albums back-to-back. I guess we've had a 'Seven séance' now. I think this is a good time for an announcement I need to make." He paused briefly, and then continued. "When the fatwa was put on Seven in 2035 he was deeply concerned for his safety and thought there was a good chance he'd be killed. He asked me to meet with him and his lawyers one afternoon about a month after the issue was made. At that time he made me the sole executor of his estate in the event that he'd be leaving us sooner than expected. In his will he stipulated that I be given one percent of his fortune, and that I assume responsibility for directing the remaining ninety-nine percent toward serving the 'cause of humanity' through some sort of humanitarian project or program. At his passing Seven was worth 7.3 billion dollars."

To the salon members, the idea of a 'cause of humanity,' which Seven had mentioned specifically in his will, was a familiar concept. And while each member would have expressed it in their own unique manner, they each understood it in essentially the same way, as fostering for the individual freedom of mind, body, and spirit; freedom of opportunity; guarantees of quality of life; encouragement to create and explore; engagement in mutual interests with humanity; the development of wisdom and transcendental awareness; and the sense and experience of peace and equality.

"If possible, I'd love for the salon to play a central role in carrying out the mission these funds are intended for," Slowbe said.

"Did you have something specific in mind?" Red Horse asked.

"Well, perhaps the salon could inform the development of a more formal, yet organic entity: a nonprofit organization or something, like a think tank or a social marketing platform— some sort of mechanism or ongoing program that raises awareness of human potential. I don't have a lot of particulars in mind, but the idea of establishing something that intersects with, and builds on, the momentum of the truth of consciousness rallies, and our own art and works and ideas, seems to make sense. I also think the *Reflective Survey on the Human Condition* is an interesting piece to utilize, or somehow incorporate, because it conceptualizes the human race collectively, as a representative human, and speaks to who and what we think we are."

"A program of human uplift is definitely needed," Monarch said, "something therapeutic, and revelatory, something eye-opening."

"The report could definitely be something to build off of," said Sangree.

"Especially given the huge amount of publicity surrounding it," Henry added.

"I'm curious, what are some of the things that stood out to you all about the survey?" Sangree asked the group.

"That the collective human is an addict, with a fairly poor self-image," Monarch stated matter-of-factly.

"But also, behind that is a nature that's brilliant and ingenious," Henry said. "And I think the survey clearly shows that an important part of our representative human's self-concept is the sense of being connected to some divine purpose, origin, or nature, and of having far-reaching intellectual and creative capacity."

"True," Monarch said.

"The self-image that the survey depicts is certainly conflict-ed and contradictory," said Henry, "the juxtaposition of spirit and ego, of the state of grace and the state of addiction, and then also of wisdom and ignorance."

"That's something that stood out to me, the juxtapositions and apparent contradictions," Slowbe responded. "But also to your point, Joan, about the inference that the collective human is like an addict...for me, whenever there is an absence of peace, harmony, and love as basic conditions of the mind and the inner self, then there is some measure of addiction. Addiction is the repetition of any unhealthy pattern, any behavior that creates a false sense of power, or the normalizing of any negative emotion or thought. It's like compulsively adhering to a distortion of truth or reality. So, yeah, addiction is the norm. Grace, I suppose, is the alternative."

"Yes, there are many ways to behave addictively, think addictively, and relate to emotions and the body addictively— it's certainly not all about drugs and alcohol," Monarch said.

"It's interesting how we always seem to blame our compul-sions, shortcomings, negativity, and character defects on the ego, as if it's some separate part of us that has its own will and personality apart from the person," Sabin said. "I call it 'ego bashing,' and I'm not sure it's particularly helpful. Too often, we fail to focus on, or even understand, the positive features of the ego structure, or to really understand its nature and the critical role it plays."

"Toussaint once told me that 'the ego is whole when it is aligned with the soul,'" Slowbe said. "That's always stuck with me. In other words, the ego function, which I think is a dimension of the person, like you said, Mia, is at the height of its capacity as an interpreter and navigator of physical reality when it has in some significant way become synchronized with a greater energy source, or system—the soul—and is thus in a better position to mitigate the influence of negativity, addiction, attachment, and fear. That's when we see the natural flourishing of all the traits we associate with the best of humanity."

"Indeed," Henry said, "the ego can blend with the Self like a bucket of water can be poured into the ocean and blend with the ocean; but the ego, when it's fearful, negative, and controlling, can also be like a piece of plastic dropped in the ocean—not in harmony with, or unaligned with, its greater environment."

"I like the analogies," Sabin said.

"Our representative human, who behaves like an addict, is also tremendously resilient...I admire that...to be able to endure this addictive condition, albeit self-imposed, over all these millennia," Sangree said in an almost playful tone. "To persevere through the self-abuse and self-destruction, the self-induced fog, the separation, all the barriers and booby traps we set for ourselves, and all the negative consequences we endure as the result of our actions, and to keep coming back. We are incredibly resilient, even if the experience often resembles a dark comedy."

There were a few expressions of gentle laughter.

"We humans are very resilient," Slowbe concurred. "We do have that going for us."

"What's interesting to me is how addiction often exists completely unbeknownst to the person, and how individuals become addicted to negative, painful, or angst-inducing sensations," Red Horse said. "Generally speaking, abiding by an addiction seems counterintuitive; for example, it doesn't necessarily make sense that a person would be addicted to stress, chaos, distraction, or a poor self-concept, but it's all too common. Of course, it does make sense that one might be addicted to power over others, anger, or drugs and alcohol, as these things generate such a rush of adrenaline or sense of euphoria."

"I found that my addictive state was a fluid mind-body-emotion condition," Henry said.

"I think that's always the case, one way or another," Sangree replied.

"Perhaps," Henry said. "There were certain negative thought patterns, which then induced negative emotional conditions, which, in turn, generated a particular physical sensation. When I first became aware of this pattern, long before I was able to let it go, I assumed that the reward, or payoff, that I received from the process was in the physical sensation that the thoughts and the emotions gave rise to. Then I began to wonder if each point in the pattern had its own addictive purpose. Physically, the sensation was like a tension or constriction in my torso area. It was an energy sensation for me. I guess I could say that the physical sensation and the emotional condition seemed almost the same to me; but it all revolved around anxiety, impatience, angst, resentment, and intolerance. I had grown so used to this cycle, it was so habitual. I realized that I was propelling the whole thing. And, no doubt, it was counterintuitive, which may, in fact, be one of the hallmarks of the addictive experience, because at the same time that I was experiencing this habitual pattern I was uncomfortable with it, even its very existence. I knew these weren't copacetic thoughts or feelings I was perpetuating, and I knew I wasn't serving myself well by holding on to, and engendering, the tension. This knowledge then, of course, created more angst and tension, like a seamless cycle. Eventually I was able to cast myself deep enough into a place of stillness that I could see how my state of being had developed its own momentum that was proceeding unabated. I had to pay very, very close attention.

"I needed to find a way to halt the pattern, to pull it back, like pulling back the reins on a wild horse, although without getting trapped into pushing and pulling in the opposite direction, into fighting the current, as that becomes a whole new exercise in generating tension and constriction. In some ways it felt like the pattern wasn't me, as if it was something independent of me that was manipulating me, but I knew that it was a part of my conscious self. I had to admit there was a part of me that was invested in keeping the cycle in place as it was. I paid very close attention to a sense of stillness and presence, as if my life depended on it. And I found that the more I practiced experiencing stillness in the present moment, the more I could effortlessly discard the pattern and tune into my natural, undistorted self—my untethered self. The nature of my relationship with energy started to transform. I like to say that I became attuned to clean energy, and clean states of being."

"In Alcoholics Anonymous it's assumed that an individual must undergo what they call a 'psychic change' in order to be liberated from the addictive patterns," Sabin said.

"Absolutely," Henry added.

"Psychic change is really what the truth of consciousness movement has been all about," Slowbe said, "and what *The World Within*, and many of our works, have been about. I suppose it's what this new project would want to invoke: psychic change."

"So, what about a name for the project? What should we call it?" Monarch asked.

"The Human Evolution Project," Henry said in an upbeat tone.

"What'd you say?" Red Horse asked.

"The Human Evolution Project," Henry replied. "Wasn't it a conversation about evolutionary thinking and human evolution that got this gathering started in the first place?"

Everyone present was familiar with the dream Sangree had told Slowbe about back in March, and with the conversation that had ensued. There were a few silent moments as everyone reflected on what Henry had just suggested.

"I like it," Sangree said.

"I do too," Song added.

Slowbe and the rest nodded approvingly, somewhat surprised at how quickly a name had emerged for the potential entity.

"That's good, Joseph," Slowbe said. "The Human Evolution Project. I like that."

By 2:00 a.m. the group had compiled a set of basic values that they felt should be infused within the culture of the project, first and foremost being an unabashed, multifaceted idealism. Adherence to idealism was an obligation, a responsibility, a sacred duty, they thought. There was no hope for discovering a universal truth, or even a great truth, unless one was using idealism as one's guide. It was a key ingredient for evolution, and had everything to do with true power and wisdom, vision and potential. On one level, idealism was the conviction that humans had the tools and resources, talent, creativity, and intelligence to fashion a world marked by peace and common well-being: the belief that a copacetic world was attainable. It implied an abiding faith in humanity, as well as a call to live what Slowbe referred to as the "beneficial life," meaning a life led in such a way so as to be simultaneously of benefit to oneself as well as to others. On another level, idealism was the commitment to the intrapersonal work of progressing toward an embodiment of love, peace, freedom, growth, expression, and enlightenment. It was the dedication to gaining real, tangible cognizance of, and communion with, the universe and the Macro Self.

The salon members sought to align the project with Singularism and the concept of immanence. They grounded their vision in the ideas of "independent spirituality" and the "trans-religious" experience. They affirmed the preeminence of the individual and the idea of the individual as a universe unto himself or herself. They emphasized creativity, and the power and boundlessness of the present moment. They embraced the pursuit of balance in all matters, including humanity's relationship with the earth.

Around 2:30 a.m. all the candles were blown out. Henry lay awake. He thought of the visible spectrum of light, of light waves and their associated colors. On one end of the spectrum was red, with the longest wave pattern. In the middle was green. On the other end of the spectrum was violet, which had the shortest, highest-energy wave pattern.

The Spectrum

A blue heron glided steadily across the early evening sky, measured and serene, its long, flowing wings slowly catching the wind like a broad sail. Below, Red Horse sat quietly on a patch of grass at Tom McCall Waterfront Park in downtown Portland. She observed the creature attentively as it traveled south, high above the Willamette River. When it eventually faded out of view she turned her attention to the waxing half-moon. Off in the distance to the east, Mt. Hood rose up, exuding an effortless self-mastery. The normal bustle of Portlanders riding public transit or driving their cars home after the workday; or walking, running, or biking along the Willamette River esplanade; or heading to a nearby establishment to meet friends for dinner and a drink, hummed in the background.

Red Horse had just spoken with her parents, John and Mary, who were at John F. Kennedy International Airport awaiting a return flight to Idaho. They'd spent the previous week in New York City and would have stayed longer were it not for the fact that Hurricane Darlene had changed course over the last forty-eight hours. New York was now directly in its path. Torrential rain had already descended upon the region. Darlene was expected to make landfall in three days. Red Horse's parents told her that flights were being delayed, and they were uncertain about when they would be departing. Since 2036, fifteen Category 5 hurricanes had come to shore along the Eastern Seaboard of the United States. Darlene would be the sixteenth, and the most northerly.

"Silence, stillness, presence," Red Horse quietly said to herself, reflecting on one of the most valuable credos that she'd received from her mother and father as she was growing up. Silence, stillness, and presence reside at the center of your being, they said, in a place of spirit; be intimate with them, be attuned to them within yourself, embody them. Within them there is dynamic, ceaseless, flowing energy; within them there is peace and power, they said. Red Horse listened carefully to her parents, and watched them, and sought to follow their example and their teaching. Over time she saw that the teaching appeared again and again in the world around her: in the tree, the blue heron, and the spider; in the mountain, the moon, and the sun; and elsewhere.

Red Horse's Array made a faint chiming sound, and she pulled the device out of her pocket. It was a message from the Oregon Secretary of State's office informing her that the articles of incorporation and bylaws for the Human Evolution Project were registered. Listed in the articles were Lillian Red Horse, president; Dara Sangree, treasurer; and Edward Slowbe, secretary; although, as far as the salon members were concerned, these titles were simply a formality to satisfy the state requirement that nonprofit organizations have a minimum of three board members.

Red Horse submitted copies of the articles and bylaws to the Oregon Department of Justice portal and filed the project as a "public-benefit corporation." Without delay she went to the Internal Revenue Service portal and requested an Employer Identification Number. Responses from both agencies came within minutes. As of July 18th, 2048, three days after the salon on Sauvie Island, the Human Evolution Project officially obtained 501(c)(3) status and was free to operate statewide, nationally, and internationally as a nongovernmental organization.

About forty yards away from Red Horse, a group of Canada geese grazed on the fresh-cut grass of the waterfront park, gradually moving from one area to the next, seemingly mindful of keeping a safe distance from any encroaching human. Red Horse glanced at them while she repositioned herself so that she was facing Logos Tower, a seventy-eight-story structure built with a glass curtain exterior wall system similar to One World Trade Center. Headquarters to Logos, Inc., a solar-energy development company, the building was located on Naito Parkway, west of the park, not far from where Red Horse was sitting. Red Horse lifted her arms upward, stretched her legs out, and bent over to touch her toes. She leaned forward for a short while before returning to an erect position and crossing her legs. She took a deep breath. This feels good, she thought to herself, as a fresh, clean burst of energy coursed through her body. Then she closed her eyes and began focusing intensely on her inner plane, and the ever-present field of electromagnetic energy. Once in her trance, she envisioned a beam of light and Logos Tower standing before her. She sat motionless for close to forty-five minutes.

When Red Horse opened her eyes again, the first thing she noticed was the group of geese suddenly taking flight. Much to her surprise, they'd approached to just a few feet from her. She watched as they flew off to a rocky area along the river's bank. She then looked back in the direction of Logos Tower. A few moments later she noticed Henry and Monarch at the north end of the park. They were walking toward her but were a good distance away, and Red Horse wasn't sure if they'd noticed her. She kept her eyes on them. Monarch, who was looking up at the half-moon, soon felt a slight breeze glide across the right side of her face. Her eyes moved downward and southeasterly, in a curvilinear path back to the terrestrial, and landed squarely on Red Horse. Monarch waved, and Red Horse returned the greeting.

"There's Lillian," Monarch said, pointing to the spot where

Red Horse was sitting. Henry, whose attention had been temporarily diverted by a reflection he noticed on the east-facing side of Logos Tower, didn't immediately reply. A large white circle of light, with smaller circles of red, orange, yellow, green, blue, and violet inside it, hovered on the skyscraper as if it was being projected upon the structure. The image had an eerie, cloud-like aspect to it. Henry looked across the river to see where the reflection might be coming from. The sun was already on its westward descent. He turned back toward the image, and before he had time to nudge Monarch to point it out to her it had disappeared.

"I'm sorry, what?" he said.

"There's Lillian," Monarch repeated, pointing again to Red Horse.

When Henry saw her, a smile spread across his face, his eyes lit up, and he waved.

Tall, broad-shouldered, with slightly greying curly brown hair and a ruddy complexion, Joseph Henry was a popular and well-respected "man of ideas," as he was often described, who was fond of noting that truth was indeed stranger, and more stirring, than fiction. There was a distinctly majestic quality about him, and an air of benevolence, especially when he spoke, due to the musical and resonant quality of his voice; and his amber-colored eyes were like lucid gemstones. One could easily imagine him atop a great mountain sitting in meditation; communicating with, and commanding, the elements; peering into distant regions beyond the firmament.

Born in Tel Aviv, Israel, in 1993, he had immigrated to the United States with his family when he was ten years old, settling in Portland. And although he was deeply enamored with Jewish culture and history, he did not adhere to the religious practices or beliefs. He thought of himself as an "unaffiliated spiritualist." On more than one occasion, much to the consternation of his family members and many in the Jewish community, he'd asserted that all peoples were the chosen ones. Most of his cosmological and metaphysical positions emerged from, or in one way or another revolved around, the experiences engendered through his meditation practice, which he'd developed while in his early teens, following the instruction of one of his uncles. Over the years it had evolved into a form of mysticism.

In late September of 2023, Henry returned to Tel Aviv for the first time since his family emigrated. One night, while he was meditating in a dimly lit basement room at his great-aunt's home, a flash of intense white light suddenly appeared before his mind's eye, filling his entire field of vision and seeming to pervade him. He was so startled that he quickly opened his eyes. Nothing like this had ever happened to him before. At first, he was inclined to believe that there was some sort of optical or neurological explanation, but the burst of light was unlike anything described on the optometry and neurology websites he reviewed in the days that followed.

A couple months after the episode, Henry was walking alone along the Wildwood Trail in Portland's Forest Park. His yearning to understand what he'd seen during his meditation in Tel Aviv still burned inside him. When the sun was close to setting, he decided to head back toward the trailhead. As he turned around, he noticed a small wood block, about three inches long, three inches high, and about half an inch thick, placed against the trunk of a cedar tree. He stepped off the trail and picked it up. In the center of the block was a carving of a single eye, with the iris, pupil, and sclera portrayed in elaborate detail with swirling lines. Engraved beneath the eye was the phrase "I searched myself." Henry held the carving in his hand and stared at it intently. At the time, he was unaware that the passage was a quote from the Greek philosopher Heraclitus. Without a shred of doubt or uncertainty, he immediately embraced the engraving as a sign, as a message for him.

To Henry, an eye symbolized many things: sentience, awareness, vision, insight, and even omniscience. He continued on the trail and contemplated what it might mean to search himself—what it would imply, and what it would entail. Perhaps part of it had to do with self-reflection and self-examination, he thought. He remembered what another Greek philosopher, Socrates, had once said: that "the unexamined life is not worth living." It seemed to Henry that searching oneself could begin with self-examination, meaning the examination of one's beliefs, behaviors, motivations, thoughts, and emotions, and even of one's unique traits and personal interests; but it went beyond self-examination, into the realm of pure exploration. If searching oneself involved pure exploration, he presumed, then this would imply that there was, in fact, something to explore, and discover, within oneself, that there was a realm awaiting exploration and discovery. He considered an idea he'd heard many years ago: to find oneself, one must lose oneself. He couldn't remember where he'd heard it, but for some reason the notion that it was an ancient Chinese saying had stuck in his mind. Nevertheless, he'd always been drawn to the phrase, and he assumed that "to lose oneself" meant that the ego would acquiesce to, or orient itself toward, a conscious structure greater and deeper than itself, the body, and the five senses.

Henry came around a bend in the trail and into a clearing where the sun shone through. He stopped for a moment. I can search my mind, he thought, I can search my emotions, I can search my beliefs; but when I search myself I am doing these things and more. When I search myself, I am venturing into a transcendental dimension. He continued walking. By the time he arrived at the trailhead, he was determined to embark on a new type of exploration, the exploration of Self. He now pondered what he needed to do to penetrate a heretofore unexplored realm that he could not clearly define or explain, the existence of which he trusted in solely based on vague, ancient rumors and a sliver of intuition. What would thrust him forward, past the atmosphere of the self that he knew and into the deep space of the Self that he sought to explore? he asked. "Seek, and you shall find," he whispered to himself.

The next morning when he awoke, he decided he would fast, as an offering of sorts, as a way of honoring his new quest. He relaxed for the greater part of the day: took naps, played his guitar, and read passages from Rumi. At 11:00 p.m. he entered his bedroom and closed the door. He sat down on a large pillow with his back against the wall. Once he was situated with his legs crossed, he twisted his torso to the left and to the right and stretched his arms upward. "I have to shut everything down," he stated aloud. He closed his eyes and turned his attention away from his surroundings and the events of the day. In less than ten minutes, his mind had become placid. Feeling centered within himself in the present moment, Henry engaged in a willing suspension of disbelief. He knew he had a body, but he suspended that focus in his mind, allowing his body to virtually disappear. He knew there was a room and a house and a neighborhood and a city surrounding him, but in his mind he allowed them to virtually disappear.

All he saw was blackness. But on this occasion, the blackness didn't seem entirely two-dimensional, as it normally did. It seemed amorphous and dynamic. There was, he sensed, a hint of depth and motion. He thought of the nighttime sky and he peered intensely, straight ahead, into the blackness. And the more intense his gaze became, the more he began to intuit a sense of depth. There is a world on the other side of the facade before me, he thought. I am seeking a world beyond the black facade, he began repeating in his mind, in anticipation. Gradually, his orientation shifted, and before long he started to feel as if he was sinking into an intuitive realm, and as if he was beginning to perceive through an intuitive eye. The blackness remained discernible for a time, but the more he took his concentration off it the more inconspicuous it became. He was starting to see through it. And then it was all gone.

What am I? he asked silently. A murmuring voice, almost haunting, and yet beautiful and comforting, rose up from within and said, "A spectrum." Henry was astonished and overjoyed by the sound of the unearthly voice and the direct response to his question. He felt no fear.

Images began to appear, some of which resembled landscapes, open spaces, and geological formations. And somehow, they seemed to be greater in magnitude and grandeur than anything he'd ever seen. Other images he perceived were indefinable to him. He had the sense of being surrounded by something that went on and on interminably from one world to another, from one realm to another, from one dimension to another, from one plane of existence to another. He continued to observe the fluctuating inner landscape for close to an hour. He heard no further sounds, just the silence one experiences when one is alone in a vast wilderness. Seconds after he opened his eyes, he saw a flash of violet light. "I am," he said to himself.

Henry induced the experience time and time again in the days and weeks and years that followed. He always referred to the dimensions on the other side of the blackness as "the kingdom" and the act of venturing into those places as "communion" or "exploration." Before long, he learned that while he was in "the kingdom," he could get direct answers to questions or obtain specific information he might be seeking— for example, insights on how to enhance his experience, solutions to problems, and information about the nature of reality and the universe, among other things. The notion that the answers lie within, or the truth lies within, took on new meaning for him. Sometimes, the information he sought came to him through the sound of a subtle voice, and other times it came to him as a sudden revelation or vision. In time, he gathered information about past lives he'd lived, and future lives he would live, although he realized that he, and all his past and future lives, existed simultaneously in a vast present moment that encompassed time and space. He also understood that there were aspects of the greater multidimensional Self that were not primarily, if at all, focused on physical reality.

Henry's knowledge of his past and future lives informed his writing, in particular, his seminal work, *The Rights of Origin*, published in 2041. Written in the genre of the philosophical novel, the same genre Sangree would subsequently adopt, it was considered by many to be one of the greatest works of literature ever written. It was his sixth novel, and it won a Nobel Prize. The story, which took place at the turn of the twenty-second century, centered around a character named Jules Charis. Growing up in the Berkshire Mountains of northwestern Massachusetts, Charis is raised and mentored by an idiosyncratic cast of characters, each of whom symbolizes a layer of Charis's psyche: his mother, a professor of Greek philosophy and a renowned expert on Socrates and Heraclitus; his father, a descendent of Phineas Quimby, the forerunner of the New Thought movement in the United States; his maternal grandmother, a retired astrophysicist; his uncle, a freewheeling, yet devout, Buddhist; and an old Nigerian shopkeeper named Angeni, who appears in Charis's life after the youth, at age thirteen, witnesses the death of his best friend. Spurred by unexpected psychological and physical events (including his mother's discovery of a lost Heraclitus text in Selçuk, Turkey; a face-to-face encounter with an albino black bear; and a dream about a conversation with the Chinese philosopher Lao Tzu), Charis, at age sixteen, begins to keep two journals, one of his dreaming life and one of his waking life. Twenty years later, he uses the journals as source material and writes a book that he refers to as a "treatise on metaphysics." That same year Charis's wife, Marcella Mantegna, gives birth to their only child, a daughter, whom they name Gaia.

Charis's book revolves around what he refers to as "the rights of origin": limitlessness, joy, fearlessness, grace, abundance, and power—all resources and states of being inherently present within the greater psychic body, entity, or soul of the human being, all inalienable birthrights that could be effortlessly realized by the individual given the right orientation, or given the proper alignment of ego and spirit. Henry's story eventually moved forward seven generations from Charis to the year 2290 and revealed how the life of one human had impacted the trajectory of human civilization.

Henry and Monarch sat down next to Red Horse.

"The Human Evolution Project is now officially a 501(c) (3)," Red Horse said. "I just completed filing with the state and the IRS."

"That's great," Monarch said. "This should be a fun project."

"Yes, absolutely," Henry said. "Thanks for taking care of these details for us, Lillian."

"Of course," Red Horse said. "So, what are you two doing down here today?"

"We were just visiting some art galleries in the Pearl District," Monarch replied.

"That sounds nice," Red Horse said. She paused for a moment and then asked, "Did you notice the lights on the side of Logos Tower a few minutes ago?"

"I did see those," Henry replied. "I couldn't figure out where they were coming from."

"I didn't notice," Monarch said.

"I generated the images," Red Horse stated.

"What do you mean you generated images?" Monarch asked.

"*Mens agitat molem*," Red Horse replied.

"Translation, please," Monarch stated, looking curiously at Red Horse.

"The mind moves the matter," Henry interjected. "It's from Virgil's *Aeneid*."

"I projected a field of light onto the side of Logos Tower," Red Horse explained. "Like a transfer of radiant energy. I've come to realize how the mind is simultaneously a vacuum, a prism, and a propulsion device, with the capacity to draw upon the highly concentrated electromagnetic energy of the soul, align the energy with physical form, and then project the transposed energy onto the external plane. It takes a lot of concentration, but it can become like second nature. There are other transpositions that can be manipulated using this process: healing power. Consciousness is always, in one way or another, the progenitor of phenomena."

"Is this what Edward did in New York?" Monarch asked.

"I believe so," Red Horse replied.

Henry looked back at Logos Tower and noticed a crowd of people gathered around the east side of the building where the lights had appeared.

"How did you learn to do this?" Monarch asked.

"I searched myself," Red Horse replied. She looked over at the tall glass building. "It takes a lot of concentration. I am . . ."

"Can you do it again?" Monarch asked.

Red Horse paused. She looked intently at Monarch and then closed her eyes. After a couple minutes, Henry and Monarch noticed that Red Horse's eyes had begun moving rapidly back and forth, as if she was experiencing REM sleep. Suddenly, a collective gasp came from the direction of Logos Tower. Henry and Monarch turned toward the tower and could see that almost the entire top quarter of the building, some twenty stories, was shrouded in a scintillating violet ball of light. Many of the crowd that had gathered not long before began to back away from the building, and Henry and Monarch noticed people looking around, apparently trying to locate a source of the light. Red Horse opened her eyes. The ball of light remained bright for twelve more seconds and then faded and disappeared.

Henry leaned forward, his curled hand pressed against his nostrils and lips. Monarch's right pointer finger was pressed against her temple and she stared at the building.

"What is this?" Monarch asked. "What does this mean?"

"It means we are much more than meets the eye," Henry said in an understated tone.

"It means that everything is amalgamated," Red Horse add-ed. "New science and technology; a continuum of conscious-ness, intelligence, information, love, creativity, and energy; a set of transcendent rights of being; an expanded framework of the Self and of the inner landscapes. We can understand new ways of actualizing and manifesting. It's all amalgamated."

Within twenty-four hours video footage of the Logos Tower lights had gone viral. And by mere virtue of the fact that Red Horse, Henry, and Monarch had been seen, and also captured on video, in close proximity to the tower during the appearance of the mysterious lights, the incident was immediately linked to the Relaxists. A few days later, public fascination reached a fever pitch when Red Horse conducted an interview on Fox News and responded to questions about the "experiment."

Beyond the Big Bang

In 2011, when Slowbe was four years old, an article was published in the journal *Nature* that reported on new discoveries from the Hubble Space Telescope. Scientists believed the images they'd recently retrieved showed the universe just 480 million years after its genesis. By 2036, images of a nascent fifty-million-year-old universe had been retrieved—a stunning development that convinced many it wouldn't be long before space telescopes captured the legendary moment of creation, the Big Bang. On August 17th, 2048, as Slowbe stepped onto his deck in the early morning hours, images and data from the Unbounded Energy Retrieval Telescope began to trickle into a small, isolated room in the Kerr Observation Center where two astrophysicists and a cosmologist, all women, stood in rapt silence, almost in disbelief.

Slowbe leaned against the deck railing. The entire horizon was blanketed in a dirty, brownish-grey haze that had drifted up from the south. A week earlier, dozens of asteroids had crashed into north central California, sparking a conflagration that, due to aggressive winds and a terrain parched by a years-long drought, spread rapidly across the landscape. Dark-orange flames, billowing black smoke, stretched from Redding to Sacramento. At almost the exact moment that asteroids were descending upon the Golden State, a hail of Israeli missiles landed on the Palestinian city of Ramallah.

Slowbe went into his kitchen. After preparing himself some tea, he opened his Array and began freewriting ideas for an article he'd been asked to submit to the online magazine *Peace and Reconciliation*: "Many say that because humans have always been at war there will always be war. I don't believe that. Peace is inevitable. The past doesn't determine, or necessarily predict, the future. Many say that it's human nature to be violent, human nature to be selfish, human nature to fear the unknown, or simply to fear. The evolutionary process is ongoing. We should be cautious when we assume that our baser characteristics are our defining characteristics. We grow. The idealist must assert that our higher nature is our truer nature.

"Health, soundness, and joy all emerge from, and are implicit in, a place of peace. This is true for the person and for the society. And so if the best life for a human is one marked by peace, then the best society is one that facilitates and secures this. If it is noble and logical for a person to make peace a priority, then it is noble and logical for society to do so as well. Peace is practical. Prosperity, self-actualization, happiness, and the fulfillment of human needs are always, in one way or another, reliant on its presence. Just as a child needs a peaceful home in order to develop healthily, each individual needs a peaceful society in order to thrive to the fullest extent. By the same token, society itself needs peace to reach its own potential as an organic system.

"It is difficult for the addict to believe in, or truly conceptualize, a sober reality. It is equally difficult for society in its current state to believe in, or conceive of, a *pax mundi*, world peace. It takes, they say, a spiritual awakening, or a psychic change. Many addicts, most perhaps, can objectively view their habit and recognize its destructiveness, as most citizens can see, for example, that war is hell. And yet, the addict, the citizen, and the society acclimate to, and accept, the hell as the status quo, and often fall back on the presumption that the behavior that maintains the status quo will never cease, and that the paradigm will never shift. Change the thought, the idea, and the belief, the stuff of paradigms, and the experience follows suit. Peace is a belief, a paradigm; war is a belief, a paradigm.

"The goal is to begin changing our expectations, toward a future that isn't violent; to begin creating environments that aren't conducive to producing unhealthy, fearful, distorted, and egomaniacal psyches. We must ask ourselves, 'What proactive measures can we take now that will increase the odds of a peaceful and reconciled future?' The 'necessity of war' paradigm is the status quo, and it can be left behind. The twenty-first century is the perfect time to begin engaging a new normal, one that rejects the idea of citizens of nations killing one another or threatening one another.

"One assertion the cynic will make every time is that 'there will always be an aggressor, self-defense will be required, and thus the war begins.' This is not necessarily true, particularly if we set about creating environments in which basic needs are met; nations and peoples do not feel threatened, isolated, or marginalized; and diplomacy is revered. The way to solve the problem of war is to address the root causes. We need to treat the problem as if it were a collective concern. If the causes are religious, we have to address that; if they are rooted in issues that happened in the past, we must find ways to heal the past; if they are nationalistic or monetary in nature, or over natural resources, we should examine these dynamics. Every citizen in the world must ask themselves the question, 'Do I want peace?' This is a 'yes or no' question, not a 'yes, but . . .' question. As opposed to preemptive military strikes we may be better served by preemptive peace processes. This would be in everyone's best interest. Diplomacy, cultural exchange, concession, open-mindedness, and belief are some of the paths to peace. We can avoid passing war on to future generations. War is not acceptable among the civilized.

"There is no separation between the inner and outer realities. Not only is the outer reality framed, colored, and defined by the thoughts, emotions, and beliefs of the person, but it is perpetually reflecting the person's psyche. Ultimately, life is internal. Each idea, each construct, each framework, each paradigm that is materialized as physical reality originates from an inner plane. Personal realities overlap with other personal realities. On one level, the world revolves around each person, with the masses and the world serving as the supporting cast and the stage, respectively, in the story of the individual. On another level, there is an innate connection linking the subjective realities of each of the planet's nine billion individuals—a collective consciousness, or collective energy, from which are born the shared experiences of history and world events. Communication and exchange of information is occurring on multiple dimensional levels, and between multiple dimensional levels, at all times. Before events appear in physical reality, on the pages of history, they exist within the realm of collective consciousness and the individual's inner reality. The bridge, the book, the building, the government, the catastrophe, the heroic moment, et cetera, are non-physical ideas, non-physical potentialities, before they appear as physical manifestations. There is tremendous activity behind the scenes. It is up to the individual to become aware of the underlying apparatus, processes, and energy that create reality. Each person is responsible for the events of their lives, as well as for the course of history. The inner invariably becomes the outer. Create world peace within. Peace within creates peace without. It may not be easy for the masses to believe, given humanity's track record, but peace is a choice, peace is possible. The development of love and peace on the inner plane is the greatest contribution an individual can make to society."

Before he got any further, Slowbe received a message from Heart Stevens informing him that the contract between the Human Evolution Project and the advertising agency Wieden+Kennedy, which Stevens had helped negotiate, was finalized. A public statement was being prepared for the

24th. Slowbe opened the attached document and began skimming over the executive summary, which described the fifteen-billion-dollar venture as an "art and social marketing project" and a "media art installation" that would be renewed in ten-year intervals "until the program was no longer necessary." An important stipulation of the contract was that Wieden+Kennedy would open an HEP-specific office and work in close coordination with the salon members, in particular with Monarch and Song because of their backgrounds in the visual arts.

To the surprise of everyone involved in the project, just two days after it was announced that the organization had been formed, and that Wieden+Kennedy and the salon members had entered into a multibillion-dollar agreement for its promulgation, Pope Leo issued a press release expressing concern that the HEP, and the example of spending such an inordinate amount of money for its promotion, would only result in "corrupting the youth." He denounced the HEP contract, and any subsequent promotional activities, as an "abominable publicity stunt." Slowbe and his so-called Relaxists, he proclaimed, were unabashed manipulators. Less than a month later, on September 18th, he announced the convening of the Third Council of the Vatican, to be held from December 3rd to December 7th. The purpose of the assembly, he declared, was to "address threats to the church and other concerning matters."

Although Leo's public statements didn't clarify what specific threats or concerning matters he was referring to, it was generally assumed that they likely included a range of factors, from the truth of consciousness rallies and the legacy of Toussaint Riviere; to Slowbe's book; to the actions of the salon members, collectively and individually; to Christianity's declining membership. Worldwide, self-identification as Christian had fallen by fifty-eight percent from 2012, with the steepest part of the decline occurring after 2027. The negative trend in religious affiliation was also found within Islam, where the decline in self-identification from 2012 was fifty-one percent.

*

Adik Abundo was a dying man. Cancer had ravaged his seventy-three-year-old body, which just six months prior had been robust and imposing. Now, his days were mostly spent confined to a large Belgian-made bed where he was propped up by oversized pillows and covered by plain silk sheets. A soft, quieting breeze passed through the open windows of his bedroom, bringing the slight hint of lavender into his broad nostrils.

For the past twenty years, Abundo had been the dominating force in the Democratic Republic of the Congo: first as an influential general in the army, and then as president. Since 2041 he'd been referred to by many central Africans as the King of Lake Tanganyika because of his victory over the combined armies of Zambia, Burundi, and Tanzania late in that year. Known as the Lake War, the struggle for control of Tanganyika left over a million Africans dead and Abundo's ships an ever-present sight on the 418-mile-long body of water—the second deepest and the second largest by volume in the world. Another great African lake, Lake Victoria, had been controlled by Uganda since 2043. In the years that followed, a menacing arms race, exacerbated by the desperation for water, emerged between the four major central African military powers: the DRC, Uganda, Angola, and Kenya.

Slowbe arrived at N'djili Airport in the capital city of Kinshasa at 4:14 p.m. on December 1st. He walked out of the terminal and quickly noticed a large man holding a sign that read "Bill Wilson." Slowbe greeted the man with a nod and then proceeded to follow him through the busy airport without either of them saying hardly a word, aside from the man telling Slowbe that his luggage was being collected.

Outside it was 110 degrees Fahrenheit. The man led Slowbe to a waiting limousine, opened the back door for him, and motioned for him to enter. Slowbe stepped into the spacious compartment. There were mirrors on the ceiling, a full bar, reclining seats, and plates of food. Slowbe's luggage was placed in the trunk. After a few moments, he heard the front doors slam shut. A voice on the speaker system said, "Please relax, Mr. Slowbe, and enjoy the ride. If you need anything, push one of the call buttons located on the armrests." The vehicle began making its way out of the airport and on to the estate where Abundo was bedridden.

When they arrived an hour and a half later, a dozen or so people, all dressed in formal attire, were standing outside. As the vehicle pulled up to the mansion, there were murmurs among them, and the brows of several of them were furrowed. The sound of the wheels rolling over the gravel driveway ceased and there was silence. Slowbe stepped out of the limousine. Noticing the rigid demeanor of the small assembly, he was measured in his greetings, offering a nod and a courteous, but reserved, smile. The group of observers, which included household staff, nurses, doctors, and political advisors, who'd been standing in the wide passage leading to the front door, parted as the man escorted Slowbe toward the main entrance. It occurred to Slowbe that the scene seemed straight out of a movie. Not a word was spoken.

Slowbe entered the residence and was relieved by the drop in temperature. Most of the curtains were drawn, and the light was dim. Nonetheless, the white marble flooring that spread out across the huge, circular foyer seemed to shine. The space was filled with plants; fine china; and several paintings, including a Gauguin, a Cézanne, a Monarch, and a Modigliani. To his left, Slowbe noticed a large sitting room with delicately crafted wood furnishings and lavishly embroidered couches and chairs. There was a bronze fountain, about five feet tall, sculpted into the figure of a young boy playing a flute. In the room immediately to his right there were several glass ornaments and more paintings. Although he couldn't make out the artists, they appeared to be African in style.

Slowbe was led to an impressive stairway that rose up about forty feet from the entrance. His hand slid along the marble railing, relishing its coolness and its smoothness. Once at the top, Slowbe followed the man down one hallway and then to the end of another until they came to two tall wooden doors with gold-covered handles. The man pushed a button and a bell rang inside the room. Within a few seconds, the doors opened and Slowbe was shown into the enormous bedroom. His escort stayed in the hallway.

The first thing Slowbe noticed when he walked into the room was Abundo lying in an extravagant bed that was situated between two sets of bay windows.

"Come over here, Mr. Slowbe," Abundo said in a deep, raspy voice. "Please sit down."

Slowbe nodded his head and walked toward Abundo, who had planned for this moment by having a chair placed next to his bed. The aides and attendants who were standing or sitting in various parts of the room stared silently.

"Thank you, Mr. President," Slowbe replied, as he took a seat next to the controversial African leader known for his inclination to joke with reporters, his comically grandiose sense of himself, his intimidating physical presence, his brutality, and the military endeavors that had secured water for his nation. Evening was settling in and, looking out of the bay windows, Slowbe could see an array of colors rising upon the horizon, one field of light lying atop the other, morphing into one another, starting with orange directly on the horizon, then turning to red, pink, aqua blue, light blue, and finally dark blue as one's eyes traced upward. Directly above, a small circular portion of the sky had turned pitch black, like a portal.

"I am very happy to see you. I trust you had a comfortable flight from Portland."

"Yes, very comfortable. It's quite a short trip these days, in terms of time." Slowbe's flight from Portland to Kinshasa had included a short layover in New York City and had taken five hours all told.

To Abundo, and many of his countrymen and countrywomen, Slowbe was the man who had "pulled fire from the sky." Also, like many of his countrymen and countrywomen, Abundo was a devout Catholic. And although he hadn't read *The World Within*, since late June he'd been expressing to his aides that he wanted to meet Slowbe. His personal assistant had attempted to make contact in July and August, leaving several video messages. Initially, Slowbe was reluctant to return the calls, but on September 25th he informed the salon members that he was planning on traveling to the DRC to meet Abundo to talk with him about the Human Evolution Project. A few days later, he contacted Abundo's office and stated that he wished to accept the president's invitation, but noted that his schedule precluded arranging anything for October or November.

"Please leave us," Abundo said to the aides and attendants scattered about the room. "I want to be alone with Mr. Slowbe. Please give us some privacy." The five men and two women made their way past the large wooden doors and out into the hallway.

"Ring if you need anything, Mr. President," said an aide as she shut the doors.

Slowbe looked out the windows at the wide African landscape.

"We saw a young male lion kill a hyena two days ago, just out there, about two hundred meters off," Abundo said, pointing his thumb toward the windows behind him. "They are mortal enemies, the lions and the hyenas. They want the same resources." He laughed and patted Slowbe's forearm. "There can be no peace between them. Is it not the same with humans?" he asked.

Abundo extended his right arm toward the reading lamp that rested on a table next to his bed. He pulled the short chain. A gentle light encircled the area surrounding his bed.

"Are you comfortable?" Slowbe asked.

"Yes...I'm fine...are you?"

"I am."

"People say you are a Relaxist, that you live in the deep, still pool, that you practice the art of relaxation. How nice. You seem very calm. Yes. I can see it in your eyes."

"But I come from a place of turmoil."

"Ah, you are a human. You come from humanity, from the earth."

"Yes, the same as you."

"The Pope thinks you are very different from me. I believe he has used the word 'unnatural.' I don't necessarily agree with everything the Pope says."

"That which is natural is largely unknown to humanity, as of yet, but you see there is great change afoot. What do you think is natural?"

"Greed, fear, hunger, violence."

"Is that your reality?"

"It's the reality of the world."

"Perhaps you'll change your mind, in time."

"It's too late for that, Mr. Slowbe, I'm a dying man."

"But you wish to be proven wrong, or to see some evidence to the contrary?"

"About what?"

"That you are a dying man, and that greed, fear, hunger, and violence are the natural states of humanity and the world."

"What do you mean?"

"Why else would you want to have me here with you?"

Abundo was silent for several moments and then asked, "Can you help me?"

"Do you think I can?"

"That is why I have been so eager to meet with you, Mr. Slowbe."

By now the black veil had crept across the sky, while a band of dark, deep-blue light remained immediately above the horizon, not yet ceding completely to the night. Millions of stars began to appear.

"Turn the light off, Mr. Abundo," Slowbe said. "And I'm going to close the curtains, if that's ok."

"That's fine," Abundo said. He leaned over to pull the light switch and the room went dark.

"I just want to be quiet for a few moments," Slowbe said.

Nearly a minute passed with no words spoken between the two men. Slowbe then placed his right hand on Abundo's shoulder. In a matter of seconds, Abundo felt an overwhelming rush of energy surge through his body and then a dull, blunt pain in his head, chest, and stomach. Shortly thereafter he lost consciousness. Slowbe walked over to the large wooden doors, opened them, and informed the attendants that Mr. Abundo had retired for the evening. One of them went over to check on Abundo momentarily before exiting the room again. Slowbe was shown to his guest quarters.

When Abundo awoke the next morning at 7:07 a.m., he felt an unusual lightness. The last thing he recalled from the night before was turning off the lamp next to his bed. He rang for his assistant.

"Where is Mr. Slowbe?" he asked.

"He stepped outside to take a walk, sir."

"Go get him."

The assistant hurried out of the room. Twenty minutes later she returned with Slowbe.

"I feel different," Abundo said.

"Call for your doctors and have them do imaging scans," Slowbe said.

Slowbe's instructions were carried out, and before long Abundo's three doctors returned to his room with results from the tests.

"We don't understand, sir, your cancer appears to be gone. We would like to do more tests tomorrow."

Abundo began crying uncontrollably. His assistant dropped

to her knees and fell toward Abundo's bed grasping her president's arm. By December 4th, every corner of the globe had heard of the remarkable occurrence in central Africa. On the 6th Abundo ordered the removal of the DRC's naval presence on Lake Tanganyika.

Genius

Although Slowbe rarely used the word "spiritual," this hadn't always been the case. In his late teens, his twenties, and most of his thirties, it was how he'd often described his poetry, the way of life he sought, and the type of truth he longed for. In many ways it had been his favorite subject to discuss. And then the concept just faded away, but the nature of reality didn't change. He was left with the memories of years of musings on the subject; various analogies and models he'd imagined; as well as journal entries, short essays, and poetry. During his college years, he'd envisioned the "harmony model" and the "infinite ocean and water molecule analogy."

With the harmony model, Slowbe conceived of spirituality as being the set of principles, beliefs, and behaviors that fostered harmony—harmony within oneself; harmony with one's fellow humans; harmony with one's natural surroundings, including the earth and the universe; and, if one was inclined to acknowledge or believe in such things, harmony with one's soul or with "God." Slowbe thought this harmony model was a fairly inclusive framework that could be broadly applied and didn't necessarily have to do with the supernatural, or even spirit, for that matter.

With the infinite ocean and water molecule analogy, Slowbe imagined the spiritual as being like an infinite ocean: no beaches, no sky above, no ocean floor, just an infinity of water.

An infinity of water that was even more than the sum of its parts. And within this vast ocean he imagined a single water molecule. The water molecule represented the physical universe, or perhaps a person. Existence as the water molecule, or within the water molecule, wouldn't appear to be aquatic; it wouldn't even seem wet, he thought. The water molecule might not be cognizant of the bigger pictures, such as the drops of water, the ocean currents, or the breadth and magnitude of the ocean itself and all its energy. Slowbe thought humans could understand the oceanic nature of things, analogously speaking, if they could somehow see beyond the prism of the water molecule. For Slowbe, experiencing the violet realm was like glimpsing a drop of water in the infinite ocean. To see the water, to become oceanic, was to understand, and be in, the "spiritual."

Slowbe likened the "spiritual," as imagined in the infinite ocean and water molecule analogy, to a concept he'd first been introduced to in a class he took on the pre-Socratic philosophers during his junior year in college: the logos. He was fascinated by the idea of the logos and, being so inclined, took creative license with how he interpreted ancient writings on the topic. Before long he'd developed his own personal conception of what the logos was. Historically, this wasn't a particularly unique exercise, because over the centuries and millennia numerous thinkers, philosophers, philosophical schools, and religious traditions had taken the principle of the logos and conceptualized it in their own way—from the pre-Socratics to Aristotle to the Stoics, from the Hellenistic Jewish philosophers to the early Christian theologians, from the Neoplatonists to the Muslim mystics and metaphysicians of the Islamic Golden Age, to the twentieth-century psychologist Carl Jung. In Slowbe's mind, the logos became the realm, or thing, or level of existence in which all paradoxes, contradictions, and seeming opposites, like chaos and order, were indivisible. It was the realm, or thing, or level of existence that transcended logic and rationality—for example, the place where there was no beginning and no end (but within which beginnings and endings could exist). His sense of the logos in some ways resembled the interpretation espoused by Plotinus, the third-century philosopher, who had described it as being the underlying state, or reality, from which all else emerges. Slowbe was attracted to the idea of the logos, in particular his vision of it, because it helped stretch his mind beyond the plainly visible and the plainly sensible and toward a more mysterious and transcendental concept of reality. It sparked his imagination and he played with the idea in his mind for a while.

The two main philosophers discussed in Slowbe's class on the pre-Socratics were Heraclitus and Parmenides, both born in the sixth century BC. Slowbe quickly developed a fondness for both of them, especially for Heraclitus, who was the first to write about the logos as a principle, and who was known in antiquity as "The Obscure," due to the paradoxical and enigmatic nature of his philosophical ideas. The relationship between Heraclitus and Parmenides was notable for the fact that the central arguments they presented seemed diametrically opposed: Heraclitus asserting that all things were in a state of becoming, or flux, and Parmenides insisting that all things were in a state of being, or changelessness.

On a winter evening, a couple weeks after the course was over, and after having spent about an hour in meditation, Slowbe collected some of his favorite quotes of the two philosophers. In a burst of spontaneous creative writing he proceeded to weave together what amounted to an informal treatise of sorts—one that intentionally framed, or manipulated, Heraclitus's and Parmenides's quotations and sentiments in a way that supported his own metaphysical beliefs. He would end up sending the composition to his class instructor several days later, after having made a few edits, but never received a reply.

"In several important areas Heraclitus and Parmenides seem to be speaking the same language. To begin with, they both assert that human understanding of reality, in most cases, misses the mark, so to speak; our eyes, clouded by delusion and misunderstanding, often fail to see the underlying truth. Essentially, they both say we overlook that which is real. 'The logos holds always but humans always prove unable to understand it,' Heraclitus says, adding that we 'fail to notice' the logos (or the truth of reality) as we live in our own 'private understanding'—a private understanding that amounts to tunnel vision, and habitually looking in the wrong direction, and being so entranced by the mirage that we are convinced it's real—this tendency being distinctly different from enlightened subjective awareness. Heraclitus also likens the prevailing human condition to being asleep, i.e., not awake to the true nature of reality. Parmenides, as well, points out that the ideas humans have regarding the nature of reality are often based on misconceptions. What Heraclitus refers to as 'private understanding' Parmenides calls 'mortal opinion.' Both are phrases that indicate the respective philosophers' notions that there are paradigms and constructs, created and perpetuated by humans, that do not reliably shine light on the actual truth. Our five senses are unreliable; our mortal opinions and private understandings are unreliable; and any description of reality based on them is, at best, incomplete.

"We are led to believe that the secondary reality is, in fact, the primary reality. I should note that when I use the phrase 'primary reality' I am referring to a reality whose fundamental feature is its infinitude, and when I am referring to 'secondary reality' I am referring to a reality that is characterized by brevity, duality, corporealness, and the appearance of separateness. I assume that the latter springs forth from the former, and that the latter is encompassed by and pervaded by the former. Both Heraclitus and Parmenides acknowledge a secondary reality, which most humans are hypnotized by, but also conceive of a deeper, more essential and fundamental reality that, on the whole, escapes our notice. 'Divine things for the most part escape recognition because of unbelief,' Heraclitus writes.

"What lies within the human, or what might our truer nature consist of, according to Heraclitus and Parmenides? Both of them point out that there is a greater reality that typically escapes our detection, and thus it shouldn't be surprising that each also suggests that there is a greater dimension of our own human nature that generally goes unnoticed. It stands to reason that if a human does not understand the true nature of reality, then they could not possibly, in the fullest sense, understand their own true nature (and perhaps vice versa). On one level, both philosophers consider humans to be mortal creatures. But they both refer to our mortal nature only when they are speaking of our delusions and misguided conceptions. There is the implication that when we dispel such delusions and misguided conceptions, what we are left with is a divine, immortal Self.

"In Parmenides's poem there are direct correlations made between the human and that which transcends night and day, between humans and immortality, and between humans and gods. The goddess in his poem tells Parmenides that the most important thing he has to learn is 'the unshaken heart of persuasive Truth.' We can assume this is something that, eventually, all humans need to know; and we should assume that it is something transcendent. Indeed, beneath the shadow of mortal opinion lies a fundamentally immortal nature. This is not to say that the body does not die, but it is to say that consciousness and personality and soul are intrinsically linked with the eternal and, like energy, are never destroyed. Parmenides's conception of the persuasive truth, i.e., the true nature of reality, is one that is characterized as being imperishable, whole, and timeless. It must be said that this, as well, is his conception of the true nature of the Self.

"Heraclitus also points to an immortal nature in many of his passages. 'You would not discover the limits of the soul although you traveled every road: it has too deep a logos.' The soul is so vast, then, that it could be described as something that extends virtually ad infinitum. Heraclitus goes on to say that 'the soul has a self-increasing logos.' It is expanding, growing, creating, developing (the universe being an excellent metaphor). But the soul is not distinct or essentially separate from what we think of as the human. The human is a function, or physical representation, of the soul. We cannot separate from, or escape, the soul, just as we cannot separate from, or escape, our personality. In essence, we are our souls. This being the case, again, we are of an immortal nature. 'Things unexpected and unthought await humans when they die,' Heraclitus writes. Clearly, he accepts that consciousness and personality do not perish. And when he says that 'immortals are mortals and mortals are immortals,' he is suggesting that, yes, our physicality is mortal, but yet we are essentially non-physical entities. Incidentally, things unexpected and unthought await humans before they 'die' as well, deep within the depths of their own being.

"The idea that all things are one is a central concept for both Heraclitus and Parmenides. Heraclitus repeats the idea time and time again, most directly when he says: 'Listening not to me but to the logos it is wise to agree that all things are one.' On two occasions Heraclitus refers to 'God.' He states that 'God is day and night, winter and summer, war and peace, satiety and hunger' and goes on to say that 'to God all things are beautiful and good and just.' Certainly, the idea of 'God' is one of the strongest statements of oneness that can be made. The logos is of oneness, of unity. It is a timeless realm, plane, or state of being. Its origin is not in the sensible world, but reflections of it, or representations of it, emerge in the sensible world and take the appearance of things that seem to be opposed, but which in fact have the same place of origin and are composed of the same 'stuff.' Night and day are actually one thing, simultaneous, but we do not know what that one thing is. We cannot see the one thing, not with the five senses. Heraclitus states that 'the beginning and the end are common

on the circumference of the circle.' This is his analogy. In
actuality, we can never see the beginning or end of a circle, and
it could be argued that no such things exist but superficially.
Parmenides also suggests that there can be no beginning or end
of reality, or God. He writes, 'Being is without beginning and
[is] indestructible; it is universal, existing alone, immoveable
and without end.' The idea of no beginning and no end with
respect to reality is something that cannot be understood by
humans using our rational faculties alone.

"Finally, Parmenides says that the 'What Is' (the Gestalt
of All That Exists, God, or logos) is uncreated, imperishable,
whole, timeless, unchanging, complete, one, and continuous.
His conclusion is that there can be no 'coming to be.' Heraclitus,
on the other hand, suggests that the 'What Is' is in a state of
flux, evolving, changing, constantly coming into being. So,
while they both embrace the idea of a Gestalt of All That Exists,
or God, or logos, the one says it is a state of Being, and the
other says it is a state of Becoming. Heraclitus and Parmenides
can be reconciled on this matter with the simple assertion
that there is necessarily Being and Becoming, simultaneously
and inseparably. The Gestalt of All That Exists is uncreated,
imperishable, whole, timeless, unchanging, complete, one,
and continuous, while at the same time creative, dynamic,
expanding, renewing, and in flux. We cannot understand how
Becoming and Being exist simultaneously by using logic, or
the five senses, or through the lens of a time/space/duality
paradigm. The oneness of Being and Becoming, like a oneness
of stillness and motion, is a truth within the logos."

Slowbe had always been naturally inclined toward
inhabiting a world of analogies and imagery; metaphors and
similes; and symbolism, ideas, and models. He was a poet. And
for a while, he embraced his notions of the logos, the infinite
ocean and water molecule analogy, and the harmony model
(among the numerous other psychic devices he would utilize
in order to help himself align with something greater than

himself, to free his heart and mind, to elucidate his intuition, and to break through the paradigm). It was both a serious and a playful exercise. So, while he couldn't truly comprehend an infinite ocean, or, rather, the reality for which it was a metaphor, he felt that something like this would always be in the now and would always be in a state of manifestation. The infinite ocean might take the form of a tree, which doesn't always look like or feel like a tree, depending on the perspective, or it could take the form of a star, which doesn't always look or feel like a star, depending on the perspective, or it could take the form of a person, or many other things that have not been discovered or dreamt of by human beings. Slowbe envisioned himself amidst the illimitable and imagined that he, too, in essence, was boundless.

His awareness of the violet realm, while subjective, had been consistent and pervasive, and it had led him to seek (with less than complete dedication during his drinking years, but eventually in earnest) the broadest possible perspective, the widest experience of consciousness, the most open mind. It wasn't difficult for him to conceive of reality as having an infinite, multidimensional, and non-physical nature, although by no means did he presume that the infinite or the multidimensional were simply an endless expanse of violet light. Over time, he grew less inclined to entertain, or rely on, metaphors, analogies, similes, labels, models, or definitions, at least intrapersonally; but he would never abandon these devices altogether. He remained a poet, one who accepted that there is a point at which the truth cannot be spoken, only realized and intuited. And even though the primacy of non-physical reality was evident to him, as evident as his own body, as evident as his own existence, he was deeply enamored with the material world and never doubted its value, its significance, or his intimate connection to it. To Slowbe, physical reality, the universe, was a marvelous facade; a truly grand, stupendous, dazzling, and hypnotizing spectacle; an animated, creative expression that was utterly real for all intents and purposes, uniquely suited for exploration and play, creativity and imagination, discovery and personal growth. It simply wasn't the be-all and end-all. Every aspect, feature, and manifestation of physical reality was a symbol, a reflection of some element of a deeper, underlying reality.

*

The sky was overcast on the mid-December evening. Song got out of her car and walked toward the trunk to retrieve her most recent painting, which, it had been agreed, would be one of the subjects of discussion for the salon. Other subjects on the loosely structured agenda included two poems by Red Horse; a new book Henry was working on, tentatively called *The Potential Genius of Humanity: A Meditation on Creativity, Vision, and Idealism*; and plans for involvement in some of the truth of consciousness rallies that were scheduled to take place in the early months of 2049. To date, rallies were planned for several African and European capitals, as well as Atlanta, Houston, Los Angeles, Tokyo, Peking, and Seoul.

Song opened her trunk, and as she reached for the canvas, she heard the sound of cars approaching. She turned and noticed Red Horse, Henry, and Sangree, each in their own vehicle, pulling into Slowbe's long driveway, one directly after the other, like a convergence. Before long, greetings and embraces were being exchanged.

Song pulled out a three-by-four-foot painting. The small group was silent for a few seconds.

"Let me get a closer look at that," Henry said as he carefully scanned the work of art, impressed by its tone and rhythm. Red Horse smiled and nodded at Song, the glint in her eyes, and her raised eyebrows, indicating that she was moved by the picture. On an almost subliminal level, it seemed to speak to a theme that had recently been weaving its way into the current zeitgeist: the idea of humans as multidimensional entities. (The subject of the current zeitgeist was itself something that had been discussed and written about extensively over the course of 2048. Most people believed they were living in an extraordinary era that somehow already felt legendary. In November, during an interview with CNN, Deepak Chopra had coined the phrase "Aquarian Renaissance" to describe the current age, noting that it seemed to be a time of reflection and awakening. "People have started to understand something I said back in 2010," he told the reporter, "that the possibility of stepping into a higher plane is quite real for everyone. It requires no force or effort or sacrifice. It involves little more than changing our ideas about what is normal.")

Henry, Sangree, Song, and Red Horse gradually began making their way toward Slowbe's front door.

"When I was a kid," Henry said, "my mother used to drive me and my brother up this way during the summer to watch the sunset. Usually, we'd go to Council Crest Park. I love the mood you've captured with this painting, Angel. For some reason it reminds me of those special summer evenings from my childhood."

"I was actually up at Council Crest earlier today," Red Horse mentioned. "There was a group of plein air artists working."

Henry nodded his head in response.

"The painting evokes a nostalgic sense for me too," Song said. "It reminds me of a feeling I vaguely remember from long ago."

"How long ago?" Henry asked.

Song noticed the clouds lying like a dark blanket overhead and a faint raindrop touched her hand. "From my time in Aleppo," she said.

"When were you there?" Sangree asked.

"For eleven months, when I was eight and nine years old," Song responded. "My father was involved in organizing humanitarian efforts there. We lived in an apartment outside the city and from my bedroom window I had a panoramic view. There was a small hill in the center of the old city called the Citadel of Aleppo, or citadel hill. It was a few miles away from where we lived, but I could see it easily from my room. I was told that some of the ruins there were almost five thousand years old, including remains of a temple to the storm god Hadad. I never went to the site, but I was always mystified by it, and I would stare at it night after night from my bedroom window. I would actually have dreams about Hadad."

Before the group got to the front entrance, Joan Monarch and Mia Sabin pulled into the driveway. Moments later, Sarah Goulle, Char Ron, Sam Glowston, Bridge Mayfall, and Caroline Abadie all arrived. It was a sudden flurry of activity.

Inside, Slowbe was on a call with a man named Dr. Isaac Johnson, who was the director of research at the SETI Institute in Mountain View, California. Dr. Johnson had mentioned that he'd been at Harvard at the same time as Slowbe, and that he'd known of Slowbe's "little secret society," as he put it.

"The Tuesday Night Tequila Club?" Slowbe asked.

"Yes," Dr. Johnson replied. "I remember you and the others would gather every Tuesday night at midnight in the basement of the dorm. If I was up late enough, I would hear the voices from your meetings coming through the vent into my room. That was freshman year. I remember overhearing discussions about 'the cause of humanity' and 'divine immanence,' and a lot of other stuff that I found really fascinating. I think I became a seeker because of what I overheard on those late nights. We met a couple times, but I wasn't very social in those days."

"I'm not sure if I recall meeting you," Slowbe said.

"Well, I read your book as soon as it came out in January and have been following your activities closely. In case you're curious, I got your phone number from Jazz McKinley, whom I happen to know. Are you familiar with the SETI Institute? SETI stands for 'Search for Extraterrestrial Intelligence.' I've been the director of research for the past eight years."

"Yes," Slowbe answered. "In fact, I'm a SETI volunteer. I have all of my computers set to your telescope array. Waiting to receive that first signal."

Slowbe heard the rumblings of his visitors entering his home. He stepped out of his office and motioned that he would be with them in just a few moments.

"Jazz told me about your great enthusiasm for astronomy and cosmology."

"Absolutely," Slowbe said.

"Since 2007, when the first forty-two telescopes were set in motion, the teams at SETI have been waiting, and searching, patiently. It's been forty-one years now. There are some things I'd like to discuss with you about this project."

"Of course," Slowbe said. "What is it you'd like to discuss?"

"I'd prefer to speak in person, if that's possible. It's regarding some ideas I've been considering, as well as some interesting findings that a few of my colleagues have recently made. Would you be able to meet with me this month?"

Slowbe didn't think long on his response. "What day did you have in mind, Mr. Johnson? May I call you Isaac? Please, call me Edward."

"Of course, call me Isaac. How about December 27th? I know that's only a couple weeks away, but I'll be in Thailand for the entire month of January, so I was hoping to meet before I leave. If you wished to stay in Mountain View for the weekend I could make lodging arrangements for you. I'd also love to give you a tour of the Allen Telescope Array."

"Will you hold for just a second, Isaac, while I check my calendar?"

"Sure," Johnson said.

Slowbe was curious, and a bit taken by a sense of adventure. He wondered what Johnson had in mind to share with him and was eager to find out. He opened the calendar on his Array and noticed that the dates were open.

"That weekend will work," Slowbe said.

"Great, it will be an honor to meet with you. I'll send you my address and information regarding lodging."

"Thank you. I look forward to meeting with you as well, Isaac, and hearing all about your work. Take care."

"Goodbye," Dr. Johnson said.

Slowbe set his Array on his office desk and went to greet his guests.

The group had made their way down to the basement level and into a spacious lounge where two plush L-shaped couches took up much of the south wall and some of the west. A large oak table was situated near the couches. Four large windows faced east, and every inch of the floor was covered with brown shag carpet. On the north side of the room there was a piano; two reading chairs; a fireplace; and a collection of oil paintings and black-and-white photographs, all but one of which had been rendered by individuals present at the salon. The collection included works by Song, Mayfall, Monarch, and Glowston. All of the photographs had been taken by Sangree. Numerous plants also occupied the space.

Slowbe and Henry slid the reading chairs over next to the oak table, and the other salon members settled into the couches as the group began to engage in small talk about the weather, the view, and news reports that the magnetic poles were shifting.

"Shall we?" Sangree said after ten minutes or so. The room grew silent, and everyone looked around at one another in recognition and approval. Glowston and Sangree closed the curtains and the room went dark. A twenty-minute period of meditation commenced.

Since her visit to Slowbe's cottage in Nehalem in late June, Song had been working on letting go of her fear of death and on orienting herself to the reality of a multidimensional Self. She was using visualization exercises and was examining, and gradually changing, her core beliefs. There were two phenomena, both drawn from her love of astronomy, that she focused on and internalized during her exercises: the image of the supernova and the image of the infinitely expanding universe. These phenomena had captivated her imagination ever since she was a child. She remembered being astonished when her father explained to her that in 2010 NASA scientists had used information gathered from the Hubble Space Telescope to conclude that the universe would continue to accelerate and expand forever. Now, when she took time to sit quietly and turn her attention inward, she would visualize within herself a supernova exploding with tremendous energy in all directions, or the universe expanding unendingly; and she imagined these phenomena as metaphors for her own Self or soul. "The Self is limitless and inextinguishable, this is my new belief," she would repeat to herself during her exercises.

Silence permeated the room. Song's mind became quiet, but then wandered briefly to a conversation she'd had with Slowbe a few weeks after her visit to his cottage. During the conversation she'd asked him what he thought it meant to surrender, or to let go. "I suppose it means a lot of things," he responded. "I think it means that I'm viewing myself as a system and I'm orienting myself squarely within myself in the present moment. For many of us it takes a great deal of practice to become comfortable with, and acclimated to, being firmly in the present moment. But, essentially, it takes one forceful cognitive and emotional shift and there you are. Also, for me, surrendering or letting go means that I'm saying yes to something. I'm saying yes to something that is not physically dense. Maybe it's useful to consider the fact that the atoms that make up our bodies are ninety-nine percent empty space. If we reflect upon ourselves in this light, it's easier to understand that we're really just energy and consciousness, and that we're not so bound and tethered as we may have thought. We are spirit, so to speak, first and foremost.

"From my perspective, in surrendering I become more integrated into the Gestalt of All That Exists—into a oneness—

and I'm saying yes to immortality, or at least to fearlessness regarding death. I'm saying yes to the idea that the soul is limitless and that I am a part of that limitlessness. I am saying yes to the interconnectedness of all things, the earth and the universe, and all creatures; and I'm connecting to myself on the deepest, most expansive, and most intimate level that I can access. I'm also saying yes to something that is the unknown. I'm trusting in something larger than myself, I'm trusting myself, and I'm trusting process. I'm accepting the seen and the unseen. Trust is a key part of this. Some call it faith. I call it trust.

"So, for me, surrendering and letting go means that I'm exhibiting some willingness to stand face-to-face with something profound and powerful, either within me or beyond me, and accepting it; like taking that plunge into an ocean—even if there are uncomfortable emotions within the ocean, or unfamiliar things. I'm saying yes to the field of energy, creativity, intelligence, information, love, and consciousness, and I'm deciding to see it all flow through me freely, without restriction. I accept that ultimately there are no walls, no separations, and I am embracing, and trusting in, this formlessness and breadth. I'm walking away from tunnel vision.

"Being in the present moment is the first step, seeing the eternal in the now, and letting the present moment be your epicenter. It's a choice. And if we aren't letting go of something, we must ask ourselves why we don't want to let go, why we want to cling to the things we cling to, and what we are afraid of. Letting go is always liberating, always positive and constructive, always about expanding. It's an affirmative process, not about pushing something away or suppressing anything. It's about settling in."

Another thought crossed Song's mind: What would it take for her to believe in the soul with the same certainty that she believed a thought was a thought, the earth was the earth, or a word on a page was a word on a page, and to consciously interact with the soul in the same tangible, practical way that she interacts with a thought, the earth, and a word on a page? Song quieted her mind and began to visualize a supernova.

Mountain View

Shortly after passing through the town of Yachats, Oregon, Slowbe entered Cape Perpetua Scenic Area. Located within the Siuslaw National Forest, the large headland area covered 2,700 acres of dense spruce, Douglas fir, and western hemlock forests, as well as rocky coastal habitat noted for its unique features— places like Devil's Churn, Cook's Chasm, and Spouting Horn, where the ocean crashed upon the shoreline with thunderous claps, creating huge plumes of water that soared upward. From the highest point of the cape, eight hundred feet above sea level, one could see seventy miles of the central Oregon coast, and almost forty miles out to sea on a clear day. The area had been named by Captain James Cook, who came upon the site on St. Perpetua's day, March 7th, 1778, as he was exploring the Pacific coast in search of a Northwest Passage.

Around 1:20 p.m. Slowbe took a left off Highway 101 and drove up a narrow, winding road and into the empty parking lot of the visitor center. He parked his Volkswagen Microbus in the uppermost portion of the lot, near the entrance to the six-mile Cook's Ridge and Gwynn Creek Loop Trail. He drank some water and ate a couple bananas and an apple before heading toward the trail. A light breeze drifted about, somehow complementing the visceral sense of stillness and silence that pervaded the scene.

Slowbe proceeded through the forest at a leisurely pace, taking in the scenery, pausing on occasion to gaze at a particularly large Sitka or Doug fir, a grove of ferns, or some other bit of forest majesty. His mind was filled with the green foliage that surrounded him, and his eyes traced the tree trunks and the boughs that spread out in abstract and illogical patterns. The forest smelled good and his body was relaxed. Patches of blue appeared through the canopy and he noticed a few thin, white, low-lying clouds.

After a couple hours, Slowbe noticed a stream up ahead where the path veered to the right behind a large rock formation. As he approached the bank of the stream he was drawn by the soft bubbling sounds of its ripples. He continued on for a while alongside the rock face to his right and the stream to his left, until the trail veered again to the right. He came around the bend and stopped abruptly. Less than thirty feet away, a male mountain lion was moving across the trail. The animal stopped when it saw Slowbe appear from behind the rock, and for several moments it stood lengthwise across the trail with its head turned toward Slowbe. Slowbe didn't think of death or pain. Amidst the adrenaline that was coursing through his body he remained calm, and he focused his energy toward the big cat. A conversation from many years ago flashed through his mind.

Long before Slowbe had gathered the wherewithal to delve deeply into the paradigm of fear, to confront it, digest it, process it, and then expel it from his being, he had concluded that fear was not an original, natural, or evolutionarily unavoidable feature of the human condition. It was something that could be transcended and discarded. One of his heroes, Socrates, had taught his students that ignorance was the root of all evil, and Slowbe had accepted this notion for many years until it occurred to him one day that perhaps fear was actually the root of all so-called evil. In one way or another, he concluded, fear was the origin of all hatred, violence, greed, self-destruction, division, narrow-mindedness, and negativity. It was fear that was the scourge of humankind. It had to be diminished and dissipated in order for humanity to save itself.

"Don't we need fear to protect ourselves from danger?" a college friend asked during a Tuesday Night Tequila gathering. "What about fear of fire, or experiencing fear if one comes upon a cougar, or something, in the woods?"

"We only need rationality in those instances," Slowbe replied. "Fear isn't required to help me determine whether or not to touch a flame. I only need the understanding that the fire can harm me, and then the rational sense to act accordingly."

"Well, what about the prospect of imminent harm, physical harm, isn't it natural or rational to fear that?"

"Not necessarily. If we have enough presence to accept the big picture of reality, then we don't have to fear anything. Fear is always about loss, pain, death, uncertainty, the unknown, or embarrassment and judgment. If we fully come to terms with these realities, either through some type of radical acceptance or some type of surrendering or letting go, or some sort of power of belief, then there's no fear—just pure spirit, pure being. I'm basically saying that fear serves no practical or fundamental purpose, and we're much better off, in every respect, without it. So, we should work to eliminate it. And I'm saying this is possible—not easy, but possible. What do you think is left when we take fear out of the equation?"

"So, if you came face-to-face with a cougar in the woods you wouldn't be afraid?"

"Well, I'm not saying I've overcome fear, as of yet. There's definitely a gap between what I'm espousing and what my actual lived reality currently is. Hopefully, I can close the gap at some point."

"Good luck with that," his friend said.

"Thanks," Slowbe replied lightheartedly, acknowledging that true fearlessness was a daunting proposition.

Of course, he never expected that he would come face-to-face, alone in the wild, with a large animal that could maim or kill him. As he stood in the forest, the irony of his past conversation and the specific reference to a cougar encounter was not lost on him.

The mountain lion turned and faced Slowbe directly. It took two steps toward him before stopping again. Slowbe stood perfectly still. The animal then hunched its back and began to growl. At this point, Slowbe gradually raised his arms in the air with his palms open and his fingers spread wide. The mountain lion crouched down slightly and ceased growling. As deeply and loudly as he could, Slowbe began chanting the "Om" sound. He kept his arms raised and palms open and stared intently at the animal. Thirteen long seconds went by. The mountain lion crouched down further and began growling again. It then took three steps backward and suddenly sprinted off into the woods. Slowbe lowered his arms. His heart was pounding intensely. He cautiously began walking backward, his eyes focused on the area where the creature had left the trail, paying close attention for any sign of its return.

Slowbe knew he'd traversed more than half of the loop trail. He figured that if he continued in the direction he'd originally been taking, it would be about an hour before he arrived at the parking lot. If he retraced his steps, it would take approximately an hour and a half walking at a good clip. He quickly decided it was in his best interest to turn around and go back the way he came. He thought about the cougar the entire way, in awe of what had transpired, and feeling an incredible sensory acuity. One of my all-time earthly experiences, he thought to himself. Ever since he was a teenager, he'd imagined what it would be like to have a close encounter with a large animal in the wild, or to bear witness to some sort of extreme natural phenomenon, to feel the intensity of Nature in that way, even though he knew such an experience could result in death or injury. Now, such an episode had come to pass; perhaps a self-fulfilling prophecy. He felt fortunate that he would be able to tell the tale with his body fully intact.

When Slowbe got to his bus, the sun was approaching the horizon. He drove back to 101, turned south, and a couple minutes later arrived at the small roadside parking area for the trail that led down to Devil's Churn. He sat in his bus facing the ocean and fell asleep.

Slowbe woke up a little before 8:00 p.m. He stepped out of his bus and was pleased to find a cloudless sky. Countless points of light glistened above, although he couldn't yet see the Milky Way. He looked forward to it becoming visible later in the evening. From the vantage point of earth, which was located two-thirds of the way from the galaxy's center to its outer rim, the Milky Way always appeared to be a distant, separate entity. There must be a metaphor or some symbolism here, Slowbe once thought. How often do we feel, or appear to be, separate from that which we are, in reality, a part of or within?

Slowbe pulled his flashlight out of his backpack, put on a hat and a winter coat, and started walking down the short trail toward the ocean. He carefully navigated the rocks and tide pools along the shore until he came to a small, crescent-shaped stretch of sandy beach about fifty yards north from where he had exited the trail. At the far edge of the sandy beach was a rugged cape, beyond which was Devil's Churn, a cavernous inlet where the ocean surged along a narrow passage of high rock walls. Slowbe decided not to proceed any further. The small swath of beach seemed a perfect spot to sit and take in the dynamic energy that surged all around him. Furthermore, he'd spotted an abandoned fire pit that was filled with glowing embers. Numerous logs and sticks were scattered about nearby. Soon, Slowbe's arms were filled with wood. He let it all crash into a pile next to the circle of stones surrounding the embers. He placed several sticks in the middle of the pit and watched them ignite. He then positioned two logs across the burning sticks. As he sat down, his thoughts returned to the mountain lion. The flames rose up, fluttering and swaying. Eventually, the Milky Way began to emerge.

The next morning, after having spent the night in his bus, Slowbe visited Devil's Churn. A few other people were gathered along the inlet. On a couple occasions the incoming tide hit the rock walls with such force that spray was thrown nearly two hundred feet in the air.

There weren't many cars on the road when he resumed his journey south on 101 toward Mountain View, California. Fog drifted across the highway. Although it was chilly, he had his driver's-side window rolled down and was enjoying the crisp, fresh morning air that rushed into his bus.

An hour and a half after leaving Cape Perpetua, Slowbe crossed over the Conde B. McCullough Memorial Bridge, which spanned the S-shaped bay where the Coos River entered the Pacific Ocean. A few minutes later, he entered the town of North Bend, at which point he began keeping a close lookout for a place to eat. Continuing on 101, Slowbe soon crossed into the adjacent town of Coos Bay and to his great surprise noticed a sign up ahead to his right that read "Grace Market." Without hesitation he tapped his turn signal. He veered into the parking lot and pulled up to a spot right in front of the entrance. An old lady with long electric-purple hair and blue-rimmed glasses was parked next to him in her antique Mustang. Slowbe got out of his bus and waved to the old lady, who was in a very gradual process of exiting her car. She cheerfully waved back.

The front door of the market made a jingling sound as Slowbe opened it. The next two things that caught his attention were that the store smelled like lavender and that it was much larger on the inside than one might guess from its outward appearance. There were three very long aisles, and to his right, as he entered, was a dining area with a deli and a huge tank that was teeming with brightly colored saltwater fish. Along the left wall of the store was a produce area and at the far end of the store was a fresh seafood section. Both sides of the entire center aisle featured wines from across Oregon's Willamette Valley, home to some of the most highly regarded wineries in the world. A sign in front of the aisle made this evident to the customer. The store also featured a large selection of cheeses.

Slowbe took a seat at a table next to the impressive fish tank. The table itself was also striking, crafted from dark-brown, unvarnished wood, and covered with a smooth glass pane. Slowbe took off his jacket, rested it on one of the chairs, and began looking over the menu.

Before long, a teenage girl with short blond hair, green eyes, and freckles approached him.

"Hello," Slowbe said.

"Hi," the girl responded enthusiastically.

She stood there smiling at Slowbe for several seconds before breaking her silence.

"Do you know what you'd like to eat, sir?" she asked.

"Let's see. How about the Claire Falkenstein?"

All of the sandwiches on the menu, it turned out, were named after notable people from Coos Bay, and Falkenstein was an abstract sculptor and painter who'd lived from 1908 to 1997. She was considered one of the most prolific and experimental American artists of the twentieth century. Her sandwich was a grilled Swiss cheese on wheat with avocado, portabella mushrooms, and alfalfa sprouts.

"Would you like anything to drink?"

Slowbe's eyes were drawn, momentarily, to a small button on the girl's sweatshirt that read "Reconstitute the UN."

"How about orange juice?"

"Ok," the girl replied. She finished scribbling the order on her notepad, nodded at Slowbe, and walked back toward the kitchen.

Slowbe sat admiring the assortment of fish that were moving about the tank. At one point he happened to glance in the direction of the front counter of the cafe and noticed the girl staring at him from behind the cash register. She quickly resumed organizing a small stack of receipts when she saw that Slowbe had noticed her. To her left, a couple heads were peeking out from behind the swinging doors that led to the kitchen. Slowbe waved at the two young workers, who smiled sheepishly and ducked away.

The girl soon returned with Slowbe's order.

"Thank you. That was fast," Slowbe said.

"Yeah," the girl said.

"I like your button," Slowbe said.

"Oh, thanks," the girl replied as she looked down at the button and held it between her thumb and her index finger.

"You must be an activist," Slowbe said.

"Yes, I am, kind of," the girl said, blushing slightly.

"That's great. Are you in high school?" Slowbe asked, pointing to the girl's sweatshirt, which had an image of a pirate beneath the words "Marshfield High School."

"Actually, I'm a freshman at the University of Oregon," the girl said. "We're on winter break. I did go to Marshfield, though."

"Oh, ok," Slowbe said, "what are you majoring in?"

"I'm not positive yet, but maybe art, women's studies, or English."

"Ah, an artist, too. I love art."

"Yeah, I'm always drawing and sketching, and I like to paint and work with mixed media. I have my sketch pad in the back, do you want to see some of my drawings?"

"Sure," Slowbe said.

The girl's eyes lit up with excitement. "Ok, just a second," she said, and she hurried away to the break room in the back of the store. Slowbe began to eat his sandwich. When the girl returned, she was holding a nine-by-twelve spiral-bound notebook with a brown cover and one hundred sheets of sixty-pound, lightly textured paper. The girl placed the sketch pad on the table and opened it to the first page.

"What's your name?" Slowbe asked.

"Amanda," the girl replied.

"I'm Edward."

Amanda nodded her head several times in quick succession. "Nice to meet you," she said.

"Nice to meet you, too," Slowbe said.

Amanda began to flip through the pages of her sketch pad, revealing images of fishing boats docked in Coos Bay; still-life drawings of blankets, glass jars, apples, and partially peeled oranges; the coastline at Coos Bay; egrets, loons, and ravens; various trees; and the Conde B. McCullough Memorial Bridge.

"You are very talented," Slowbe said encouragingly.

"Thanks," Amanda replied.

"Have you taken lessons or are you mostly self-taught?" Slowbe asked.

"Well, I did take an art class at Marshfield, but I'm mostly self-taught."

Amanda continued turning the pages at a steady pace.

"The Colosseum," Slowbe said in a surprised tone.

"I was in Rome last summer with my family."

"Wow, that's cool."

"Yeah, it was incredible. My favorite part was getting to see the ceiling of the Sistine Chapel. I think it's the most amazing work of art ever. I was in the chapel for four hours. The Colosseum was amazing, too. It's so beautiful, although it made me a little sad each time I saw it because I thought of all the horrors that took place inside its walls. It's such a contrast, the beauty and majesty of the structure and the violence that occurred within it. Have you ever been to Rome?" Amanda asked.

"Yes, I have, it's a fascinating place."

"Yes, it is."

Amanda turned through several more pages of drawings from her trip: St. Peter's Basilica, the Tiber River, the Forum.

Eventually, the theme of the drawings shifted again.

"These are just a bunch of eyes," she said.

"I like them," Slowbe replied, "they're very mysterious."

"I better let you get to your meal," Amanda said.

"Ok," Slowbe said, "it was nice chatting with you, Amanda, and thank you for showing me your art."

"You're welcome. It was nice talking with you, too," Amanda replied.

She took a few steps toward the front counter and then stopped and looked back at Slowbe. "I went to a truth of consciousness rally in San Francisco a few weeks ago, that's where I got the button," she said.

Slowbe smiled and nodded approvingly. Amanda looked at Slowbe for a couple more seconds. Her countenance suggested to Slowbe that his affirmation was meaningful to her. She turned and passed through the swinging doors that led into the kitchen and was soon out of view.

Slowbe took a little while longer to finish his sandwich. He drank the rest of his orange juice and placed a fifty-dollar bill beneath the empty glass. The jingling sound of the front door caught his attention again as he left the market. The fog was starting to clear, and large patches of blue sky were opening up.

Over the next few hours, Slowbe passed through the towns of Bandon, Gold Beach, and Brookings, crossed the border into California, and drove past the towns of Crescent City and Klamath, before entering Prairie Creek Redwoods State Park. Shortly after entering the park, he came to a sign that read "ocean beaches," at which point he turned onto a gravel road that led him into the forest for a bumpy, meandering, slow-going six miles to Gold Bluffs Beach Campground, the second stopping point on his journey to Mountain View. Thirty minutes passed before he arrived at the forest's edge. He emerged into a serene picture, tucked away like some magical little sanctuary, with sandy beaches dotted with colorful pebbles, and sand dunes, tall grasses, shrubs, and odd little misshapen trees filling in the landscape between the ocean and the redwood forest. Not far to the south, goldish tree-lined cliffs rose up along the coastline.

Of the twenty-five campsites available, only three appeared to be in use, so Slowbe pulled up to one closer to the ocean, as it was first come, first serve during the winter months. After taking some time to settle in, and also walk along the shoreline, where he spotted two seals bobbing among the waves and a group of pelicans soaring overhead, he ambled toward the West Ridge and Prairie Creek Trail, about a half mile from his campsite. It'd been almost three years since he'd been among the redwoods. He'd held a special reverence and affection from the moment he first encountered them in 2038. This was his fourth visit. To him, the redwoods were like wise, ancient elders, towering and powerful and undaunted, that spoke in elegant, nuanced vibrations. Slowbe listened carefully as he walked in their midst.

In the late afternoon, when he was back at the beach, he saw several female elk grazing in the distance north of his campsite, and more pelicans. The sky and the ocean glowed with golden light as the sun set. The following morning he started the final leg to Mountain View.

It was just after 5:00 p.m. on Sunday, December 27th, when Slowbe arrived at Dr. Johnson's ranch-style home. Tall rhododendron bushes, cherry trees, a scarlet oak, a California valley oak, and a giant sequoia adorned the three-acre property. The lawn appeared freshly cut, and there was a flower and herb garden along the front of the house. Slowbe could smell the mint as he approached. He rang the doorbell and took a couple steps back. Seconds later Dr. Johnson opened the door and greeted Slowbe with a broad grin and a firm handshake. Slowbe was surprised by the intensity of the man's blue eyes, which seemed to affirm the presence of a formidable personality residing within what was an outwardly diminutive stature.

Dr. Johnson showed Slowbe into a spacious, sparsely decorated living room and offered him a seat in one of two brown leather high-back chairs that faced each other across an antique coffee table. On the coffee table were a silver container and a small clay bowl full of mustard seeds. Alongside the chairs was a row of east-facing awning windows that offered a view of the giant sequoia. The former classmates exchanged pleasantries and Slowbe provided a brief account of his three-day road trip.

"Do you mind if I smoke, Edward?" Dr. Johnson said.

"I don't mind at all," Slowbe replied.

Dr. Johnson opened up the silver container. Inside it was a pipe and a pouch full of fresh tobacco. He filled the pipe purposefully and with great care. It was apparent to Slowbe that there was an element of ritual involved. Dr. Johnson opened the window directly to his left and lit his pipe. A plume of grey smoke gently swirled and spiraled, responding to every subtle nuance of the light breeze that came through the window.

Dr. Johnson looked at Slowbe. "You've been in the news a lot this year," he said.

"Yes," Slowbe replied.

"It would almost appear as if by design."

"You could say that."

"There's your book, of course, which I have read, and would definitely love to discuss with you while you're here. There are the rather, I must say, enigmatic incidents in New York City and the Democratic Republic of the Congo; and then this salon group you're associated with, the Relaxists; the Human Evolution Project and the huge marketing campaign behind it; and also the speculation that one or more of the Relaxists were somehow responsible for the unexplained occurrence at the Logos Tower in Portland. I'm curious to know if you consider each of these developments ends unto themselves, or if they are, collectively, a means to an end, part of some larger overall objective."

"I would say they are a means to an end, as well as ends unto themselves."

"Could you elaborate?"

"Well, it's kind of like the relationship between creativity and creation. I don't think you can have one without the other; and while there is a symbiotic dynamic, they both have an intrinsic value that is independent. On one level creativity is the process and creation is the manifestation; process is the means and manifestation is the ends, respectively. But creativity is also an ends in that it is elucidative and generative, and creation is also a means in that it opens the door to new experience, and even new creation. Creativity and creation each function as both means and ends, and at the same time one always begets the other. I want to live and act in a certain way, and be a certain way, and engage reality in a certain way, which aligns with a positive long-term vision for humanity. In my own way, through my processes, personally and collaboratively, and through the things I manifest or help manifest, I'm not only advocating for a vision of human potential, but I'm also living that vision to the best of my ability with each new day. I'm not only promoting a paradigm shift, but I'm also living the paradigm shift as best I can. And frankly, I envision a race of enlightened beings. That's the change I want to see in the world; that's the big-picture, long-term vision: humanity's development into a race of enlightened beings. I personally believe that that's the evolutionary track we're on, despite any current divisions, setbacks, shortsightedness, or narrow-mindedness. The shorter-term vision is a peace among nations. So, as a way of life, as a means and an ends, my mission is to seek out, express, and embrace my own uniqueness, abilities, and subjective experience; to be of assistance to others and support community and collaboration; and to align myself, to the greatest extent possible, with the realm of the infinite, with my soul, or Macro Self. I believe there's a river of universal truth that we can all touch."

"You have an optimistic view of humanity and human potential."

Slowbe looked at Dr. Johnson with an almost imperceptible smile. "I do," he said.

"Do you think creativity and creation are always the result of a creator?"

"Well, ultimately, I think one of the fundamental themes of

every human life is *I create*. Through our actions, our thoughts, our emotions, our beliefs, and the energy we emit, we create the events and experiences that surround us. We may as well get attuned to the power and breadth of our agency as creators, because the fate of our individual and collective experiences rests on this awareness. We're responsible. Now, I have to admit that my natural disposition is to see reality through an artistic lens. I see life as an exercise in imagination and expression, within which learning and discovery occur. I write poetry and music, but I view my entire life itself as being like an art project, as experimental art. I think our personalities and our lives are expressions, creative expressions. We create...on so many levels; it's certainly one of the hallmarks, perhaps *the* hallmark, that defines us as beings. Now, if we're looking specifically at the features of human civilization and we ask the question, 'Are creativity and creation always the result of a creator?' then the answer would certainly be 'Yes, there is always a creator.' For the most part, every aspect of our society is created by individuals or groups of individuals. But I think the creator/creativity/creation model exists beyond human experience and civilization, although I don't think we need to have a hard-and-fast definition of what would constitute, or qualify as, a 'creator.' It could be energy, it could be the expanding universe, it could be consciousness, it could be an atom, or it could be something we've never thought of or can't imagine. Maybe all these things are essentially one and the same.

"It seems safe to say that all that exists is a creation, and that something is always being created. And it would seem that existence is always in the process of creation. Perhaps that's the nature of things. From my perspective, it's all a creative act, it's all a creative process, down to the last iota, whether we're aware of it or not. Even destruction would fall under the umbrella of creation and creativity, because there's something new or different or changed as a result, and energy is involved. I probably have one of the broader definitions of creativity."

"What's your definition?" Dr. Johnson asked.

"The process by which something is changed or created via the expression of energy."

"So, an electron spinning around a nucleus, a red blood cell delivering oxygen, a star going supernova, water evaporating, a black hole exerting gravitational force, the gears of a clock moving, a leaf falling from a tree, and so on and so forth, all creative acts?"

"Absolutely."

"Do you believe in God?"

"Well, yes, I think there is an all-encompassing, all-pervasive presence that transcends infinity and eternity—and I describe it in those terms, as transcending infinity and eternity, to highlight that its nature is beyond our comprehension. I think of it as a sentient, independent idea; as a sentient Gestalt of All That Exists; but also as a presence whose being extends beyond all that exists, like a whole that's more than the sum of its parts. The only other things I would assume about it are that it creates and it loves. To me, love is the adhesive that connects all things and, ultimately, the impetus behind all creativity and creation. But basically, I try to avoid entertaining any mental images, definitions, or frameworks regarding the idea of God, aside from what I've just mentioned. I just don't think it's something that's possible for the human mind to fathom, although we shouldn't feel like it's something that's outside of us, or external to us. Any sense of connection to it is always going to be intuitive, perhaps psychic. I usually don't use the word 'God,' simply because the term is so wrapped up in religious dogma and anthropomorphic characterizations. I'll refer to it as 'Creator' when I have to, during conversation; but I prefer to not even name it."

"One thing we can probably say for sure," Dr. Johnson added, "is that of all there is to know, and of all that exists, we are aware of, at best, infinitely less than an infinitesimally small amount. And that will never change. The good thing is that we'll never run out of things to learn or discover."

"That's certainly true, whether we're talking about our mortal lives or our immortal lives," Slowbe said matter-of-factly. "With respect to God, obviously there will never be scientific proof, but there doesn't need to be, although scientific proof regarding the existence of realities or dimensions beyond the physical universe could likely occur at some point."

"I don't think there necessarily needs to be a conflict between science and the idea of God, or Creator," Dr. Johnson said, "but I take for granted that the physical universe that we know comes complete with scientific explanations, and I feel it's crucial that scientists abide by their creed and seek only scientific answers to the mysteries of this universe. It's their responsibility to society."

"Yes. It's worth contemplating, though, what, if any, might be the limits of scientific explanation, or the limits of science as a construct," Slowbe said. "I do believe that the realm of science extends beyond this universe and this dimension; and I think that if we dig deep enough into our universe we start entering into, or overlapping with, other planes of existence. But I also believe in what I would call the 'psychic universe,' which may or may not fall under the purview of science. My basic premise is that our physical universe is not all there is. Generally speaking, though, I agree that all things in the physical universe have a scientific explanation, even if we may need to develop new sciences, new technologies, and even new ways of thinking, in order to answer all our questions about its nature. There are about five or six areas where I'd be particularly curious to see where the science goes."

"What would those be?" Dr. Johnson asked.

"The origin of life, the nature of consciousness, the origin of the Big Bang, dark energy and dark matter, black holes, and the existence of dimensions beyond our own."

"I'm very interested in those mysteries as well. The first two might take centuries to figure out, hard to say. I believe we'll have a full understanding of dark energy, dark matter, black holes, and the truth behind the Big Bang in the near future, in the next decade or so."

"My guess is that more complete scientific knowledge around the nature of consciousness will end up pointing to, or possibly confirming, evidence of a multidimensional nature of reality, or, conversely, evidence for the multidimensional nature of reality may lead us to new understanding on the nature of consciousness. We'll see which comes first."

"Interesting," Dr. Johnson said. "That may be."

"I'm fascinated by the prospect of what scientific discoveries, and technological advances, lie ahead in this and future centuries. They will definitely continue to shift and expand the paradigm we operate within. I also think there'll be explorers, discoverers, who'll shed light on the psychic universe in ways that will fundamentally alter our understanding of ourselves and reality. The discoverers will help us remember, so to speak, what we are and where we come from."

"Are you one of these discoverers?" Dr. Johnson asked.

"I'm a herald," Slowbe said.

"The Pope certainly seems to consider you a threat. He's very critical of you."

"Well, I've never criticized the Pope, religion, or anyone's religious beliefs."

"But your whole program implicitly undermines religion. And I'm sure it was no coincidence that the happenings in New York City and the DRC, which both garnered immediate and massive news coverage, occurred at roughly the same times as highly publicized papal events. You've kind of stolen his thunder on a couple notable occasions this year."

"I think it's the tide of history that's undermining the Pope and the religious establishment. Perhaps he sees me as a symbol."

"So, what happened in New York City and at Abundo's estate?"

"A convergence of belief, mental energy, and force of soul," Slowbe said. "Atoms respond to consciousness." There was a momentary silence, and the expression on Dr. Johnson's face seemed to indicate that he was processing Slowbe's response and preparing a follow-up question. "I have a question for you, my friend," Slowbe said.

"Please," Dr. Johnson replied.

"What do you believe about the universe?"

Dr. Johnson raised his right eyebrow and chuckled slightly beneath his breath. He leaned over, emptied his pipe, and began to load it with fresh tobacco.

"I'm a theorist, and so I believe very much in the power of imagination," he said, "but first and foremost I believe what the science tells me, although that's been subject to quite a bit of change in recent years. As we make one new startling discovery after another, the cosmological paradigm keeps shifting. I like to think that I have an open mind. There are many things I can't explain, even things I've experienced that I can't explain, but as a rule I don't come to conclusions about the natural world nonscientifically; however, I allow myself license to speculate. I do believe there's a fundamental cosmic creativity and a cosmic narrative. I see story in the universe and I feel deeply connected to that story. The universe is within us, it is us, and we are it."

"Yes," Slowbe said.

"I think of our universe as a probable universe, with multitudinous other probable universes overlapping ours. I don't believe in the idea of the Big Bang as the one and only genesis, or that it emerged from nothing."

"Interesting," Slowbe said in a surprised tone. "There's always context."

"Well, the science may be starting to back that up. In August, my close friend Joy Evers and her team at the Kerr Observation Center received the first transmissions from the

Unbounded Energy Retrieval Telescope. The UERT is a very unique instrument. Like all the great telescopes, it allows us to travel back in time to retrieve information about the universe, but what's different about the UERT is that it's designed to detect a particular instance in the cosmic narrative: the moment when the four primary forces—gravity, electromagnetic energy, weak force, and strong force—appeared to be united as one phenomenon. This only happened once, and for a very short period of time, less than $1 \times 10^{(-43)}$ seconds after the birth of the universe, or the Big Bang. When the transmissions came back and were initially examined, Joy and her team saw something that wasn't supposed to exist where they were looking: indications of an energy field that they believe is the environment, so to speak, out of which the primordial particle emerged. In addition, the environment they detected resembled light, or electromagnetic energy; and they are looking at evidence of what might be electromagnetic wavelengths with much smaller spatial periods than those previously known to science. These findings won't be made public until much more analysis has been conducted, and there are more transmissions expected next year—likely for years to come."

"That is incredible. Wow."

"When Joy informed me of these developments, she mentioned you."

"How did I come up in the conversation?"

"You, and quite a significant number of others now, millions of people, myself included, have described a field of light that can be observed, or experienced, internally. According to the traditional laws of physics, this shouldn't be possible because, as far as we know, there isn't an internal energy source that would produce such a thing."

"Ah, but there is," Slowbe said.

"The UERT's data suggests a similar phenomenon, the existence of light without a definable, physical source. The findings of Joy and her team have two major implications:

1) the Big Bang particle emerged from something, a pre-universe environment, and didn't just materialize out of nowhere, and 2) electromagnetic energy, or light energy, may be multidimensional in nature, and thus much broader in scope than we previously thought. The team believes electromagnetic energy existed before the Big Bang, even though it also appears as one of the four primary forces in the physical universe. But, specifically to your question, Joy asked me if I thought the electromagnetic energy that you and so many others report observing and the electromagnetic energy that appears to be showing up in the transmissions from the UERT could come from the same source."

"What did you say?"

"Well, I was surprised by her question. I told her I thought it was interesting to consider the idea that delving into the depths of consciousness, or into inner realities, and delving into the origins of the universe may lead one to the same place, or to similar places. It's possible, I suppose. I actually like the hypothesis. For the time being, though, scientists don't really have a good enough understanding of what consciousness is, and it may be a long time before we do; and we have a lot to learn about where the universe really comes from as well, or, as you put it, what the context of the universe is; but the recent findings are leading us in an interesting new direction."

"Just going back to another point real quick, I'm curious: So you do think we'll eventually have the science to explain the origin of biological life?"

"I don't know," Dr. Johnson said. "There's a part of me that doesn't think we'll ever solve that one."

"What about the other part of you?" Slowbe asked.

"I recognize that the world of tomorrow is beyond my wildest imagination, and that the science and technology and discoveries of the centuries to come will seem miraculous or godlike if compared to our times, just like our times would seem miraculous and godlike to someone from the Middle

Ages. So, anything is possible. We may find proof of how life began on earth, or we may find that it originates elsewhere. I don't know. Who knows, we may become masters of this universe and someday, in tens of thousands of years, evolve to a different dimension." Dr. Johnson paused briefly. "You might find it interesting that I don't believe there's life elsewhere in the universe, intelligent or otherwise."

"Now that's...that's rather shocking to hear you say. Why have you come to this conclusion? It goes against the consensus of the scientific community, not to mention the aims of your career."

"Indeed, it does," Dr. Johnson said. "The SETI program has been in operation since I was an infant, and despite our extraordinary instruments, we haven't detected even a faint hint of intelligent life. Over the course of the last several years, I've simply come to believe that the odds of life emerging are infinitesimally small, despite the size of the universe, despite the existence of water across the galaxies, and despite a plethora of planets in habitable zones. I believe that life emerging on this planet is a cosmic fluke—an anomaly of epic proportions."

"I've always thought that the notion of life existing elsewhere in the universe and the notion that we were alone in the universe were equally improbable."

"I'm thinking about more important things now, like peace on our home planet. We live in a dynamic and conflicted time. I believe we're at a great crossroads. And as you know, over the last decade the anticipation around first contact with intelligent life from other planets has absolutely reached a fever pitch. There's been this steady flow of reports about new planets being found in habitable zones; and basically, humanity is expecting news of extraterrestrial life to come at any moment."

"It seems to be very much in the forefront of our collective consciousness," Slowbe said.

"What do you think would happen if news hit that intelligent life had been discovered, or had contacted us?"

"The social and psychological impact would be immeasurable. It would be an instant paradigm shift. I can imagine that type of revelation actually influencing nations to put aside their differences, because all of a sudden we're earthlings, and not Russians, or Israelis, or Chinese, or Mexicans; we're the race of humans; we're suddenly reinvented in the cosmic order. Given the level of anticipation that currently exists, it's likely the news would be readily accepted by the public. That'd be my guess, but it's hard to say for sure what the reaction would be. The discovery could possibly be used as a rallying point for peace and unity on the planet."

"Exactly. Can you help me?" Dr. Johnson asked.

"Help you what?"

"Make this happen."

"What do you mean?"

"I can arrange for SETI observatories to appear to receive radio signals from, say, the Pleiades system, and in a way that would make the hoax unidentifiable. The transmissions would be real for all intents and purposes. I need you to help publicize the importance of the discovery, to make it a rallying point, like you said. You and the other so-called Relaxists, with the HEP, have attained such an enormous level of international prestige and influence that your voices connected with the news would help achieve the desired effect."

"What exactly is the desired effect?"

"Adding fuel to the peace movement. Peace treaties. World peace."

"You'd be willing to discard your commitment to science, and possibly have your reputation ruined should the deception be exposed, all on the chance that it would have anything resembling this desired outcome?"

"I'm not discarding my commitment to science. This is an anomaly. "

"Is it ethical?"

"At worst it's a practical joke with a poignant message—no

worse than the *War of the Worlds* broadcast or the great moon hoax of 1835. At best it leads society to reexamine itself and possibly leads to a global peace treaty."

"The *War of the Worlds* broadcast caused a great deal of outrage when the truth came out, and many of the listeners were traumatized."

"But we're not talking about an invasion taking place. And like I said, it's foolproof."

"I'd be lying if I said I wasn't drawn to the idea, but I don't think I can help you with this project."

Dr. Johnson emptied his pipe, rolled up his bag of tobacco, and placed it in the container. Slowbe glanced at the bowl of mustard seeds.

"Are you hungry, Edward?"

"I am."

"There's a Greek restaurant downtown I'd like to take you to, and perhaps afterward we can stroll along Stevens Creek for a spell."

"That sounds great."

The two walked toward the front door and exited the house. Slowbe looked up and saw the Seven Sisters shining brightly.

Guiding Principles

"It may be cynical to think that the best way to achieve a peace among nations, or a peace paradigm, would be to subject the whole species to an elaborate hoax," Slowbe wrote in a January 21st, 2049, journal entry as he flew over the Indian Ocean en route to Seychelles, an archipelago nation made up of 115 islands located a thousand miles off the coast of Kenya. "But then, humans engage in numerous self-deceptions," he added, "one of which is the false belief that we don't have the capacity to bring about a sustainable peace. Isaac Johnson thinks the scheme he's considering could lead humanity to a deeper sense of collective identity. If the deception is used to eradicate a limiting or negative belief, then perhaps so. I suppose a person could be tricked into believing in themselves and in their own power and grace; and if no one is harmed, then maybe it doesn't matter what means are taken to get to the positive belief."

After Slowbe concluded the brief journal entry, he began to reflect on the fact that it was the one-year anniversary of the release of *The World Within*. Over eighty million copies had sold worldwide. Set in a universe-like realm called Meta, the novel, or meditation, as Slowbe referred to it, revolved around a being named Person and its relationships with Body, Ego, Conscious Mind, Inner Self, and Soul, who were portrayed not only as entities that Person interacted with, but also as systems, and as the contexts of Person's experience. The narrative described in vivid and colorful detail the various processes through which Person developed agency within physical and non-physical dimensions, accessed the powers of Soul, used mental energy and belief to create reality, became centered within a limitless present moment, and learned to see itself in the other entity-systems. Over the course of the meditation, Person evolved from a paradigm marked by the appearance of separation between itself and the five entity-systems to a paradigm of no separation. Love, uniqueness, and creativity took on new, deeper meaning. Eventually, Person was self-actualized as part of a singular multidimensional system that the omnipotent narrator referred to as a Macro Self.

A soft, rippling sound could be heard from the deck of Song's forty-five-foot cabin cruiser. The cloudless sky was bright blue and a light breeze swirled around the anchored vessel. Sunlight glistened against the translucent, turquoise waters. To the east and south, three large tropical islands could be seen: Silhouette Island, where Song owned a twelve-acre property; North Island; and Mahé Island, the largest island in the Seychelles archipelago and home to the capital city of Victoria. Red Horse, Slowbe, Sangree, Monarch, Henry, Sabin, and Song had flown into Seychelles International Airport on Song's Gulfstream the day before, on the 21st, for a ten-day retreat that had been planned since the first week of January, when it was announced that the signing ceremony for the recently negotiated African Great Lakes Region Peace Treaty would be taking place in Victoria on the 27th.

"How many miles offshore do you think we are?" Sangree asked.

"About ten," Song replied.

Sangree and Monarch stood at the port side of the cruiser.

"Are you ready?" Sangree asked as she looked at Monarch.

Monarch smiled and nodded, and almost simultaneously, they both dove into the warm, balmy water. Slowbe and Red Horse soon followed.

Sabin, Henry, and Song sat leisurely in the stern of the boat.

"I watched Daniel Eagle Staff's inaugural address again this morning," Sabin said.

"It feels like we're at a turning point," Henry said.

"It does feel that way," Sabin responded.

On November 3rd, 2048, Daniel Eagle Staff, an enrolled member of the Muscogee Nation, became the first Native American elected President of the United States. The election was a landslide victory for the charismatic Democrat from Oklahoma who was known for his penetrating oratory and, in recent years, for his frequent references to the historic nature of the times. During a speech he made in February of 2047, two months before he announced his candidacy for president, Eagle Staff commented that "we live in a time of great trauma and great uplift, great destruction and great creative genius; a time of great discovery and great opportunity for change." He went on to posit that a number of circumstances had converged to create a "perfect storm," the result of which was the presence of an unprecedented level of psychosocial tension within the human species. "Humanity is at the ultimate crossroads," he said.

Eagle Staff had grown up in the foster care system in Oklahoma. Between the ages of seven and eighteen he'd lived in nine different foster homes. Despite the instability and suffering of his childhood and adolescence, and the absence of any normal support systems, he went on to earn a law degree and a PhD in history from the University of Michigan by the time he was thirty. For the ten years prior to his 2024 election to the Oklahoma Senate he taught history full-time at the University of Tulsa. He continued to do so part-time while serving in the state capitol. In 2032, he won a seat in the United States Senate, and eight years later he began the first of two terms as governor of Oklahoma. Eagle Staff was sixty-four as he prepared to move into the White House. In twenty-four years he'd never lost an election.

The new president had the good fortune of beginning his first term at a time of low unemployment, rising median wages, and a renewed sense of the United States as a dynamic, creative entity. The economy was surging after having suffered through the Second Great Depression, which struck in 2036 and lasted through 2044. A Gallup poll taken two weeks before his inauguration showed that the economy was not among the top five concerns of Americans. The poll also showed that for the first time most of the issues of concern or interest to Americans were international in nature, a trend seen in other countries as well; these issues included re-establishment of the United Nations, solving the global water crisis, environmental protection and conservation, overpopulation, and artificial intelligence. Also making the top ten was space exploration.

Sabin and Red Horse both knew Eagle Staff personally. In 2007, when Sabin was ten months old, her parents moved to Ann Arbor, Michigan, to begin their graduate studies. Shortly thereafter, Jonathan and Winter Sabin met Eagle Staff and his wife, Michelle, at a gathering of self-proclaimed futurists called the Horizon Club. The club gathered once a month and was invitation only. Average attendance was about twenty-five individuals, primarily consisting of U of M students. Over the course of the next seven years a close, lasting bond was formed between the Sabins and the Eagle Staffs, and Daniel Eagle Staff became like an uncle to Mia Sabin, and Michelle Eagle Staff like an aunt. Red Horse first met Eagle Staff in 2041 at a water protection conference in Tahlequah, Oklahoma, capital of the Cherokee Nation.

"He has a lot of charisma, and he's just an incredible orator," Song said.

"Yes," Henry said.

"This address might actually go down as one of the great ones," Sabin said.

"I was pretty transfixed," Henry said. "He's probably the most gifted American orator since Barack Obama."

"I think he surpasses Obama," Sabin replied.

"Perhaps," Henry said.

"One part of the speech that jumped out at me," Sabin said, "was when he was talking about solar technology and how it's starting to transform society, and he said we're becoming a 'sun-based society.' The first thing that came to my mind was the idea of the sun as symbolizing the soul. That's the image I've always held. Obviously, he was talking about energy, and 'environmentally sophisticated trends' is I think how he put it, which is great; but the phrase 'sun-based society' just captured my imagination, as if he was subliminally referring to a soul-oriented or soul-based society."

"I liked that line, too," Henry added. "Sun-based society. What really shocked me, though, and a lot of people, I guess, was when he was referring to 'the progress of our species' and he mentioned that the work of 'nonprofit organizations like the Human Evolution Project and Water Protectors, and movements like the revolution of consciousness, speak to the deepest yearnings of our times and of the human spirit.' That was very unusual, to name names like that in an inaugural address."

"Yeah, that was very surprising when he mentioned the HEP," Song said.

"Definitely. Who knows, maybe he took a cue from Abundo having expressed support for the HEP when the date for the treaty signing was announced," Sabin said with a hint of curiosity.

"I'm gonna dive in, ladies," Henry said. He got up and walked to the starboard bow of the cruiser, where several pairs of flippers and snorkels were stacked. He put on the gear, tightened the drawstring on his chartreuse swim trunks, and jumped into the ocean. Monarch, Red Horse, Slowbe, and Sangree were well beneath the surface of the water mingling with colorful fish and sea turtles.

There was a long silence as Song and Sabin both drifted off

into their private spaces, surrendering to the warmth of the sun and the pacifying breeze. Song closed her eyes. Sabin reclined and gazed into the blue sky. Her mind drifted to Pope Leo. He was 93 years and 141 days old, and now the oldest person to ever preside as Pope. The milestone had been a major news story around the world for the past week. Despite his advanced age, the austere pontiff was a marvel of health and energy, and many considered it possible that his reign could last another twelve years, at which point he would be the longest-serving Pope in history. Some papal observers suspected that he would love nothing more than to surpass St. Peter for the longest papal reign, and that his stubbornness just might keep him alive long enough to reach that goal. The previous September he'd completed his twenty-fifth year in the papacy, and in March he would pass his namesake, Leo XIII, to become the fourth-longest-reigning Pope, behind St. John Paul, Pius IX, and St. Peter.

Sabin was fascinated by Leo, not only because he was the first American Pope and a reformer who'd increased the power of the Holy See despite dwindling church membership, but also because of the notable efforts he'd made to bridge religious divides. She was also intrigued by his sheer force of will and his regal countenance, as well as by the enmity he'd publicly expressed toward Slowbe. Sabin viewed Leo as a man of deep contradictions, who was, without question, a towering historical figure. And there was the coincidental link he had to another American religious figure.

"Do you know who Andrews Norton is?" Sabin asked, breaking the silence.

"Isn't that the Pope's birth name?" Song replied.

"Wow, I'm surprised you know that," Sabin said.

"Me too. I don't know where I heard that."

"Do you know who the other Andrews Norton is?"

"The other Andrews Norton?"

"The nineteenth-century Unitarian minister and theologian."

"No, I've never heard of him," Song said.

"He lived in New England from, like, the 1780s to about the 1850s. He was a lecturer at Harvard and Bowdoin for a number of years and was widely published. He was sometimes jokingly referred to as the 'Unitarian Pope' because he was so influential and domineering, and such a vocal proponent of mainstream Unitarianism. By the standards of the time he was pretty liberal, but in the late 1830s he was involved in highly publicized conflicts with the New England Transcendentalists, whose ideas he considered to be bordering on the sacrilegious—even though he himself didn't believe in the virgin birth. One event in particular incurred Norton's wrath and sparked the great dispute. In 1838 Ralph Waldo Emerson, himself an ordained Unitarian minister, delivered an address to the graduating class of Harvard Divinity School in which he critiqued the failures of what he referred to as 'historical Christianity,' arguing that personal intuition was a better guide to moral and virtuous behavior than religious doctrine, and expressing doubt as to the necessity of belief in the miracles attributed to Jesus. The firestorm that ensued completely took Emerson by surprise. He was called an atheist, which was a very severe term at the time, and an infidel, among other things. For several years all of New England, and especially Boston, was embroiled in a theological and philosophical controversy that pitted Norton and his supporters against the Transcendentalists. And the person who bore the brunt of most of Norton's criticism was Emerson, who was regarded as the leader of the Transcendentalist movement."

"That is amazing, and now we have another religious leader named Andrews Norton involved in the public castigation of another prominent mystic," Song said.

"Exactly. History repeating itself."

"Last week the Pope said he would never read *The World Within* and that he thought Edward was a false prophet and a charlatan."

"He's spared the rest of us though, hasn't he? Even Lillian."

"Yeah, that's interesting."

"Maybe he sees Edward and the book as epitomizing the shift away from religious establishments and doctrines."

"Perhaps, although the trend has been occurring for decades, and I don't recall him ever criticizing Riviere. But it does seem as if *The World Within* is like that one storm that breaks the dam, or at least severely threatens to break it."

"Yes. It's raining very hard now, and the waters are rising, so to speak."

"Do you believe in the miracles attributed to Jesus?" Song asked.

"Well, some of the miracle stories described in the New Testament are certainly fictional," Sabin said, "but I think the historical Jesus had full awareness of the mechanics behind the process of mind over matter. And it would only take one or two instances of him manipulating physical reality for a whole array of stories to emerge. I'm sure he exhibited what would be considered supernatural powers, perhaps on more than one occasion, perhaps on numerous occasions, and this would have, of course, completely dumbfounded the people of his time and place. I think Jesus was an example of a person in the natural state, as a fully integrated Macro Self, and so I suspect he did have powers, abilities, and insights that seemed miraculous, or seemed to defy logic and reason. It's likely that he healed people, or at least was skilled at facilitating the power of personal and collective belief in such a way that stimulated an individual's belief in their own healing. I think all of this could be said for Siddhartha Gautama as well."

"It's interesting to reimagine the human being as being inherently supernatural, by nature," Song said.

*

Victoria, Seychelles, was abuzz as leaders from eleven African nations—DRC, Zambia, Tanzania, Burundi, Rwanda, Uganda,

Kenya, Angola, Central African Republic, Sudan, and South Sudan—gathered on the grounds of State House, the official residence of the president of Seychelles, for the signing of the historic peace accord that would eliminate all nuclear weapons in the region, create shared water collection and treatment systems, and formalize a commitment to nonaggression. The outdoor ceremony, scheduled to commence at 1:00 p.m. and set to be livestreamed, was expected to draw thousands of spectators to State House and over a billion viewers online.

Slowbe and the other salon members spent the morning perusing the winding streets of Victoria: down Liberation Avenue and Bel Air Road, to Revolution Avenue and past the Arul Mihu Navasakthi Vinayagar temple, and along Albert Street toward the clock tower at the intersection of State House Avenue, Albert Street, Francis Rachel Street, and Independence Avenue. Signs that this was a day of celebration were evident throughout the city. Brightly colored banners hung from nearly every building in the central area of town, welcoming the signatories. Mimes, musicians, artists, fortune-tellers, poets, dancers, jugglers, and costume artists wearing elaborate outfits and donning flamboyant masks filled the sidewalks and street corners.

Just before noon the group arrived at an attractive cast-iron clock tower called Lorloz, located in the center of town. Modeled after Little Ben in London, England, the structure had been built in 1903, the same year Pope Leo XIII and the artist Paul Gauguin died. After admiring it for a short time, the group made their way to a newly opened restaurant called Blue Rendezvous that was directly in sight of Lorloz, at the slightly curved intersection of State House Avenue and Francis Rachel Street. Located on the second floor of a two-story building that featured grey pillars and white covered arches, the restaurant had a covered patio that provided shade for the diners and views of the bustling, picturesque intersection. Bougainvillea trees, frangipani trees, umbrella trees, and various palm trees;

mignonette, pappus, and hibiscus plants; and brightly colored orchids could be seen up and down the thoroughfares, and lush, dark-green hills rose up on the western edge of the city in bold contrast against the extraordinarily blue sky. The whole scene was awash in light and color.

The group settled in at a rectangular table made of glass and copper. On the sidewalk near where they were seated, a street performer was singing and playing his guitar. A loud car horn sounded at the intersection and a man waved his hand out of the window and yelled at the group, "Hey!" The musician, curious about the sudden commotion, looked in its direction, and then turned back toward the group, smiled, and continued playing his song. Moments later, a short, beige-skinned man with brown hair approached the table.

"I was just leaving the restaurant and saw you all out here," he said as he stood in between Red Horse and Slowbe. "I wanted to introduce myself. I'm John Washburn."

None of the salon members had ever met Washburn in person, but they were all very familiar with his journalism and other writings, and each had a favorable opinion of him. They also each understood that he had contributed to their collective notoriety, and thus their collective efforts, by coining a moniker that had become widely recognized. It was a brand that they didn't resist because they felt it set a constructive tone.

"Hi John," Slowbe said, as he extended his arm and shook hands with him, "I'm Edward. So pleased to finally meet you. What a surprise."

"Lillian," Red Horse said as she shook Washburn's hand.

The rest of the group expressed warm greetings through various physical gestures.

Washburn had been in Victoria since January 3rd on sabbatical from the *New York Times*. His travel plans had been made prior to the announcement of the ceremony, and since he was already on location he'd agreed to cover the event. His main purpose for being on the island was to work on content for a book—part sociology, part history—about the dissolution of the UN following the 2036 bombing, and about recent trends that seemed to be creating favorable conditions for its restoration. The contract he had with Simon & Schuster required that a draft be completed by April 15th, and he was planning on staying in Seychelles through March to write.

In the twelve years prior to 2036, the United Nations had been steadily coming apart at the seams. The beginning of the unraveling could be traced back to the addition of Japan, Germany, and Canada to the Security Council in 2024. In 2027, four more countries—India, Brazil, Nigeria, and Saudi Arabia—petitioned for inclusion and were denied, despite earlier assurances from the United States and China that, if they supported the 2024 group, they would have a clear pathway to be added within three years. All four countries responded to this perceived slight of exclusion from the Security Council by ceasing payment of their UN dues, though they remained members of the General Assembly.

By early 2028 India, Brazil, Nigeria, and Saudi Arabia had removed their soldiers from UN peacekeeping activities in Africa and the Middle East, putting substantial strain on the countries that were contributing troops and forcing a reduction in the number of new missions that could be undertaken. A diplomatic crisis ensued, including calls for the four countries to be expelled from the UN. By the end of the year, the disturbance had been quelled, but morale among UN staff and leadership had been greatly diminished. The four rebelling nations remained members in name only.

Four years after the "UN Rebellion," another crisis emerged at the United Nations: China and the United States both withdrew from the 2024 International Air and Water Pollution Accord. News of their withdrawal was particularly unsettling to the public because of the circumstances that had led to the treaty's signing in the first place. In February of 2019, data collected by the Global Burden of Disease project showed that

10.5 million people around the world were dying per year as a direct result of air pollution. As if on cue, a sharp increase in birth defects among children in both first- and third-world countries was observed in a 2022 report. Another study that year revealed massive fish and insect die-offs and an increase in deformities in fish and mammal populations around the world. Then, in March of 2023, the World Health Organization issued a report showing that the number of human deaths due to pollution for each of the previous two years had risen to over thirty-five million.

A third crisis shook the UN in 2034 when Israel launched a devastating attack on the West Bank and the Gaza Strip, nearly annihilating Hamas. The already fractured UN, having put a "temporary freeze" on all peacekeeping the prior year, was further divided by this new crisis. Its lack of response to the ordeal in Israel felt like the silence of death, both to those who hated the organization and to those who believed in its potential and in the original mission stated in the preamble of its 1945 charter: "To save succeeding generations from the scourge of war, which twice in our lifetime has brought untold sorrow to mankind; and, to reaffirm faith in fundamental human rights, in the dignity and worth of the human person, in the equal rights of men and women and of nations large and small; and, to establish conditions under which justice and respect for the obligations arising from treaties and other sources of international law can be maintained; and, to promote social progress and better standards of life in larger freedom; to practice tolerance and live together in peace with one another as good neighbors; and, to unite our strength to maintain international peace and security; and, to ensure, by the acceptance of principles and the institution of methods, that armed force shall not be used, save in the common interest; and, to employ international machinery for the promotion of the economic and social advancement of all peoples."

"Quite a festive scene," Washburn said as he clasped his hands behind his back.

"Yes, it's wonderful," Red Horse added.

"When did you arrive on the island?" Washburn asked.

"We all flew in on the twenty-first," Red Horse replied. "And you?"

"I've been here since the third," Washburn said.

"Please sit down and join us," Slowbe said.

"Thank you," Washburn said, "I'd love to, but I'm actually on my way to State House for the ceremony. Covering it for the *Times*."

"Been getting some vacation time in? Is that why you arrived early?" Henry asked.

"Well, I'm officially on sabbatical, working on a book. I'll be staying in Seychelles for a few more months. So, kind of a project-focused vacation."

"What's your book about?" Sangree asked.

"The UN," Washburn said.

Sangree nodded her head slightly.

"Are you all here for the ceremony?" Washburn asked.

"Well, yes, but primarily as a little getaway," Red Horse said. "We wanted to be here to take in the atmosphere surrounding the treaty signing, but we're not planning on attending the ceremony. Perhaps some of the festivities afterward."

A young, heavyset woman approached the table with a pad and pen in her hand. A look of surprise swept across her face as the identities of the individuals seated before her came into focus. "Hello," she said, "do you know what you'd like to order?"

After receiving some recommendations, the party decided they would share plates of coconut curry, Ladob, grilled vegetables, and fresh fruit. They each chose iced tea to drink, with the exception of Slowbe and Red Horse, who ordered water.

"I'm surprised that your presence here has gone under the radar," Washburn said.

"There has been a lot of coverage of the Relaxists, hasn't there?" Monarch noted lightheartedly.

"Tremendous, it seems almost nonstop," Washburn said.

"We didn't leak anything," Red Horse said.

"I see," Washburn replied as he chuckled.

"I doubt it will remain under the radar though," Monarch added, looking at Washburn with a slight grin.

"Probably not," Washburn replied.

The musician started playing an old Steely Dan song called "Kid Charlemagne," which caught the attention of Slowbe, Henry, and Red Horse.

A small yellow bird landed on the pavement next to the musician. It took a few steps around the man's guitar case and then flew off.

"The weather here is incredible, isn't it?" Washburn said.

"I haven't seen a cloud the entire time we've been here, and the temperature has just been perfect. Warm sun, cool breeze," Red Horse said.

"Quite the change of pace from Portland, where there's been record-setting snowfall this month and last," Monarch said.

"It seems like everything is hyperbole these days," Washburn said, "except that the exaggerations are real life, everything is 'worst ever,' 'record breaking,' et cetera, et cetera. The flooding of the Thames last month was the worst in the country's history. Darlene last year...when it made landfall was the strongest hurricane ever recorded. The drought in California is one of the longest and worst on record, and on and on. So many devastating natural events. Our times are surreal, even the art, science, and technology...the sociopolitical."

"Things seem heightened, elevated," Red Horse said. "There are a lot of intense forces seemingly coming to a head, all bumping up against each other, bound in a sort of crucible—incredible dynamic tension."

The musician packed up his guitar and proceeded to make his way down the street.

"I would love to talk more, but I have to run. Perhaps we can meet sometime before you leave the island. It's been a pleasure seeing you all," Washburn said.

"If you'd like to join us tomorrow evening for dinner, we're staying on Silhouette Island," Song said. "I have a property there."

"That would be fantastic," Washburn said.

"Do you have a business card?" Song asked.

"I do," Washburn said as he reached for his wallet.

"I'll send you my number and the address," Song said. "Does 6:00 p.m. work for you?"

"Yes," said Washburn. He bowed his head slightly to the group and walked away.

*

Song's property on Silhouette Island was located at the foot of Mont Dauban, a densely forested 2,464-foot peak near the village of La Passe on the eastern side of the island. Prior to being purchased by her father, the French country-style home made of tan brick had been owned by members of the Musk family. Song stayed at the residence multiple times per year, usually for no more than a couple weeks but on occasion up to a few months, if she was working on a major piece or group of pieces. On the second floor of the residence was a large, well-lit room that served as a dedicated art space. It was full of paints, canvases, easels, and brushes and had three rows of ceiling lamps and two large copper-topped bay windows that looked out over the pristine waters surrounding the island, which in 1987 had been declared a marine national park. Song mentioned the protected status at dinner the night after the treaty signing. A long conversation on the state of the world's oceans ensued: the enormous garbage patches floating in each of the world's five major ocean currents, the smallest of which being the size of Rhode Island; the extinction of numerous fish and marine mammal species; loss of seventy-five percent of the world's coral reefs; massive ocean deserts along the North American Atlantic Seaboard; ocean acidification due to carbon dioxide.

Later in the evening, close to midnight, Washburn and Slowbe stepped outside for a short walk. The nighttime sky seemed unusually animated as the stars flashed and sparkled with excitement.

"When I consider the great paradigm shifts in history," Slowbe said, "those moments when our understanding or perception of reality fundamentally expanded, I often come back to Edwin Hubble's discovery that ours is not the only galaxy in the universe; in other words, that our galaxy is not the universe—which had previously been the accepted model, or belief system. In virtually one fell swoop, with the observations from his telescope, we went from living in a static universe of one galaxy to realizing that we lived in a perpetually expanding universe with countless galaxies in addition to our own. We now know the number to exceed 300 hundred billion. Literally and figuratively, it amounts to a massive expansion of consciousness. I believe the paradigm shift we're currently in the midst of is akin to this. The conception that the ego, body, and mind are the entirety of the Self is parallel to the view scientists had of the universe prior to Hubble's findings. Humanity is gradually understanding that the ego-mind-body 'galaxy,' so to speak, is part of a much, much larger system of personhood, Self, and consciousness. We should think of the human entity not as a single static galaxy—only mind, body, ego—but as an ever-expanding universe with multitudes of galaxies and dimensions, i.e., levels of Self and self-awareness. It's like a shift from an ego paradigm to a soul paradigm—the personal equivalent of the shift from a one-galaxy cosmology to a cosmology of hundreds of billions of galaxies within an ever-expanding universe."

"The process of uncovering and discerning what actually is, what exists by nature, what the natural state is, or the true state of things, is ongoing," said Washburn. "The scientific method, testable evidence, still remains the gold standard; so, in a way, scientists have a corner on defining what is real, what is natural, and what exists."

"They do, in a way. Their approach to verifying what is true and real should be applied as universally as possible; and we should be guided by reason, logic, and evidence as much as possible. I don't advocate for blind faith, but, of course, there's much to be said for subjective and empirical truth, subjective and empirical reality, and intuition. All these things are valid. To a significant degree, our understanding of reality will always be subjective," Slowbe said.

"'It is precisely the most subjective ideas which, being closest to nature and to the living being, deserve to be called the truest,'" Washburn said, smiling. "Carl Jung."

"I can't say I disagree," Slowbe said. "I think that as we move forward into the future the gap between science and what is currently perceived as spiritual, or mystical, or supernatural will continue to diminish. A lot of this will have to do with scientists developing new instruments to observe and measure energy and consciousness, and light."

"Imagine how much greater our understanding of what is, and what is real, will be a couple hundred or a thousand years from now if we stay on the same trajectory of scientific and technological advances and discoveries—and on a progressive trajectory of psychic advances and discoveries, for that matter," Washburn said.

"Or two thousand, five thousand, or ten thousand. And really, there's no reason to dismiss the idea that our species might be around in a hundred thousand years or more, perhaps much longer...on earth, in other solar systems or galaxies, perhaps eventually evolving into other dimensions."

"I suppose evolution is a never-ending prospect, always full of surprises, always venturing into the unknown."

"Yes, and humans can be very intentional about their own evolution, to a large extent," Slowbe said.

"You're optimistic about the future of humanity," Washburn said.

"Oh yes, very," Slowbe replied. "We just need to heal, and take the blinders off. On the whole, we're not fully aware of who and what we truly are, in my opinion, and we've wrapped ourselves in a thick blanket of fear, disbelief, and negativity that keeps us at odds with the truth. Another analogy I've used is that our nature is like a breathtakingly enormous mountain that's primarily submerged underwater, but whose tip pierces the surface, like an island, into what we call physical reality. Many of us mistakenly believe, or are convinced, that the tip is all there is. More and more brave and inquisitive hearts are shedding the blanket and taking the plunge into the deep waters and are gaining a better sense of the true breadth and scale of the mountain. They're finding out for themselves by experimenting, by searching themselves and obtaining their own evidence, by using belief and intuition as something like psychic navigational tools."

"I guess the tip of the mountain is like the ego, mind, and body."

"Yes. And not to discount their significance and importance, or their beauty and power. It's just important to get things in perspective, and to be purifying those systems on an ongoing basis because they can easily become a quagmire of negativity, fear, and disbelief."

"I like the analogies," Washburn said. "I guess the goal is adherence to that famous maxim inscribed at the Temple of Apollo at Delphi: 'know thyself.' But we should add that this includes actually knowing what thyself is."

"One of the guiding principles I've used is that it's not

about me, per se, or my ego; it's all about allowing the soul free rein and expression in my earthly life," Slowbe said.

"That seems to imply some sort of surrender or acquiescence, which is a very disorienting and unappealing prospect to the ego."

"Yes, on both points. The ego will fear losing itself, losing control, which is why it must be trained to understand that this process is in its own best interest, that its own purview and powers are greatly expanded under this arrangement of acquiescence."

Train the mind, Washburn thought to himself.

Self, Relationship, Creation

Leo lay in his bed at the Papal Palace of Castel Gandolfo staring blankly at the last page of *The World Within*. It was getting close to 11:00 p.m. He'd been in possession of the copy for over eight months, since his arrival in New York City for the Religious Reconciliation Assembly, when he'd instructed one of his minders, a man named Gavin Smythe, to purchase the book for him and to maintain the utmost secrecy regarding the matter.

Despite the fact that his heart was beating more intensely than usual, a deep sense of calm had overcome him, and everything within him and around him somehow seemed harmonious. He closed the book, having consumed the entire work over the course of three consecutive evenings, and placed it on the nightstand immediately to his left. The reading lamp next to his bed produced a soft, almost pastel-like light and the faint scent of frankincense wafted about the room.

Leo had arrived at the palace on February 25th for a three-day retreat and in the morning would be returning to the Vatican. Overlooking Lake Albano, a small volcanic-crater lake, and the hill town of Castel Gandolfo, the luxurious estate, traditionally the summer vacation residence of Popes, was frequently visited by Leo and featured ornate and beautifully landscaped grounds where he loved to take walks, particularly on crisp winter days.

For a time, the palace had ceased to be a papal residence. In 2016, Pope Francis, rejecting its ostentatiousness, had granted the town permission to turn it into a museum. But twenty years later, in the fall of 2036, Leo publicly stated his desire for the site to return to its original function. With almost no additional persuasion on his part, the museum was decommissioned and work began on remodeling the palace to serve as living quarters once more. On Leo's birthday in 2037, a celebration was held to mark completion of the project. Adding to the fanfare, the board of directors of the Capitoline Museums in Rome donated a painting that carried special significance: *A Portrait of Pope Urban VIII*, painted in 1627 by Pietro da Cortona. It was Urban VIII who had ordered construction of the palace in the seventeenth century.

Leo looked over at the portrait, which hung on the west wall of the bedroom, directly in front of him. Urban's eyes stood out to Leo. Briefly, Leo's mind drifted to Galileo Galilei's *Dialogue Concerning the Two Chief World Systems*. The book, published in 1632, had created a firestorm in Rome with its arguments in favor of the Copernican system over the Ptolemaic system—in other words, in favor of the idea that the planets revolved around the sun over the idea that the earth was motionless and at the center of the universe, the latter view being supported by literal interpretations of the Bible and over a thousand years of church theology. Adding insult to injury, the foil in *Dialogue*, a character named Simplicio, who pathetically attempts to make the case for an earth-centered universe, was widely seen as a satirical characterization of Urban VIII and his views. Advancing the more scientifically sound Copernican view was a character named Salviati. Urban VIII's response to the whole affair was to put Galileo on trial for heresy, of which he was found guilty; demand that Galileo recant his view that the earth and planets revolved around the sun, which he did not do; put Galileo under house arrest for the rest of his life; and place *Dialogue* on the *Index of Forbidden Books*, where it remained until 1835.

Leo lifted his blanket back and got out of bed. He slid his feet into a pair of sandals and ambled toward the closet, where he retrieved his jacket. He then stepped outside onto the stone balcony overlooking Lake Albano. It was cold and there was a slight drizzle, but he barely noticed. He walked toward the southeast edge of the balcony and placed his hands on the rough, four-foot-high stone wall. Light from a full moon made its way through cracks in the dark, tumultuous cumulonimbus clouds; and as he looked down he could see the rows of circular hedges, the small pools, the large rhododendrons, the cone-shaped trees, and the white gravel pathways that adorned the grounds.

The light drizzle soon became a heavy rain, and the moon slipped entirely behind the clouds. A few lights from residences at the lake's edge could be seen in the distance. Suddenly, there was an enormous flash of lightning that lit up the band of clouds hovering above the Alban Hills some five miles east. Moments later a loud thunderclap roared overhead. Leo loved the sound of thunder and the sight of lightning, and his eyes scanned the sky anticipating the next electrical outburst. His face, hair, and clothes began to drip with moisture. Then, like an unexpected sensation from a bygone era, he recalled that the night before his papal inauguration in 2023 he'd had a dream about Akhenaten. He couldn't remember any details of the dream, other than seeing the image of Akhenaten approach him, and he wondered why this memory had now returned to him after so many years. Again, a large section of cloud cover east of the palace flashed with electricity. Leo scanned the sky for several minutes and then leaned over the balcony wall and set his eyes on the lake below. Another lightning burst filled the sky, followed by a tremendous thunderclap. And then the rain stopped. The moon was made visible again by a break in the cloud cover and a beam of light spread across Lake Albano.

Leo returned to the bedroom and immediately took off his clothes and let them drop in a pile next to the door leading to the balcony. After stepping into the bathroom and drying himself thoroughly, he got back into bed, pulled the blankets over his body, and propped up his pillows so that as he lay on his back his head was slightly elevated. He turned off the reading lamp, and the room became pitch black. Leo closed his eyes and placed his right index and middle fingers over his right eye and placed his left index and middle fingers over his left eye. He began to concentrate intensely on his sense of himself within himself, to the exclusion of the room and world around him. After several minutes, with his mind quieted and focused, he began to repeat these statements: "I am calling out to my inner self. Please make your presence known to me. I acknowledge your presence." He continued to repeat the mantra in his mind for almost thirty minutes until, without warning, he was overcome by an experience he'd never known before—one that instantaneously altered his cosmology, his worldview, his beliefs about the nature of reality and personhood, and, ultimately, his theology. Seven days later, on March 6th, he resigned his office as Pope, citing only "personal reasons."

In the fall of 2076, a commentary written by Leo, entitled *magnus ab integro saeclorum nascitur ordo* (typed in all lowercase letters) and dated March 4th, 2049, exactly four months before his death, was discovered in the Vatican Apostolic Archive by researchers. The title, a passage from Virgil's *Eclogues*, translated from the Latin, meant "the great order of the ages is born afresh."

"The conversation regarding inner illumination has established itself in the mainstream narrative and, seemingly, the collective conscious. The now widespread occurrence of individuals alleging to have accessed an open, illuminated inner space and, as a result, gained insight and awareness, information, answers to questions and solutions to problems, a sense of liberation, and even psychic or metaphysical powers, is a historical phenomenon.

"Most people have noted that their initial experience of inner illumination occurred directly following a period of inwardly focused concentration during which the individual beseeched their higher self, higher consciousness, or inner self to make itself known to them. Almost without exception, individuals have described this 'calling out' or 'seeking' as taking the form of a repeatedly stated declaration that is bolstered by the expectation that their call will be answered.

"For the initial experiments in summoning awareness of non-physical planes, the terms 'higher self,' 'higher conscious-ness,' or 'inner self' appear to be more potent references (within the context of a seeking mantra) than the terms 'soul,' 'psyche,' or 'spirit', although the latter three have also been used to posi-tive effect. In essence, and for all intents and purposes, each of these six expressions means the same thing; and they all point in the same direction. Many people have commented that they used the term 'inner self' simply because it was the term used in the well-known account of Edward Slowbe's first contact. Words have a psychological effect. The word 'self' intrinsical-ly implies the personal, the intimate, the real; and using it in conjunction with the word 'inner' suggests something directly connected to the person, already present within the person, yet beyond the ego and the corporeal.

"Prior to attempting the experiment, there is a foundation that must be established: a general acceptance, or at least a sense, that the individual is a multidimensional entity, not just a physical body and an ego. The person must become convinced that awareness of other planes of existence, and other dimensions of the Self, are available at their fingertips, as naturally and fundamentally as any birthright, as naturally as the ability to breathe. The process of arriving at such a conviction can take a short or long time. It often requires use of imagination to stretch the mind, and use of a catalyst to help one reshape one's beliefs about what is possible and real. Edward Slowbe's book is a remarkably potent resource for these purposes. Proper utilization of the following tools will increase the likelihood of first contact: belief, meditation, sense of exploration, courage, supplication, concentration, open-mindedness, temporary suspension of focus on the material world, desire, intuition, visualization, and consideration of the infinite.

"Traditionally, people fear things deemed not of this world, like gods and ghosts and spirits and 'God.' To varying degrees, people fear the unknown. They fear death. An individual needs courage to face something not of this world, courage to stay present in the face of something unknown, even if there is some fear of the experience. Inner illumination, other dimensions and planes, soul, or God may not be of this world, but they are in no way separate from this world, in no way separate from the individual, or separate from humanity.

"There is a certain period of the evening, between 10:00 p.m. and 3:00 a.m., that seems particularly conducive to setting upon the initial process of coming into awareness of real inner vision. The individual should establish a calm, reflective mood within themselves, either by reading something profound or inspirational, gazing out of their window at the nighttime sky, practicing deep breathing, focusing on the present moment, or by some other similar means. How the proper mood is set is unique to the individual, but they should make sure they are in a physically comfortable position and in a dark, quiet space (dark so as to be less distracted by external light) before closing their eyes and beginning their experiment. When the individual is first starting to induce the experience on a regular basis, it is beneficial to have the sense of looking up. Psychologically speaking, looking up is associated with gazing into/toward vast spaces, e.g., the sky, the universe, or even God. Therefore, lying on one's back on a bed, or in a reclining chair, is recommended. The experiment begins with the inward focus and the calling out. Because the experience of inner illumination, by all accounts, occurs directly as a result of a concerted seeking, or asking, the prevailing assumption about its nature is that it is, in fact, an aspect of the soul, and/or part of a larger Macro

Self system, making its presence known in response to a direct request.

"Every individual is unique, with a unique inner landscape, and a unique personal reality. Given human diversity and subjectivity, and the presumed infinitude of reality and of the soul, it is not surprising that a wide, varied range of observations have been made with respect to inner vision. And yet, every human is formed in the same way that every other human is formed, made of the same stuff that all other humans are made of, and connected to the same things that all humans are connected to. Therefore, it is also not surprising that many common experiences have been reported.

"When the threshold is crossed, when the guise of blackness is lifted, like lifting a veil or a curtain, individuals almost uniformly describe a domain marked by violet light and the sensation of being within, or surrounded by, an expanse. The degree of depth that is perceived, and the vibrancy of the illumination, varies from episode to episode and from person to person. Many describe observing pulsations within the violet realm, like ripples in a pond, or strobe lights, in addition to innumerable other phenomena. The basic idea is that behind the appearance of blackness, which most people see when their eyes are closed, lies an entire realm that the individual can nurture a relationship with and develop an orientation around. In order to acclimate to, normalize, and enhance this experience while it is happening, it is important to keep the body as relaxed as possible and to stare intently into the violet space, as if one is gazing at a particular area in the sky. These practices help keep one's focus on the present moment and the present environment, and help reiterate the facts, and the beliefs, that the inner realm that is being experienced is as real and valid as the one perceived externally and that it should not be feared.

"Following the first several experiments, people have generally found that they no longer need a 'mantra of calling' in order to open the illuminated space; a dark external environment and the intentional, inward focusing that brought about the initial experience are sufficient to bring it about again. And many have explained that they eventually began to witness traces of the violet realm even with their eyes open. This can occur in well-lit or darkened rooms, although it occurs more readily when there is less external light. Others have described the violet realm emerging in place of physical features, like walls or ceilings, when the individual's eyes are open; but, for the most part, this only occurs when they are actively attempting to conjure the experience as an exercise in concentration.

"Although the experience of intersecting with the violet realm while the eyes are open is not as common as having the experience while the eyes are closed, it is a common enough occurrence that a second set of assumptions about its nature have been proposed, namely, that the violet realm is 1) a unique dimension that is distinct from, yet associated with, the dimension of physical reality, 2) a type of portal, gateway, or conduit between physical and non-physical realms of existence, and/or 3) a primary, underlying reality that is pervasive and supersedes the physical, like a substructure realm out of which physical reality emerges. Some go further and equate it with divine immanence and the infinite. One thing is self-evident: the presence of electromagnetic energy.

"The electromagnetic spectrum is defined as 'the range of frequencies of electromagnetic radiation and their respective wavelengths and photon energies,' or as 'the entire range of wavelengths or frequencies of electromagnetic radiation extending from gamma rays to the longest radio waves and including visible light' (radiation being 'the emission of energy as electromagnetic waves or as moving subatomic particles'). In physics, the terms 'light' and 'radiation' are virtually synonymous; and therefore, both refer to the entire spectrum of electromagnetic energy, visible or not.

"There are seven colors that exist in the narrow band of visible light within this spectrum: red, orange, yellow, green, blue, indigo, and violet. The color emitted depends upon the size of the wavelength. The color with the widest wavelength in the spectrum of visible light is red. From there the wavelengths of each subsequent color are progressively shorter and thus higher in photon energy. Violet has the shortest wavelength, and the most concentrated energy, of any color. Gamma rays have the shortest, highest-energy wavelengths on the entire electromagnetic spectrum as it is currently known.

"In my opinion, the non-physical planes that many are beginning to explore and access are imbued with light of far shorter wavelengths and more concentrated photon energies than what have heretofore been detected by science. When the human brain intersects with these planes it automatically translates what it is experiencing into a framework that it can comprehend in physical terms, namely, visible light. Although the dynamic of interacting with non-physical realms or entities is not a linear phenomenon, one can imagine that if a line was traced from right to left on an electromagnetic spectrum, from inconceivably small wavelengths moving toward the wavelengths of visible light, the first color to appear would be violet.

"Light transcends physical reality. It is not exclusively of this world. At a certain point, the spectrum of light crosses a threshold from physical reality into the asomatous. When the mind crosses that threshold, it will sense that it is surrounded by the color with the shortest wavelength and the highest-energy photons. While the term 'violet realm' is convenient and makes sense on a surface level because of how the brain interprets the experience of non-physical reality, the incorporeal is not a realm defined by, or made up of, violet light, although it is a plane wherein there exists light energy."

Poetry

Slowbe stepped onto his deck, where Sangree was setting up her tripod. The sun was minutes away from rising into view, and orange, red, and blue light rushed ahead, filling the horizon. Across the Willamette Valley, brightly colored leaves underscored the fact that it was the fall equinox. Mt. Hood, the main focus of Sangree's attention, looked serene, its sharp white slopes starkly contrasting the flamboyant morning sky.

"They found a six-foot amethyst statue at the Amarna site," Slowbe said. He approached Sangree and showed her some of the pictures featured at the Archeology News portal. "It was in a previously undiscovered chamber of Akhenaten's tomb."

Sangree spent a couple moments carefully looking over the images, then put her eye on her camera viewfinder and began to adjust the focus.

"Beautiful. Looks like a heron," she said.

"It's called 'the Bennu.'"

"The Bennu," Sangree replied with an inflection that suggested her unfamiliarity with the name.

Slowbe glanced again at the Archeology News portal and read aloud a few passages from the article on the discovery.

"It's an ancient Egyptian deity—representing creation, rebirth, and the sun—often referred to as 'the one who came into being by himself' or 'lord of the jubilees.' It was an important figure in Egyptian mythology, associated with the gods Atum, Ra, and Osiris, and was the sacred bird of Heliopolis, a city located in what's now the northeastern side of Cairo."

"Well, I'd say the discovery is a rather auspicious sign for the upcoming Global Reconciliation Summit," Sangree said lightheartedly, "especially given that it's being held in Cairo."

"The name of the Bennu bird," Slowbe continued, "is derived from the root *bn* which means 'ascension' or 'to rise.' It says that, according to tradition, the Bennu had a life span of five hundred years, and when it was near death it would build a nest of myrrh and other spices and set it aflame with a clap of its wings. The Bennu would be consumed by the flames and then reborn out of its own ashes to begin a new life cycle. Following its rebirth it would embalm the ashes and fly with them to Heliopolis, where it would deposit them at the altar of the temple of the sun."

"That sounds very similar to the Phoenix from Greek mythology," Sangree replied.

"Actually," Slowbe said, "the Bennu is thought to have been the inspiration for the Phoenix myth."

Sangree snapped several photos in rapid succession. The sun was now parallel with Mt. Hood, and the light on the horizon was red and yellow, gradually turning to blue as one's line of vision moved upward.

"When I was in eighth grade, my class went on a tour of the UN headquarters. In the Security Council chamber there was a huge mural painted by Per Krohg, a Norwegian artist; and the main image was of a Phoenix being reborn, rising from its own ashes," Slowbe said. "I remember the tour guide mentioning that the presence of the Phoenix in the mural symbolized society being rebuilt after World War II. That was the first time I'd ever heard of the Phoenix."

Sangree couldn't remember when she'd first seen images of the Phoenix, or heard about it, although she vaguely remembered a book from her childhood about a golden firebird.

"But I'd never heard of the Bennu until now," Slowbe added.

"I hadn't either," Sangree replied.

The discovery was the first significant find at the Amarna site since 2007, when a small cemetery was uncovered. And while amethyst jewelry had been found at numerous archeological sites from the ancient world, the excavation of a statue made entirely of the violet-colored gemstone was unique. But what was a statue of the Bennu doing in a chamber of Akhenaten's tomb? Akhenaten had denied the traditional pantheon of gods and deities in favor of one god, the Aten, represented by the sun, and he had imposed this belief on the society he ruled and had built a new capital city, Amarna, dedicated to the worship of Aten. The Bennu, while being associated with the sun, was also inherently linked to Atum, Ra, and Osiris. Perhaps, archeologists conjectured, Akhenaten found meaning in the Bennu because it aligned with his reverence for the sun and the idea of rebirth. Maybe it was placed in his tomb at the time of his burial by someone who admired him but who also maintained a reverence for the old ways and wanted the Bennu to journey with Akhenaten into the afterlife. Nonetheless, the discovery didn't have any bearing on the widely held view among scholars that Akhenaten was the first monotheist in history.

It was Akhenaten's adoption of monotheism, considered heretical by many generations of Egyptians who came after him, that Slowbe found most fascinating about the enigmatic pharaoh. How does an individual suddenly conceive of the idea of one God when all that had ever existed in one's familial upbringing, in one's nation, in one's culture, and in the whole prior history of humankind, was a polytheistic belief system? Slowbe had wondered. Akhenaten had somehow seen a vision outside of the paradigm he was born into, and to Slowbe, there was no greater feat, no more exciting occurrence, than the envisioning or grasping of a new paradigm.

Slowbe closed his Array. The light breeze that had been moving across the valley all morning had stopped. With the sun seeming to stand directly before him, Slowbe found himself harkening back to the dream he'd had when he was sixteen years old, of him walking down the stairs in the middle of the night and into his mother's library; standing in the soft, glowing light; looking at the photographs of his dead grandmother; finding a book called *The Book of Aten*, and reading it in its entirety. It was a vivid, precious memory. Like a primer on being in relationship with the soul, the dream had introduced him to the idea of a limitless realm within, and of having, as a birthright, access to the vast resources, power, and information therein. He had awoken convinced that reality was infinite and multidimensional in nature, and that his own true nature, as an entity, was in concert with this. There was something more, more to who and what he was, more to it all, more than met the eye. Slowbe was thankful that his young self, the sixteen-year-old Edward Slowbe, had the courage and curiosity to dive into the great unknown, to explore, and to set in motion a process of discovery.

"Can I take a look at your photos?" Slowbe asked.

"Of course," Sangree replied. She took a step back from the tripod and slid her index finger across the camera display screen twenty or so times until she arrived at the first picture she'd taken that morning. Slowbe leaned forward as Sangree stepped slightly to the side of the camera and began the slide show, giving Slowbe about five seconds to take in each photo.

"Wow, these are great," Slowbe said after having looked at the first few. Sangree didn't respond, and continued on to the next photograph. Before long she'd gotten through all of them.

"I like these," she said, "really nice light."

"Yeah," Slowbe replied.

"I've taken a lot of photos of Mt. Hood the last couple days," Sangree said.

"Any particular reason why?" Slowbe asked.

"Trying to capture the moment it blows," she said in a dry, matter-of-fact, yet joking way.

"Oh, ok," Slowbe said, laughing.

In the previous three weeks two earthquakes, both above

magnitude 6.0, had been recorded beneath the mountain. Such tremors weren't unprecedented, and didn't necessarily indicate an imminent explosion, but this was the strongest seismic activity to have occurred since 2002, when a magnitude 4.5 earthquake was measured. The fact that these recent earthquakes had been so strong and had happened just two and a half weeks apart spurred a great deal of speculation, as well as some apprehension, that the mountain was going to erupt at any moment.

"It's overdue, right?" Sangree said.

"Probably," Slowbe said.

"Actually, it's just really captured my attention lately, visually, with all the new snowfall," Sangree said. "It looks stunning."

The mountain's appearance had indeed changed recently. Although the last few days in Portland had been balmy and cloudless, this pleasant weather had been preceded by twelve consecutive days of rain and cold, during which time Mt. Hood had accumulated almost three feet of snow—a September record made even more bizarre by the fact that the region had hit one hundred degrees earlier in the month. When the skies cleared in Portland, and Mt. Hood came back into view, it not only appeared to have increased in size, but it also glistened, boldly and conspicuously, in the sunlight, like a jagged, pristine, snow-white monolith.

"I'm going to get a glass of water," Sangree said.

"Sure," Slowbe replied.

Sangree made her way toward the sliding glass doors.

"Have you been reading this?" she asked, glancing at the copy of *A Legendary Time Mind* by Mia Sabin that was placed on the circular glass table next to Slowbe's hammock.

"Yeah."

"What do you think?" she asked.

"It's great. I've really enjoyed it."

"Interesting title."

"'Time mind' is the literal translation of the German word *zeitgeist*."

By all accounts, Sabin's work brilliantly illuminated the intersection of the social, political, scientific, technological, philosophical, and artistic developments of the mid-twenty-first-century experience; and within a week of its September 13th publication it had moved to the top of several best-seller lists. It wasn't Sabin's only notable piece of writing in 2049. The other was a fourteen-hundred-word editorial, published in the May 1st issue of the *New York Times*, that proposed a global forum on world peace—an idea that members of the HEP had briefly discussed with President Abundo in the days prior to the signing of the African Great Lakes Region Peace Treaty.

On May 8th, during an interview with the BBC, Abundo became the first head of state to publicly support the idea. In the same interview, to the surprise of millions of viewers watching the livestream, he offered a personal account of the interaction he'd had with Slowbe in December of 2048, which he believed had resulted in his cancer suddenly going into complete remission. Abundo described the experience as *the* watershed moment in his life, one that compelled his subsequent peacemaking efforts. "In the realm of energy," he said, "anything is possible. I have come to believe that there is something fundamentally supernatural about our true nature. If we are to live up to our potential, we must have the right environment within which to develop. There must be peace. And we have the power, creativity, and intelligence to create this in our lives and in our world. Let us walk in a noble light, and respect our divinity."

Ten days after Abundo's remarks, when President Eagle Staff, leader of the most powerful nation on the planet, replied "yes" to a reporter's question about whether or not he would participate in a forum on world peace, it was as if a clarion call had sounded. Over the remainder of the month, the truth of consciousness movement took on a new ebullience, and a new aura of ascendancy, as the frequency of rallies, the number of cities where they occurred, and the number of people involved exceeded anything seen in the twenty-four years since its inception. Every day from May 19th through the 31st, there were at least a dozen rallies taking place in different locations around the planet; and it was estimated that between seven hundred and eight hundred million people around the world were involved. It was like a volcano that had been rumbling and releasing smoke and ash, possibly for years, centuries, or millennia, finally lighting up the sky with glowing balls of light.

Sangree returned to the deck with a glass of water.

"Have you written any poetry lately?" she asked.

"Not in the last couple months," Slowbe said, "but I've recently started work on another book."

"Really?" Sangree said in a surprised tone. "I didn't know you'd been planning on doing that."

"Not a lot of planning has gone into it so far, but the general idea first came to me when I was driving out to Portland in '36, the day after Arongeaz Everyman bombed the United Nations."

"What's it about?"

"Well, it's called *The Flourishing Individual*. It's a novel, a philosophical novel; that's the genre I'm going to continue writing in. The main idea in the book is that the true purpose of a society is to foster environments that allow for the full, healthy expression and actualization of the individual. And then, in turn, healthy, actualized individuals give back to society in one way or another, instinctively. There are a lot of ideas going into it, but the story is about a twelve-year-old girl named Grace who lives near the Mississippi River, and about what she learns from the river and what the river means to her—the river as storyteller, metaphor, conduit for various teachings. And it's about the messages she's getting from society, past and present, and how she has opportunities to process these messages with other characters that she spends time with by, or on, the river. The backstories of the other characters will be important to the narrative; their themes all kind of converge at Grace."

"Interesting," Sangree said. "How much have you written?"

"A few paragraphs," Slowbe said, grinning.

"Ok," Sangree said as she smiled and nodded her head, "it's a start."

"It's a start," Slowbe repeated. "Starting is the hardest part. I'm excited about being in the process. I've crossed the threshold. I'm in the book now."

"When is the story set?"

"2076. One year in her life."

"That's great," Sangree said. "Congratulations on starting the new project. I look forward to reading some when you're a bit further along."

"Ok," Slowbe said.

Sangree looked at her camera. "I think I should write something," she said.

"You should," Slowbe said. "What do you think you'd want to write about? Would it be a story, or a memoir piece, or something else?"

"I don't know, maybe a satire, something about misnomers and misconceptions."

"Hmm. What types?" Slowbe asked.

"Well, all sorts, I guess; maybe around labels that humans have placed on one another, the language we use, false beliefs. Have you ever heard of Carl Linnaeus?"

"Yeah," Slowbe said, "the eighteenth-century Swedish scientist who popularized racial color codes; he identified Asians as the yellow race, Native Americans as the red race, Europeans as the white race, and Africans as the black race, although I think sixteenth-century Portuguese slave traders were the first to refer to Africans as black."

"Perfect examples," Sangree said with slight laugher. "First, of course, it's a biological fallacy that there are different races of humans. There's just one human species, with different ethnicities, cultures, nationalities, or geographical origins. Right? It's just recently becoming more widely known by the general public that race is strictly a social construct, and not an inherent physical or biological condition. And obviously, there's no such thing as a human whose skin tone is literally black, literally white, literally red, or literally yellow."

"True," Slowbe said. "We don't really hear people being referred to as red or yellow that much anymore, but when those terms are used to describe Native Americans or Asians it's considered a racial slur. It's interesting that we continue to cling to this black/white dichotomy, referring to people as being black or white, and for some reason those labels aren't considered racist by the mainstream; but they definitely are."

"If you look at what the colors white and black have symbolized over the millennia," Sangree said, "at least in Western civilization, in the church, in fairy tales, in popular culture, et cetera, it's no surprise that Linnaeus assigned Europeans and people of European descent the color most associated with goodness, angels, purity, et cetera, and that he would assign Africans and people of African descent, who were being enslaved at the time, the color most associated with evil and sinister things. The black/white dichotomy would actually justify slavery, since in the minds of Europeans of the time, and people of European descent, peoples associated with the color black must be sinister, and lowly, and not close to God, and thus deserving of enslavement, the exact opposite being true for those associated with the color white. It set up a vicious hierarchy, one that certainly benefited the Europeans and those of European ancestry. I mean, it benefited them then and it benefits them today. If you're referred to as the color that has all the best, most noble connotations, that's a good thing for you, no doubt. Language has a powerful impact on psychology and how we internalize and experience reality.

"In modern times there've been studies showing that African American children are harmed by being referred to as black, simply because they're surrounded by so many instances of the color black joined to a negative concept or thing, or symbolizing something negative; and then they themselves are called black. What are their little minds to conclude? You look in Webster's dictionary and it's incredible all the negative connotations associated with the color black, and all the positive connotations associated with the color white; and then we refer to humans in such terms. It's problematic. And, you know, like you mentioned, Native Americans aren't commonly referred to as red anymore, but they are referred to as Indians, even amongst themselves; and it's because a European guy, Columbus, thought he was in India when he stumbled upon Indigenous peoples in the Caribbean and so he called them Indians and it stuck as a label for all peoples across the entire North American and South American continents. It might be difficult to shed the residue of colonialism if one identifies oneself using the colonizer's labels.

"I think we should use ethnicity, geography, indigenous names, and maybe nationality, to describe humans, not symbolic color codes or names rooted in historical errors and ignorance, or names rooted in racism and hierarchies. And I don't have any problem with Europeans, obviously, but it's silly that they've been the ones to determine labels for everyone, whether it's Indian, black, white, yellow, red, and so on. Peoples should reject identifying themselves with labels that colonizers, oppressors, or slave masters gave them. It's internalized oppression. It gives power away. It helps perpetuate a hierarchy and power structure rooted in the past. On the other hand, people should grow out of identifying themselves with labels that bolster a facade of superiority. In a way, it's all about referring to ourselves in the most accurate and realistic terms possible.

"There are so many examples of how our sense of identity is shaped by labels or beliefs that don't accurately reflect reality, even down to how we perceive ourselves as physical entities. You know I like to point out that our bodies are almost ninety-nine percent empty space, and how, relatively speaking, there's as much space between the atoms in our bodies as there is between the stars in the universe. It might be an epic misconception to think that we're even solid mass at all or that we, as entities, are our bodies; we're more just concentrated, sentient energy. It takes a little reimagining, but it's realistic. So, anyway, maybe I'll write some sort of satire about a group of people who exist in a hall of mirrors and never get a true sense of who they are because they can't distinguish between themselves and the facade they're enmeshed in—between themselves and their own misconceptions and misnomers."

"Kind of sounds like Plato's analogy of the cave," Slowbe said.

"It does, doesn't it?" Sangree said. "Maybe I can make parallels in some way, kind of like what James Joyce did with his novel *Ulysses*—how he made parallels between his story and Homer's *Odyssey*. I don't know, we'll see. I have to come up with an actual story."

"Well, I think it would be great if you wrote something along these lines," Slowbe said. "Sounds like there might be some overlapping themes with what I'm working on: reflecting on the messages we get from society, how we internalize or reject or process or navigate them, and how all of this impacts our sense of identity for better or for worse—and what liberation looks like."

"How far have you gotten in *A Legendary Time Mind*?" Sangree asked.

"I'm almost done," Slowbe said. "I just need to finish reading her epilogue on the Holy Land Peace Accord."

In mid-April, reports began emerging that Pope Leo was in Isfahan, Iran, staying as a guest of the Grand Ayatollah, Mohammed Al-Fin. Prior to this revelation, Leo hadn't been seen in public for close to a month, and the reports that were coming out suggested he'd been in Isfahan the entire time. It was a shocking revelation. Had the Pope converted to Islam? Had he been on a vacation or retreat? Was he ill and/or convalescing? What was the nature of his relationship with Al-Fin? Then, on April 23rd, a thirty-three-page essay called "The Necessity of Peace," co-written by Leo and Al-Fin, was released. Shock quickly turned to disbelief.

The essay brazenly asserted that there were only two moral codes in the universe that demanded observance: love and peace. It argued that any view of religion, politics, civic life, or morality that in any way distorted this basic truth, or attempted to rationalize around it, was an affront to the divine nature of humanity and a direct threat to humanity's survival. Furthermore, it argued that true understanding of these moral truths could only be found within. The human species must begin to reorient itself, to redefine itself, and to assume far greater responsibility for its own collective fate, the essay declared; and this also, it was maintained, applied to humanity's relationship with the earth.

A week after the essay's release, Leo and Al-Fin held a joint press conference in Isfahan. Adding to the suspense of the occasion was news that had broken the day before: the Pope and the Ayatollah would be traveling to Jerusalem to help negotiate peace talks between the Israelis and Palestinians.

The press conference began promptly at 1:00 p.m. in the Chehel Sotoun palace. Leo and Al-Fin were seated next to each other at the center of a long, rectangular table covered with a brown, gold, and white-embroidered tapestry. The reporters sat in front of them, filling five rows of chairs. Al-Fin's personal assistant, a short, rough-skinned man named Farhad Ahmadi, was tasked with selecting which of the thirty-seven reporters to call upon.

"Thank you for joining us today," Ahmadi said from behind a podium to the right of Leo and Al-Fin. "Let's get straight to your questions." He pointed to the lady in the beige pantsuit seated in the front row.

"Banafsha Alvi, BBC. Your Excellency, how long have you been in Iran?"

"I arrived in Isfahan on March 15th and have been here since then."

"Many people are, of course, surprised to find that you have been in Iran. What made you decide to come here?" Alvi asked.

Leo paused and turned toward Al-Fin, raising his right eyebrow.

"The Pope and I became good friends during the Religious Reconciliation Conference last year," Al-Fin said, "and when I heard he'd abdicated the papacy I contacted him and offered him use of my private residence here in Isfahan as a retreat."

"The invitation was well timed," Leo added, "and it appealed to me not only for the opportunity to engage in discussion on theological and spiritual matters with the Ayatollah, which we very much enjoyed doing during our time together at the conference, but also for the opportunity to spend some time in an environment very different, and removed, from what I had been accustomed to, and very much out of public view."

"How long do you plan on staying in Isfahan?" Alvi asked.

"I don't know," Leo replied.

Ahmadi pointed to a man in the fourth row who was wearing a dark-green shirt and brown pants.

"Jackson Stephenson, *The Australian*. Who proposed the idea of working together to write 'The Necessity of Peace'? What was the motivation for writing it? And how did you agree upon its content?"

Al-Fin glanced in the direction of Leo. A couple seconds passed before Leo spoke.

"As you know, the Ayatollah is a great lover of peace. The oration he gave at the Religious Reconciliation Conference, 'On the Meaning of Salam,' was one of the greatest I've ever heard. In the time I've known him, it has been evident to me that the idea of peace is his favorite subject to talk about. So, naturally, not long after I arrived in Isfahan it became a recurring focal point of our discussions. We started considering the idea of co-authoring something on the topic a couple weeks after

I arrived. We knew that such a document would necessarily represent a break from the respective traditions that we come from, but we eventually decided to proceed. We are both very encouraged by the treaty signed in Seychelles, but we are also concerned about the barriers to peace that remain for the individuals, communities, and nations of our world. The recent one-hundred-year anniversary of conflict between the Israelis and Palestinians also served as impetus for the work."

"The Pope and I spent many hours discussing peace, religion, human nature, human potential, and the urgency and wonder of our times," Al-Fin said. "The Pope also came to me with a challenge, which I will elaborate upon at a later date, but which has since changed my life. Through these discussions, and hours of prayer and meditation, and through what I will refer to as 'communion,' we were able to fashion content for the essay."

"What do you hope comes from this document?" Stephenson asked.

Once again the naturally gregarious Al-Fin deferred to the more reserved Leo.

"Something different," Leo said rather abruptly. There were several moments of silence as the press pool waited for him to continue. It soon became evident that he wasn't going to elaborate, and that Al-Fin wasn't going to add anything.

"Next question," Ahmadi said, pointing to a lady wearing a turquoise blouse and green pants who was seated in the first row.

"Fatima ibn Firnas, Al Jazeera. Supreme Leader, identification with a religion has declined by over fifty percent since 2012, and this decline has been particularly notable with respect to Christianity and Islam. Does this essay undermine religious institutions, or religious authority, by saying that moral truth can be found within?"

"It may or may not," Al-Fin said. "Perhaps it depends on the disposition of the reader and how they interpret the idea. For those who are already non-affiliated and who seek spirituality and wisdom independently of a religion, the notion may affirm something they already believe to be true. For those who would never be swayed from their religious affiliation, I don't believe it will affect their adherence to religious authority, or their belief in it. Religious authority exists only insofar as believers are willing to assign it. It is a social construct. It's not inherent. The bishop or the imam is no holier than the housekeeper or the handyman. What the Pope meant when he said we want to see something different is that we believe our times demand that we reexamine age-old paradigms that have governed how we view ourselves, society, our relationship with the earth and the universe, and even reality itself. As far as the impact of the idea on religious authority, I'm sure you will be surprised to hear that I'm not particularly concerned about that. There are some things that are more important."

"Jesus taught that the kingdom of God is within," Leo said, "so that may be a proposition to consider, or flesh out, with respect to your question."

"Supreme Leader, will you remain the Ayatollah?" Ibn Firnas quickly interjected.

"It is time for me to retire from these duties," Al-Fin said.

Ahmadi pointed to a man in the second to last row who was wearing blue jeans and a beige sports jacket.

"William James, *Boston Globe.* Your Excellency, are you still a Christian?"

"I am a follower of Christ, and nothing more," Leo replied.

"And Supreme Leader," James quickly added, "are you still a Muslim?"

"I am, shall I say, an evolving Sufi," Al-Fin replied.

"Next question," Ahmadi said. He pointed to a lady in a black dress seated in the middle row.

"Shakari Mali, *Dainik Jagran.* Can you confirm the reports that you will be traveling to Jerusalem to help negotiate peace between the Israelis and the Palestinians?"

"Yes," Al-Fin said, "those reports are accurate."

"You will be arriving in an unofficial capacity, and without the weight that your former stations carry. What authority do you bring to these peace talks?" Mali asked.

"I can respond to that," Leo said. "We don't come with any authority, per se, other than many, many years of experience, and a unique understanding of, and perspective on, the historical, sociopolitical, and religious factors at play in the Holy Land. The Ayatollah and I reached out to the Israeli and Palestinian governments to offer our services in helping to support a cease-fire and peace talks, and both sides responded enthusiastically."

"I would just add that there are certain liberties that come with not holding an office," Al-Fin said.

"When are you planning to arrive in Jerusalem?" Mali asked.

"May 15th," Al-Fin replied.

"Will you attend the truth of consciousness rally on the sixteenth?" Mali asked.

"Yes," Leo said.

Al-Fin and Leo then looked at Ahmadi and nodded.

"That is all the questions that we have time for today," Ahmadi said abruptly. "Thank you."

There was complete silence as the two elderly men stood up and departed the room.

Sixteen days later close to forty thousand people assembled in the Old City, a walled, .35-square-mile area within Greater Jerusalem, which was home to several important religious sites: Islam's Dome of the Rock and al-Aqsa Mosque, Christianity's Church of the Holy Sepulchre, and Judaism's Temple Mount and Western Wall. Al-Fin and Leo arrived at the rally at 12:00 p.m., an hour after the event had commenced. There was no entourage accompanying them, and both men were dressed in plain clothes. As they waited for the first speaker of the day, Saudi writer and feminist Noor Adar, to take the stage, their presence began to draw the attention of others in the crowd. Not everyone recognized them though, and, for the most part, the two enjoyed the afternoon somewhat unaffected by their celebrity. Nevertheless, by the end of the day, they had been photographed and captured on video numerous times. Before the rally concluded at around 4:00 p.m., many images had gone viral.

That evening Al-Fin and Leo had dinner together at the King David Hotel, where they were both staying. They discussed the day's events while periodically referring to their Arrays. They agreed that the experience at the rally had gone better than hoped in that they'd achieved their objective of having news of their participation flood the internet, and yet they'd been able to have the experience without being overwhelmed by people wanting to exchange greetings or otherwise interact with them.

Over the next several days there were more public appearances at local markets, parks, schools, and hospitals, although these were guided and more formal occasions. On May 20th the Israeli and Palestinian delegations, as well as Leo, Al-Fin, and U.S. secretary of state Arlene Stance, gathered at the United States embassy in Jerusalem for the first day of talks. Although the timeframe for achieving a cease-fire was open-ended, the goal that the parties established from the outset was to come to an agreement within seven days. The atmosphere in the rooms was positive and conciliatory and there was an unexpected display of good faith. On the fourth day, the two sides came to terms. Initially, the news was greeted by the public with great skepticism—hundreds of cease-fire violations had occurred in the past, the historical and religious enmity was too great, the agreement would be undermined in some way, the two groups were incapable of maintaining a peace, there would always be conflict in the Holy Land.

The conditions laid out in the cease-fire stipulated that following a month of cessation of hostilities, formal peace-treaty talks would commence. These talks would be led by the former Pope, the former Ayatollah, and the president of the United States. Al-Fin and Leo remained in Jerusalem as the truce held for one week, then two, then three. And then, at the end of the fourth week, President Eagle Staff arrived. In Jerusalem, and around the world, there was an unusual, surreal sense: a tangible feeling that a threshold had somehow been crossed, that the wind had shifted, something was new, different. Diplomats and politicians, businessmen and businesswomen, farmers and fishermen, artists, educators, laborers, mothers and fathers began to believe that peace in the Holy Land was finally drawing nigh. On June 27th it was announced that terms for the Holy Land Peace Accord had been agreed upon. Humanity breathed a long-awaited sigh of relief; and yet, there was some incredulity, a sort of cognitive dissonance. Many people thought to themselves, How did this happen? Is this real? Others were overcome by the symbolism of the moment and wept in joy. To many, strife in the Holy Land had been a microcosm of, and the most poignant representation of, humanity's long ordeal with war and pathological discord. The moment pointed to humanity's healing from its collective psychic trauma, and the ushering in of a new era.

The treaty consisted of twelve points: 1) a unified Jerusalem would be the capital of the state of Israel; 2) an independent Palestinian state, with its capital at Ramallah, would be created and would include the entirety of the West Bank and the Gaza Strip, the Lachish region, Har Adar, areas of the Judean Desert, and areas around Afula; 3) the right of the state of Israel to exist, and recognition of its existence as a Jewish state, would be officially declared by the Palestinian government, and the right of the state of Palestine to exist, and recognition of its existence, would be officially declared by the Israeli government; 4) the Palestinian government would receive twenty billion dollars per year for ten years from the United States government for economic, health, education, and infrastructure development; 5) Israeli citizens living in the West Bank could remain in Palestine but would live under the laws and jurisdiction of the Palestinian government; 6) the states of Israel and Palestine would develop and adopt policies acknowledging their unique relationship as "mutual benefit states," including safety and protection agreements, economic exchange, ease of passage for Israeli and Palestinian citizens across the borders of the two nations, unrestricted access for Palestinians to holy sites located within Israel, and programs to increase the number of Arabic/Hebrew bilingual speakers living in the two nations; 7) water from underground aquifers in Palestine would be shared with Israel until such time as a joint Israeli/Palestinian Water Commission, with assistance from the United States, had developed water-collection, saltwater-purifying, and water-distribution systems to ensure water supplies for all citizens of the two nations; 8) a seventy-mile railway and highway tunnel from the West Bank to Gaza would be constructed with financial contributions from Israel, Palestine, and the United States and with ownership and maintenance of the tunnel under the joint control of Palestine and Israel; 9) a Truth and Reconciliation Commission would be created to develop strategies for healing historical mistrust and to acknowledge both the harm done by Palestinian displacement and the harm caused by Palestinian terrorism against Israel; 10) the right of Palestinian refugees or their descendants to return to Israel would be forgone as a policy goal, but Palestinian citizens and refugees would receive special consideration if they desired to emigrate to Israel; 11) Palestine would create a public safety force to secure order within its borders but would not maintain a standing army or allow any military-grade munitions within its territory; 12) the United States would enter into a protection agreement with the Palestinian government to aid in securing its sovereignty against internal or external threats.

*

"I heard from Isaac Johnson the other day," Slowbe said.

"Really?" Sangree replied.

"Yeah, he sent me an email. He said he'd made all the

preparations to carry out an elaborate, foolproof hoax that would convince society and the scientific community that SETI had found irrefutable evidence of intelligent life in the Pleiades system."

"Wow, amazing," Sangree said.

"But he said he's decided against following through with it."

"Huh," Sangree said. "Did he say why?"

"No, but maybe it has something to do with the fact that leaders from nearly every country on the planet will be at the Global Reconciliation Summit in November. There's so much excitement surrounding it, and what it could lead to."

Slowbe and Sangree shared several moments of silence before Sangree's attention was caught by a new visitor.

"Another hummingbird," she said, pointing up to her left.

Slowbe glanced over and in a flash the bird was gone.

"How do you think the world would react to news of irrefutable proof of intelligent life on another planet—you know, if the evidence was accepted by everyone?" Sangree asked.

"That would really be an incredible reorientation. I think it would bring us together as a species. It would probably alter our sense of ourselves and affect how we arrange our society."

"I agree," Sangree said.

"That was Johnson's grand plan," Slowbe said.

Enlightenment Matters

Slowbe entered the unincorporated community of Imnaha, Oregon, located along Oregon Route 350 near the confluence of the Imnaha River and Big Sheep Creek. In the hour and a half since he'd left Joseph, Oregon, he'd only seen a few other cars on the remote, narrow byway. He was now at the easternmost settlement in Oregon, population 171 according to the 2040 census, and it felt like the end of the line. What do people do for a living around here? he thought to himself as he drove past a small, rustic-looking post office with a white exterior, a grey tiled roof, and a round black chimney. A commemorative plaque next to the entrance indicated that it had been built in 1885. Up ahead to the right was a brown, log cabin–style building, the Imnaha Store and Tavern. A Coca-Cola sign jutted out from the storefront and there were a couple cars in the adjacent parking lot. Slowbe approached the building at about fifteen miles per hour. For a fleeting moment he considered stopping to make a purchase, but soon the establishment was in his rearview mirror and his tour of Imnaha was nearly concluded.

Outside of town, not too far in the distance, was a high ridge where the road seemed to disappear. Slowbe drove toward it for a few miles until he got to an intersection where a waypost read "Hat Point 23 miles." Beneath the words was an arrow pointing south. By now, he could see that the road he'd been on veered into a gap between two ridges and down into a valley. Slowbe pulled his bus to the side of the road, right in front of the waypost, turned off the ignition, and stepped out. Surrounding him was a lonely and engrossing landscape of high grasslands, canyons, and mountain valleys, sparsely dotted with trees and shrubbery. He leaned against his bus, taking note of the remarkable serenity of the place. The sky was clear blue, not a cloud in sight, which boded well for stargazing later in the evening, he thought. Slowbe took a couple pictures and got back into the vehicle. He turned onto the unpaved Hat Point Road and proceeded cautiously at about twenty miles per hour. The winding, gravelly road was full of rocks and pits and bumps and ascended at a sixteen percent grade for the first six miles, after which it continued to gain elevation, albeit more gradually. On his way he passed by grassy meadows with yellow and purple wildflowers; through groves of dry pine trees; past enormous, jagged boulders; and along harrowing, narrow ridges where, looking east, Hells Canyon, the Snake River, and the Rocky Mountains came into view. On several occasions he stopped to walk around and admire the scenery.

An hour after he started on the road, he arrived at his destination. At 6,982 feet above sea level and 5,600 feet above the Snake River, Hat Point was the highest point on the Oregon side of Hells Canyon; and due to its elevation and location near the Oregon-Idaho border, it was said to be the place where the sun first rises in Oregon. Slowbe got out of his bus, stretched his arms upward, and took a deep breath, grateful for the silence and the fresh, clean air. It was close to 6:00 p.m., and his was the only vehicle in the small, undeveloped parking area. Across the way was a path, and next to it a sign that read "Hat Point Lookout 100 Feet." To his left was another trail that entered a grove of pine trees and led to a group of primitive campsites. Slowbe headed up the moderately steep trail to the lookout. Once at the top, he could see the Snake River below, flowing north through Hells Canyon—the deepest gorge in

North America—and the Rocky Mountains stretching out to the east as far as the eye could see.

Two weeks prior to his road trip Slowbe had purchased a telescope. It was the long-overdue fulfillment of a childhood dream. The first thing he could remember aspiring to be was an astronomer. Perhaps soon, he thought, with his telescope and the guidebooks he'd purchased, he might be able to legitimately call himself an amateur stargazer. Since making the purchase, he'd used the telescope almost nightly from the perch of his deck; and so far, he'd made close observations of Venus; Mars; Saturn and its rings; and Jupiter and its four largest moons, Io, Europa, Ganymede, and Callisto. But there was also a special, unique focus of his sky watching, and it had to do with why he'd been inspired to buy the telescope in the first place. At 11:17 a.m. on July 26th, 2050, Alcyone appeared in the skies above Portland. Located in the Pleiades star cluster in the Taurus constellation, approximately 440 light-years from earth, the celestial body had gone supernova. The stunning phenomenon was quickly identified as one of the brightest stellar events ever observed, drawing comparisons to the supernova reported in 1006 that was described as having a quarter brightness of the moon, and the supernova reported in 1054 that was said to be four times as bright as Venus and visible during daylight hours for twenty-three days.

Slowbe had driven all the way to Hat Point not only for the adventure of exploring a place he'd never been before, but also for the opportunity to be in an environment with no light pollution, where the views of Alcyone, the Pleiades, the Milky Way, the Andromeda Galaxy, and beyond, would be especially lucid. He wanted to take it all in, as much as he could. In the new age of telescopes, the common man or woman could readily obtain an instrument, such as Slowbe's, that would allow them to see celestial objects over twelve billion light-years from earth. The more complex devices of the age had shattered expectations and the status quo. In addition to the groundbreaking findings of the Unbounded Energy Retrieval Telescope, the Robert Song Electromagnetic Spectrum Array had also accomplished what previously seemed impossible. Over the course of two months, from mid-March to late May of 2050, it had collected data showing that dark energy, which accounted for roughly sixty-eight percent of the composition of the universe, did in fact exist prior to the Big Bang, and therefore transcended the parameters of the universe as it had heretofore been understood. It was more conclusive evidence that the Big Bang and the known universe were simply features of a much, much larger system—perhaps infinitely larger.

Among the items Slowbe had brought with him on his trip were instructions on how to locate the Andromeda Galaxy and instructions for locating the Lagoon, Trifid, and Omega nebulae, located in the Sagittarius constellation. But his main objective was to get the Pleiades star system, and its already legendary supernova, in his finderscope. He was continuing a long tradition. Since ancient times the Pleiades had captured the attention and imagination of stargazers from many cultures. The Celts, Babylonians, Greeks, Maori, Persians, Chinese, Maya, Cherokee, Aztec, Sioux, Arabs, Indians, and Aboriginal Australians, among others, had all recorded observations, and many had created mythologies around them. The cluster of stars was also mentioned in Hesiod's *Works and Days*, Homer's *Iliad* and *Odyssey*, and the books of *Job* and *Amos*. In 1610, Galileo Galilei became the first to view them through a telescope. Coincidentally, Slowbe discovered after a little research, this was around the same time Alcyone had gone supernova, given the approximately 440 years needed for its light to reach earth.

Slowbe spent a couple hours at the lookout, relishing the grandeur of the sprawling vista, including Alcyone directly above, before deciding to set up his camp. He got on his feet. Without bending his knees, he leaned forward and placed both his palms on the ground, holding the position for about fifteen seconds. He then spread his legs and leaned his body to his right, grasping his ankle with both hands before making the same motion to his left. He straightened his legs and reached upward with his hands clasped. After taking in one more view of the panorama, he headed back to his bus to gather his backpack, tent, and telescope. Soon, he was settled in at the campsite, his tent propped, his sleeping bag unfolded, himself situated in his small travel chair next to a pine tree, and his copy of *Walden* resting on his lap. It was a quarter after eight. Slowbe opened to the chapter entitled "Brute Neighbors," which began with a fictional dialogue between a poet and a hermit in which the hermit considers whether he should continue with his meditation or go fishing with the poet. It went on to describe the various animals, the "brute neighbors," that Thoreau encountered during the two years, from July 1845 to September 1847, when he lived in a self-built cabin in the forest near Walden Pond, on land owned by Ralph Waldo Emerson, outside Concord, Massachusetts. Upon finishing the chapter, Slowbe crawled into his tent and fell asleep.

His alarm went off at 11:00 p.m. One of the first things that crossed his mind when he awoke was that he was very glad he'd remembered to bring a jacket and sweater. He lay in the darkness, in the warmth and comfort of his sleeping bag, excited to venture out into the starry night, but content to remain lying down a while longer, to just be, with only a breath and a clear, open mind, in the sublimity of the present moment. In the seemingly motionless silence, a majestic violet sheen, visible across a swath of the tent's interior, subtly ebbed and flowed, undulating like a fluid heartbeat. Eventually, Slowbe leaned over and reached for his flashlight. The orange dome-shaped tent was soon completely illuminated. He sat up and began to dig around in his backpack for something to eat, settling on a couple apples and a handful of mixed nuts. When he was done eating, he quickly finished off a one-liter water bottle. He was thirstier than he'd realized. It occurred to him that he hadn't had anything to drink since leaving Joseph.

Slowbe slipped out of his sleeping bag and put on some additional clothing. He gathered his telescope and flashlight, pulled open the zipper of his tent, and placed the items on the ground in front of the tent. He crawled out on his hands and knees and casually glanced upward through a gap in the intersecting boughs of the surrounding trees. To his amazement, in the split second when his eyes captured the view of the sky a comet flashed before him—a large ball of light trailed by a long, bright-white streak that looked as if it had passed within earth's atmosphere. "Wow," he said out loud. He'd never seen one that appeared so close.

Slowbe headed toward the lookout with his telescope and flashlight in hand. With each step his anticipation grew. At the edge of the grove of pines, he glanced upward to his left. There it was. It looked like a small, incredibly luminous moon, far brighter than it had appeared on the days and evenings when he watched it from his deck in Portland—brighter than it had appeared just a few hours ago. He paused for a moment, then continued on to the lookout. As soon as he arrived, he began setting up his telescope. An exceptionally clear view of the Milky Way, which appeared as a dense, pale, yet shimmering ribbon of stars stretching from the horizon in the south, across the center of the sky directly overhead, all the way to the horizon in the north, provided the perfect backdrop for the extraordinary astronomical event shining conspicuously above.

Slowbe stood alone on the high rim. He wondered if he'd ever seen so many stars in the sky. He thought about the scale of things; the size of the Milky Way and the universe; the immense energy released by the supernova; the fact that nearly all the elements that composed his body had come from supernovae like the one he was bearing witness to, whose materials would spread out into the galaxies and form the basis of other physical bodies and objects in epochs to come. The death of the star was also a birth, a progenitor of things yet to be. Slowbe felt a connectedness in the moment, and an overwhelming sense of the power and breadth of the here and now. "A meeting place," he said quietly, referring to a passage from *Walden*, from the chapter entitled "Economy," in which Thoreau describes the present moment as being a meeting place of two eternities: the past and the future. Slowbe agreed that the present moment was a meeting place, but thought of it more specifically as the epicenter where all things—the temporal, the brief, the eternal, and the infinite—exist simultaneously. In the larger, deeper scheme of things there was only a single, dynamic, limitless, all-encompassing present moment. *This* was where he dwelled and had experience and was sentient and was found and had power and created and was created. He had always been, and always would be, in the present moment. It was the only place that had ever existed, or ever would exist, in this world or any other, in this life or any other, in this reality or any other.

It had taken him years to become completely fixed and centered in the now, even though he had long known, on an intellectual level, that the only way for him to fully experience the power and breadth of his own being, the only way for him to thrive, and to truly be aware of reality, was to be anchored in the now—a clear-minded, untethered now. Sobriety—mental, emotional, and physical—had helped him develop the wherewithal and the willingness to "let go of life as it arises," as he put it, and to not allow recent or distant memories, or the near or distant future, to preoccupy his mind. Let the instant life happens come and go like a fountain that continually rises into the consciousness and then falls into the ether, and you will always be in the dynamic now, he told himself. To consciously be in the process of becoming, one must be grounded in the state of being, he thought.

Prior to his final resolve, much of his waking life, though not all, had been spent in sometimes subtle, and sometimes overt, vacillation between a perceived future and a perceived past. Although it was not uncommon for this vacillation to be couched in hope or nostalgia, all too often he had allowed his mind to dwell on worry over potential events and experiences, or on memories of trauma and negativity, or to simply drift into a pattern of obsessively recounting the day's conversations and episodes. He knew that these tendencies detracted from his ability to wield the generative power available in the present moment, and that patterns repeated in the mind fulfill themselves in the conditions of life.

Human experience was like a movie reel, he thought, and because humans are, for practical, legitimate reasons, primarily oriented around a time/space construct, the mind and ego interpreted only one episode, one frame of the movie reel, at a time, even though the entire movie reel (i.e., the whole human life) existed at once in a multifaceted, overarching present moment, which was how the soul experienced it—as if it were holding the entire movie reel in the "palm of its hand," or in its "mind" like a single thought, or in its consciousness as one "night's dream." In order to ensure that the residue of past or future frames didn't bleed into the now and distract from the clarity of the now, Slowbe had to practice letting go of each frame as it "passed" and practice letting go of any habitual focus on potential "future" frames. He would meditate upon, and internalize, images and metaphors that helped him feel a visceral sense of presence: a rushing geyser, a sonic boom, a precise point, a circle, a beam of light, a supernova, a still pond, a flowing river, the ocean, the universe, oneness. On a daily basis, multiple times per day, he would repeat to himself out loud, "The present moment is the point of power, the point of power is now," or he would say, "All is now." He also used breath. He would take slow, even inhales, pulling in air through his pharynx so as to cause a dull hissing sound. As he breathed in, he would pay attention to the sensation of his chest expanding and his lungs filling with oxygen. He would continue until no more could enter, hold the breath for several seconds, and then exhale in the same slow, intentional manner. Without fail, the exercise relaxed his mind and body, and everything would settle to the riverbed. Often, he would meditate upon the present moment as being the point where his physical self and his soul coalesced.

Slowbe imagined that he, the experiencer, was a windowpane, nearly invisible. On one side of the window was the outward plane that his five senses and his belief in science deemed real: the physical plane of body and earth and sky and cosmos that he saw all around him wherever he looked; a fantastic realm of stars and galaxies and nebulae, and planets and black holes, and dark energy and dark matter; of molecules and atoms and quarks and the Big Bang, and wrinkles in the space/time continuum that possibly led to other dimensions; and recondite domains beyond the Big Bang. This side of the window, the outward plane, was an expanse of immense wonder and mystery, virtually infinite, that extended as far out into the distance, and as deep into the subatomic, as Slowbe's imagination could conceive, and far beyond that. It was associated with an array of hypotheses, assumptions, theories, laws, and proven facts. It consisted of many well-defined properties and processes. And it exhibited a semblance of predictability amidst overwhelming chaos. Every day the sun rose in the east. A small miracle.

On the other side of the window was a plane of existence that generally went unnoticed and unexplored due to the fact that the outward plane, which seemed to surround the individual, was the dominant, original, founding paradigm in the minds of humans, utterly consuming and hypnotizing. The inward plane existed beneath, or behind, the veil of the outward plane; yet it also pervaded, and supported the structure of, the outward plane. From the human perspective, knowledge of it was almost entirely subjective and empirical. It could be gleaned with intuition, the mind's eye, and, in certain instances, with the physical eyes. It was vivid, beyond time and space, infinite on infinite levels, and was, in fact, more real than the outward plane. With some exceptions, it was indescribable, although concrete information, and insight, and answers to questions pertaining to daily life, and knowledge regarding the nature of physical reality, and knowledge of other dimensions, could be obtained therein. In truth, there was no separation between the inward and outward planes. The "worlds" on each "side" of the window were accessible to all, by nature and birthright. To discover the world within, one simply had to look in another direction, re-focus one's attention, and reorient oneself. Each person could conduct their own experiment and find out for themselves.

Slowbe aimed his telescope in the direction of the supernova and placed his eye on the finderscope. He made a few adjustments to the position of the instrument and the focus of the lens. Alcyone came perfectly into view. It pulsated and flickered, seeming to tell a story, revealing the inherent joy of existence. He observed it for several minutes and then moved his head away from the telescope and again gazed at the celestial body with his naked eyes. He closed his eyes and imagined an outline of himself against the nighttime sky, with stars as the points of the outline. He imagined the stars exploding into a brilliant flash of light that spread outward indefinitely. The Self was limitless. The universe, and everything in it, was a rendering, a reflection, a physical representation of an underlying reality. He placed his eye back on the finderscope. Briefly, he thought of the young girl from two years ago on the Eagle Creek Trail. The girl named Adeline. "The path is cleared for her," he whispered.

Alton Spencer is a writer, poet, musician, and songwriter based in Portland, Oregon. He holds a master's degree in social work.